STILL OF WINTER

An Unsettling Reads Anthology

Edited by

ROBIN KNABEL & H. DAIR BROWN

Unsettling Reads, LLC

First paperback edition February 2023

First ebook edition February 2023

Editing: Robin Knabel and H. Dair Brown

Book design by Robin Knabel and H. Dair Brown

Photograph and cover design by Robin Knabel

ISBN (paperback): 9798376727973

ASIN (ebook): B0BW6M4MM5

Published by Unsettling Reads, LLC

www.unsettlingreads.com

STILL OF WINTER

AN UNSETTLING READS
ANTHOLOGY

EDITED BY

ROBIN KNABEL & H. DAIR BROWN

CONTRIBUTORS

CONTENTS

This book is dedicated to the nemophilists, the lovers of trees and haunters of woods.

"Nothing burns like the cold. But only for a while. Then it gets inside you and starts to fill you up, and after a while you don't have the strength to fight it."

—*A Game of Thrones* by George R.R. Martin

FOREWORD

In winter, there's a stillness—a silence. As wet snowflakes fall, sounds are muffled. A hush lingers in the air. Bare trees reach upward from the frozen ground, grasping with their spindly branches. Swaying in the frigid breeze, brittle bark creaks and moans as the trees whisper ancient secrets to one another. Sentries, standing in the stillness. Watching. Learning new stories to share with each other long after we have gone.

This winter, we want to celebrate these majestic beings and what happens when the stillness is disturbed.

Within these pages are works by authors, poets, and photographers from around the world, each with a unique perspective on fantasy, horror, and sci-fi genres. We are humbled by the pieces we received from so many talented people, and we are proud of the works we are sharing with you. It is our sincere hope when you've finished reading, you'll add a few new creative individuals to your arsenal.

—Robin & Dair

 **Fantasy**

 **Horror**

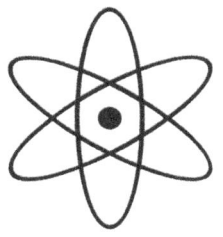 **Sci-Fi**

PART 1

LETCHWORTH VILLAGE CEMETERY, THIELLS, NEW YORK

Jennifer Woods

Jennifer Woods studied photography in New York City. She shoots urban landscapes and macro photography.
jwoodsphoto.com

THE BURIED CITY

John Joseph Ryan

after Toba Khedoori's drawing,"Untitled (Cityscape)"

Snowed-in, derelict city at the base
of white mountain, her drawbridge lost
rising in dense, lowering fog.

Two sets of prints disturb the empty streets.
The snow raven, the blood dove
shred the grey air, leave glimpses

of black boughs, clutch trinkets from
the ice before they flee: fragments
of skulls the frozen graves have heaved.

John Joseph Ryan's work has appeared in *River Styx*, *McSweeney's*, and *Suspense Magazine* (U.S.), and in international publications such as *Mystery Magazine* (Canada), *Channel Magazine* (Ireland), *Grievous Bodily Harm* (Australia), and *A-Z of Horror: 'L' is for Lycans* (U.K.). John's collaborative noir short, "Hothouse by the River," was published by the University of Iowa Center for the Book. He is also the author of a best-selling crime novel, *A Bullet Apiece* (Amphorae Publishing Group, 2015), and he contributed a chapter on Walt Whitman and Abraham Lincoln's relationship to the textbook *Teaching Lincoln: Legacies and Classroom Strategies* (Peter Lang, 2014). John lives in St. Louis, Missouri.

MELODY

J.B. Kish

Embarrassment aside, I recently choked to death on the wet floor of a crowded cafe. A couple of strangers used CPR to humiliate me back to life, so now I'm here all over again. The doctor suspects CPR broke two of my ribs, which could explain the unfamiliar weight I'm carrying, like a backpack full of stones I can't slip from my shoulders.

"Possibly," he mouths, chewing on a pen. He's dubious, I think, and cannot account for my interesting souvenir from the void. *Killed by a scone and resurrected several pounds heavier* might not be covered in medical school. I tell him it feels like a leech, and when the ASL interpreter explains, the doctor drops his pen.

My brother Isaac snaps his fingers in front of my eyes because I'm lost in the mystery of it all.

He's parked the jeep on Widow Maker Hill, so we get out and trudge across the snow. If there're any children living in the valley, I don't see them, which is unfortunate. On a day like today, my brothers and I would spend hours sledding down Widow Maker. Then we'd march single file up its spine like a band of Wild Things on the hunt for mischief-making. I'd lead the pack, of course, because their only sister must prove herself on a rolling basis.

Isaac points down the hill and says something. He's being lazy and not using his hands, so I slug him in the shoulder. I only catch about half of what people say from lip reading and he knows it. So he signs, but his finger gloves muffle the words. Finally, I get the gist and smirk. *If memory serves,* I sign, *you jumped on the back of my sled. That's the reason we crashed in the first place.*

He smiles, shrugs. His way of saying, *We'll never know.*

The melody of it all is a somber one. I probably remember that day more vividly than he realizes. It is the first time I recall asking my brothers to speak up. I could see their mouths moving, but the sound of their words died before reaching my ears. Being a small child, I didn't understand.

A couple miles out, our family cabin sits in an untouched clearing. Fifteen acres of bare land surrounded at the edge by a ring of woods. In all this winter between us, nothing stirs. We may as well be looking down from the heavens.

In front of the house, a single oak stands disconnected from the surrounding woods. Isaac calls it Lover's Tree: the spot where our mother proposed to our father. It's not until I see the tree up close that I feel the mysterious weight of my experience lift. The moment I step down from the jeep, I don't sink as far into the snow. The phantom weight has unexpectedly gone, and I have no idea why.

Close your eyes, I tell myself, letting the moment come to me. I inhale deeply. The air tickles my skin, the hair on my neck dances playfully, and I relax into a vivid sense of peace beneath the shade of Lover's Tree. The melody here has always been powerful.

"What's wrong?" Isaac asks with both his hands and mouth.

I'm not sure I know how to reply. *Better*, I say. *I feel...
better.*

"I told you," he answers with a grin. "This cabin is
medicine."

ACTUALLY, THIS CABIN IS EMPTY.

I search the kitchen while Isaac builds a fire. When he
finishes, he sits at the breakfast nook and watches me.

Mom and Dad always leave mac and cheese, I grouse. *In
case someone shows up without groceries.*

My brother shrugs and signs, "Must have forgotten." His
words are clearer without gloves on. "I'll run into town and grab
some food. Keep an eye on the fire."

Buy beer? I ask.

"And maybe some scones?" he replies.

For a careful moment, we stare at one another as I decide
whether to laugh at his lousy joke. I flip him the bird. He smiles,
grabs the keys, and waves goodbye.

IT'S AN HOUR INTO TOWN AND BACK, ESPECIALLY IN THE SNOW. I
add enough wood to keep the fire busy and consider taking a
stroll around the property. But first, there's an old Walkman in
my father's desk with a pair of cheap SONY headphones that I
place around my neck. When I click play on an AC/DC cassette
tape, a companionable vibration appears in my throat that makes
me smile. This place—the cabin, Lover's Tree, my father's dusty
office—it all performs for me. It's a composition of emotions
both new and experienced: when all the right feelings come
together and lead me by the hand. I've found that, in the end,

everything has a melody in this way, if only I look for it hard enough.

Outside, the afternoon sun has just barely kissed the tree line, and I savor the few rays that fight so hard to find my cheek. My boots sink into the snow a full six inches as I plod my way to the edge of the property, where I begin tracing the woods in a grand circle. I'm so focused on the canopy that I nearly miss the other tracks at my feet. At first, I think the creature they belong to must be big. The tracks aren't narrow like a deer's. They're wider and more forceful, made by something like a bear's paw— or a human foot? As silly as that sounds, I must admit, it really does look like someone's out here with no shoes on.

I pause the cassette tape, and for a long while, let nature play out in front of me. I'm looking for the person who made these, but the air is perfectly still and I'm freezing. I push forward, following the footprints, mostly because they're heading in the same direction.

It's easier on my calves to walk inside the tracks, and I assume the footprints will veer off any moment. But after several minutes, I think that this person might not be a passerby. They're moving too steadily around the edge of our property. In fact, it's as if they are purposefully circling my family's cabin.

Nervous, I pause and worry someone got the jump on me. But that's being too delicate: there's no hiding in the snow without leaving a sign. These tracks head plainly in one direction, and I'm clearly coming up behind whoever's here. So, I force my heartbeat to slow and think rationally. It's a hunter, which is annoying because our property is distinctly marked.

After twenty minutes of searching, I've come full circle, back to the spot where I first found the tracks. This hunter, whoever it is, has walked the entire perimeter of our home and not deviated. So how does someone enter and exit a circle without leaving a trace? I'm frightened by the question, and my heart beats painfully against my broken ribs. I stuff each hand into my pockets but cannot find my phone. Of course. I left it in the jeep like an idiot.

IF I COULD TRIPLE LOCK THE DOORS AND WINDOWS, I WOULD. I'm gripping a large kitchen knife next to the fire because it's been five hours, and Isaac hasn't returned. The sun's gone down, and the only thing I see outside is my nervous reflection in the windows.

I'm not sure how I manage to fall asleep, but I'm awakened by something running a finger along my forearm. When I open my eyes, I don't know what frightens me more: that something touched me or that the sun has risen. I rush around the freezing cabin but cannot find my brother.

Outside, Lover's Tree stands proudly in our yard with no sign of the jeep. But beneath the tree, a fresh pair of footprints cuts through the snow like a comet hurtling toward me. Wide-eyed, I follow its trail from the tree to the window, where someone clearly watched me sleep.

I take a shuddering breath—shake my head in wild disagreement—open the door and run for the highway. But as I approach the woods, something vibrates powerfully beneath me. The feeling is so startling that I trip over my feet and tumble. Snow caked on my face, I spot the foot tracks at the edge of our property. There are more now. Dozens more. Whoever is stalking me spent the night walking circles around my cabin. There are at least fifty rings now. And something about them doesn't look right. Carefully, I inch forward on my belly and peer down into a single footprint.

A great, black expanse yawns back at me, and its very presence defies explanation. All around, these tracks have perforated the snow, which somehow hovers above an impossibly large cavern.

The cavern is an all-too-familiar void. There is no melody here, I realize with horror. This place is death.

Shaking, I reach down inside one hole and curl my fingers up and out another. The sight of my own hand wiggling back drives me to my feet. From beyond the circle, something catches my eye, and despite my need to run—anywhere, in any direction—I force myself to be still.

Whatever I saw, it's fighting to take form in front of my eyes. A soapy bubble that is there one moment before popping from sight. Finally, I catch a glimpse of Isaac! He comes in and out of focus—pacing at the end of the drive, one hand on his head, another dialing his phone. He looks terrified and then abruptly he is waving down a state trooper, who eases his car to a stop before ambling toward my brother.

I'm saved! I wave my arms to get their attention! But as the men walk in my direction, they pass over the threshold of tracks and disappear. I watch two pairs of phantom shoe prints eat into the snow before fading away just inches from where I stand.

Is this a nightmare? Did I hyperventilate and pass out? It doesn't make sense. Some functioning part of my brain speculates: *it's the tracks.* They must be a kind of barrier between us. Between a *here* and a *there*.

You have to run.

I sprint as hard as I can. I time my steps to leap through the veil, but then I'm shaken from my stride by the feeling of ground coming undone beneath me. Everything is loose, like it's going to collapse in on itself. I want to keep going, but that's suicide, so I'm forced to turn back for the cabin. And when I look up, my stomach drops.

Something is waiting for me at the cabin door.

I feel the vibration of a scream exit my mouth. Tattered rags drape the barefoot creature, which has the flesh of overworked leather. A pair of bright red lips flap over its white teeth and pink gums, but hardened boils conceal the rest of its face. Both of its hands float in the air on either side of its body, wrists bent forward. The thing stands perfectly still—except for those fingers, which look like they are individually tracking me.

I know this creature.

My leech.

What do you want? I speak sharp and fast with each hand. I want this thing to know how much it repels me. When it doesn't answer, I sign even harder: *What do you want with me?*

The creature finally chuffs in response, and the vibration crawls along the snow into my shoes. In slow, lumpish movements, its hands stretch out and sign:

Your.

Melody.

Its flapping lips smile.

Panicking, my only choice is Lover's Tree, so I sprint to it. Up I climb, ever aware of the thing that's watching me. I move toward the furthest branch. If I can get high enough, I might be able to get above the threshold. Maybe I can flag down my brother. I move confidently from one branch to another, but below, the creature climbs after me. I scream and kick at it wildly, but it grabs hold of my ankle firmly. Then my leg.

I fall several branches, and it crawls onto me, onto my back —the weight of my experience returned. My off-balance passenger. My leech that never really left. It simply hopped off and took a stroll.

As the fabric of our property succumbs to perforation, I understand I've been on borrowed time. I was humiliated back to that sticky floor of the café, and now my leech is returning me to the void.

Everything is falling. The cabin plummets and the tree I cling to spins freely. I reach up, my fingers splayed toward the sky. I grope for one more limb, hoping that I might find something. That Isaac might grab my hand in return. But as I cry out for him, I'm pulled backward, down into the void, several pounds heavier. A warm finger slides along my jaw and hooks my cheek.

There is no melody where I'm going.

Originally from the Southwest, **J.B. Kish** moved to Portland, Oregon, in 2012. He is the winner of the 2020 Ooligan Press Write to Publish Award for Fiction, and his writing has been featured in *Metaphorosis* Magazine and *Cosmic Horror Monthly*. jbkish.com.

OLD GROWTH

Harrison Shimens

Time runs differently among the rolling hills of the Niagara escarpment. Tucked away between the suburban cities of Southern Ontario, the ancient deciduous forests grow and die each year, only to be reborn the next. The liminal stage between life and the unknown, the forest's prolonged dying, is when the land is at its most beautiful. Vibrant crimson and golden leaves ebb and flow in the first wintry breeze of the season. They detach, falling to the ground to rot, as the trees remain dormant through the winter. Waiting.

Crossing the border between Dufferin and Simcoe counties in his red pickup truck, Bent pondered life outside of the city. His thoughts tumbled in his mind like ice in a glass of bourbon. An image of stowaways aboard a pilgrim's vessel came to his mind: huddled bodies, damp and afraid. Except these were not aboard some New England-bound ship. These hid away in the wilderness, between the cities. Stowaways of time.

The road seemed endless. Windows down, Bent inhaled the fresh country air in deep, purifying breaths, the pungent twang of manure in his nostrils. He smiled as he listened to a local radio station, feeling a bit like a stowaway himself.

It was the first time Bent had ever taken a job outside of the city. When the client approached him, he couldn't resist taking the offer. More accurately, he couldn't afford not to take it. So intriguing was this opportunity that he got into his car at 4 P.M. on a Friday to drive two hours north, just to make initial observations for the job.

"The sooner we start, the sooner it's done," he told his crew.

They questioned his decision. "Take the weekend and relax for once!" they said.

"I can relax when I'm dead," Bent responded with a wink and a wicked smile.

A carpenter by trade, Bent earned his ridiculous nickname through a process of etymological devolution. It started with Benjamin, and as a result of ruining a few good nails, to Bentjamin. From there, his coworkers realized what a mouthful "Bentjamin" was and Bent was born. A rabble of young men who work with their hands had a way of making stupid nicknames stick like glue. And besides, he kind of liked the way Bent sounded. It conjured up images of all those nails he had ruined. Sturdy pieces of metal turned crooked at the hands of an untrained apprentice.

But that was years ago. Since then, he'd managed to create one of the most successful contracting businesses in the city. He'd even won an award for "Top Contractor" by a local newspaper.

"It's because I love my craft," he told the reporter. "And because I love to work hard."

It was true. The throbbing beneath his thickly calloused hands told him he had brought something good into the world. He created something new that someone would enjoy. Each success atoned a ruined nail.

He wondered if the pride he felt was what a mother felt like: life created through your own body's sacrifice. His very own children of stone and wood; a brood that had touched hundreds of homes in the city. By the time he finishes this job, his brood will have put roots down in Simcoe County. A growing family. Bent smiled. A pile of dried, grey leaves whirled in a flurry as his truck sped past.

Rolling down a steep hill, the truck turned down a gravel path at the bottom. There was no signage, no indication of any sort of human structure nearby. But according to the map on his phone, this was the place.

The stones crackled under the heavy tires of the truck. Hunched over his steering wheel, Bent tried to see if there was anything up ahead. The trees arched over the road. It was beautiful, in a suffocating sort of way. The smell of decomposing trees flooded through the truck's open window. Thin grasping branches skidded along the sides of the van like spiders teasing their prey. Bent was glad he paid extra for the ceramic coating on his truck.

The road went on, and Bent ruminated on how he'd get the rest of the materials out here on Monday when the crew would join him. It was a big job. The icy tumbler in his mind jostled.

"A total reno," Bent was told at his office. "Just shy of a demolition. I'll need it done for skiing season. Can you do it?"

Bent had already agreed to the job in his mind–the moment the man offered the exuberant sum at the start of the conversation, in fact. But, as a good businessman should, he kept a stoic look until the deal was made. To make the request even more interesting, the man paid in cash. First half now, second half after the job was finished. Receiving such a large sum in cash made Bent feel like a movie villain.

The truck rolled to a stop with a snap, crackle, and pop. Sitting, with the engine running, Bent looked through the windshield at a deliberate circular clearing carved out of the woods, bordered by tall maple and birch trees. In the center of the clearing was a single-floor building with crusty brown paint peeling like dead skin. A large unlit neon sign sat atop a thirty-foot pole that simply read: *MOTEL.*

"Well," Bent said, "let's see what we've got."

He slammed the door of his truck. The noise echoed through the clearing, sending a family of birds into flight.

The woods surrounding the motel were dense, and the state of the building concerned Bent. Moss overtook the roof, which looked ready to collapse.

"I guess he did say it was just short of a demo." Kicking some twigs with his heavy boots, he walked up to what he presumed was the front office. The cool metallic keys jingled as he took them out of his breast pocket. A chill moved down his spine as he unlocked the door.

Sucking on his bottom lip, he peeled away some of the brown paint to assess the age of the place. Built in the sixties, by his approximation.

"I've already had an electrician at the place," the man had told Bent. "So, when you arrive, you should have light. Just need to hit the circuit breaker. No heat yet, though. That's a whole other headache."

A dank must forced itself up Bent's nose, and moist air dampened his clothes. It was like stepping into a greenhouse. The first tingle of perspiration formed on his exposed forearms. Collapsed ceiling tiles and pink insulation scattered the floor, while the last vestiges of sunlight poured through foggy windows.

Flick. As expected, the light switch on the right side of the door didn't work.

Stepping around overturned furniture that looked as old and decrepit as the building itself, Bent moved toward where the utility closet was supposedly located. Methodically navigating the rubble, he noticed the walls were still haphazardly littered with artwork. Oil paintings of Northern Ontario nightscapes similar to something by the Group of Seven. In the dark, they almost looked like windows.

There were also portraits. Were they the family that owned this land? They had a haunting quality. There were eight portraits total, each featuring a gaunt individual with a macabre, torture-stricken face. Some old, some young, some women, some men. All in the same disturbing style.

Every one of them had roots wrapping around the frames, burrowing into the canvas of each painting. Bent's eyes were drawn to one in particular. Roots poked out from each of the subject's eyes.

"Creepy," Bent shuddered. "How on earth did everything in this room get turned up'n over, while these stayed firm in place?"

Bent figured they were nailed to the wall. "They'll be gone soon enough." By the end of the following week, the place would look as if it had been razed to the ground and completely reborn. One more nail redeemed.

Trees rustled in the wind, cutting through the silence as if to interrupt his thoughts.

Was it already starting to get dark? It felt wrong to Bent, but then again, the winter sun always dipped below the horizon sooner than expected. A sense of urgency took over Bent, like a child who had just turned off the lights and was racing to his bed to avoid the monsters that only appear in the dark.

He opened the utility closet door and knocked over a fire axe. Beside the axe, he found an old mop that had been snapped in two, a red toolbox with a couple of 'peace sign' stickers on it, and mounted on the wall directly in front of him was a stone grey fuse box.

Inside, he saw old-style fuses that looked like little glass bulbs and black switches with taped-on labels next to them. *Lobby.* He flicked the switch. Nothing. Leaning out of the closet and peeping around the door, he saw the bulb-less light fixture hanging from the ceiling.

A notepad opened in his mind and made its first entry: *lightbulbs.* Power, but no lights, apparently. He figured he may as well flick all the switches, then make his rounds before dark to see if any bulbs survived.

Wind rattled the glass windows, making them chatter gleefully. Outside, darkness descended with a sense of urgency. Bent retrieved a penlight from his pocket and snapped the other switches into place. *Room 101, Room 102, Room 103, Lounge, Room 105, Room 106, Room 107, Room 108, Main Sign.*

Backing out of the closet, the open door at the other end of the room seemed farther away than when he had wandered in. He used his flashlight to take in a better view. The light illuminated only a small portion of the room at a time, and the scattered legs of furniture cast long shadows on the walls. Deep wells of darkness filled the space behind the overturned furniture and the front desk. Cast upon the paintings that clung to the walls, the light brought a pale glow to their white eyes, except for the one with roots protruding from its sockets. Only darkness there.

After a minute of navigating rubble like a mouse in a maze, Bent stepped out of the lobby into fresh air. A sudden feeling of relief fell over him, and he was glad to be outside again. He took off his hat. The wind chilled the sweat on his forehead. The sun was beyond the horizon, and its blood-red rays made the clouds blush. Only about twenty minutes of light left, maybe less, this deep in the woods.

ZZT. Bent turned quickly and saw that the *MOTEL* sign was on. Humming, its red neon glow flickered slightly. *I should probably turn that off,* he thought, but after looking back into the lobby, something in the back of his mind told him not to. He shrugged. *Might make a good night light at least.*

Bent visited all the rooms and found only two bulbs in Room 108. Both were shattered. He underlined *LIGHTBULBS* twice in his mind and capitalized the letters for good measure.

The darker the sky became, the more uneasy Bent felt about coming up early to check things out and spend the night. The back of his truck was all set for it, though. Heavy blankets, a pillow, a bag of hot Cheetos, and his laptop with an action movie preloaded. However, as the prospect drew nearer, primordial anxiety grew within him.

The harsh red glow of the motel sign became more prominent with each passing minute. It blanketed the entire clearing in a crimson that reminded Bent of emergency lights.

ZZT. It flickered on and off, which yielded a complete blackness, like some kind of reverse flash on a camera. Knowing that the only sources of light were his truck, his flashlight, and that flickering red sign made him uncomfortable. He was used to the city, after all. *God, I miss light pollution.*

Concluding his investigation of the rooms–almost all of which were completely overgrown with weeds–he walked back toward his truck. His mental notepad jotted notes the whole way as he got lost in his thoughts.

The light flickered off. In the darkness, Bent became alert. Waiting.

Bright again. Just as his mental notepad was opening again, he noticed something. A figure stood at the boundary of the woods.

In his shock, Bent grunted a low defensive sound like a gorilla. The red aura of the sign flickered brightly, and Bent could see that it was a short, stout tree. *How could a tree look that much like a person?*

"Jesus Christ," Bent exhaled.

Now more aware than ever of his surroundings, he crept past his truck to the edge of the forest, toward the shape he'd seen. The tree stood about seven feet tall. If Bent had known anything about the native flora, he would have identified it as white ash. He took note of its eerie similarities to a gaunt man. A peculiar area of twisted bark gave the tree a kind of visage, which wore a gnarled grimace. Standing near the tree bathed in deep crimson light, Bent's heart beat fast in his chest.

The light blinked off again, and Bent watched the grimace shift in the near darkness. Fear rose in Bent's throat and sat there like a tumor.

ZZT. The light returned. Just a tree. He backed away and heard his own voice inside his head. *The quicker we start, the quicker it's done.*

Bent made his way back to the truck and settled into the back seat, the tantalizing profit dancing in his mind.

The *MOTEL* sign buzzed off and on like a lullaby as Bent fell asleep.

SOMETHING SCRAPED THE SIDE OF THE TRUCK. BENT JOLTED awake. The truck was flooded with light from the sign. A large gust of wind dropped dead leaves onto his windshield, and something pushed his truck with enough force to rock it like a cradle.

"What the hell!?"

ZZT. The light flickered off.

Scanning the darkness through the back window, Bent's terror took over. His heart pounded in his chest, and slick sweat pooled in his clenched fists.

The ground was writhing. Dark masses shifted through the

clearing, and he could hear the creaking of the trees drawing closer and closer to his truck.

Another crash launched him forward, smashing his face into the window. A warm rush of blood flowed from his nostrils. Still holding his nose with one hand, he braced himself with the other. As if struck from behind by a vehicle, another impact rocked the truck. Turning to see what had hit him, Bent caught a glimpse of that gnarled grimace.

ZZT. The light flickered on, and everything was doused in red again.

A tree with a cold human face peering from behind its leaves. An ancient entity, twisted in malice, was rooted outside his door.

"This—this can't be happening—" another crash. The windows on the left side of the truck shattered. Blinding white panic took over, and Bent rushed out of the truck. He felt movement beneath his feet. Thick roots tore through the ground. Not far behind each set of roots was a dark mass of wood, lumbering toward Bent in the red night. There was something so human about it.

Frozen in terrified awe, a sharp pain tore through his left foot. He let out a scream that made his voice crack. A thin razor-sharp root had shot through his foot, and blood began pooling in his shoe. He pulled free from the wooden spike, and it writhed back and forth like an earthworm. The woods moaned, a baleful sound, as if satisfied to have tasted his blood. A primeval bellow vibrated through the air. The hunt was on.

Bent dashed toward the lobby, dodging the crawling roots underfoot. The door slammed shut behind him. He could hear the earth being torn apart by roots and the creaking of strong wood.

Adrenaline worked its biological magic, and the pain in his foot subsided. But he knew it would return. Bent recalled the time he'd fallen off his bicycle as a child and dislocated his shoulder. Tilting his head down, he found his shoulder directly below his chin. There was no pain, no shock, only the thought: *that isn't supposed to be there. That isn't right*, and the mindless shifting of his shoulder back into its socket. And that's when the pain hit.

That isn't supposed to be there. That isn't right. The thought pulsed in Bent's mind like a migraine. *Trees can't move. That isn't right.*

The leak in his foot brought him out of his thoughts. There had to be some way out.

He felt around in his pocket for his cellphone. Gone. Left behind on the truck's driver's seat to charge overnight.

Outside, the *MOTEL* light flashed off and on, each burst of red light brought the shadows of the creatures closer and closer. Terror peaked in Bent, but in a moment of clarity, he could see something outside the window. A beacon of hope, bathed in blood red.

The path! The path was open! The forest hadn't closed the only way in and out of this clearing in the woods. Bent thanked God for bulldozers and chainsaws.

A memory flashed behind his eyelids: *the axe.* Limping, he made his way to the utility closet. Bent felt watched by the pictures on the wall. Avoiding the gazes of the haunted portraits, he grabbed the fire axe. It had a sturdy wooden handle, but a cloudy silver head dulled by time.

The tinge of red-hot pain entered his foot again, and he wiped the flow of blood from his nose. Emboldened with an animal instinct, he prepared to fight for his life. *I just need to get in the driver's seat.*

The sound of crumbling plaster took Bent off guard.

He turned and saw the portrait of the morose man with roots penetrating his painted eyes. The roots were writhing, pushing through the painting, splitting it apart. The roots kept pushing through, tearing the picture to shreds. Behind the portrait, the

23

plaster wall crumbled and fell apart, sending a large cloud of dust into the blighted air. Bent coughed furiously.

Emerging from the dust cloud was a horror Bent could hardly conceive. *This isn't right.*

ZZT. Darkness. *ZZT.* Light.

A human skeleton, animated by contorting roots and plant matter, danced toward Bent. The roots protruded from the eye sockets, each surveying its surroundings like the tongue of a snake. Its jawbone hung ajar, and its toe bones scraped limply against the porcelain floor tiles. The creature shambled over the broken wood and plaster toward Bent.

Bent scrambled desperately over furniture toward the front door. Axe in hand, he bolted forward, ignoring the pain in his foot. For a brief moment, he thought he felt the frail grasping of tiny roots against his jeans. He let out an animalistic howl and threw open the front door.

ZZT. Shadows. *ZZT.* Monsters.

The fear and rage converged. The axe raised and came down countless times. Each blind strike sent splinters into Bent's hands and face—whether from the old wooden handle or the creatures, he didn't know.

Up and down, up and down, the head of the axe plowed deep inside the trees. On and off, on and off, the light of the *MOTEL* sign buzzed. Bent couldn't count the entities. He couldn't even tell where one ended, and the next began. Ripping his feet free from twisting roots, he gained distance slowly. The world disappeared into the flickering red light.

When Bent grasped the driver's door handle, the world manifested itself again. He opened the door, threw the axe inside, and got in. He saw his phone, knocked to the floor, but still charging. Hope welled in Bent's chest. He turned the key, and the heavy engine roared to a start. The headlights illuminated the splintered masses he left behind in his wake. They continued toward the truck, mangled and twisted, no longer looking like people.

The truck thrust into drive. With a scream of the tires and a turn of the wheel, Bent drove onto the path. Trees at the mouth of the path were tighter than before, but his powerful truck blasted through them. As he drove farther down the pitch-black road, the trees let up and the throat of the path widened.

Bent let out a wild howl like a hyena. He felt pain in his nose, foot, and splintered skin.

In his rear-view mirror, he could see the shapes of the monsters. They stood still, watching as he escaped.

The *MOTEL* sign flickered on.

After thirty minutes of driving, Bent knew something was wrong. The way in had taken no more than fifteen minutes, and he was driving slowly then. Could he have missed the road? There was no way. He was driving out to a rural highway. It would have been impossible to miss. Frustrated, he smacked the steering wheel and let out a desperate cry as time slipped by, the needle on the gas gauge dipping lower and lower.

Bent drove another thirty minutes, then another, until a dull acceptance washed over him.

In the distance, directly in front of him, he saw that dim flickering red light. Gnarled wooden figures stood still. Waiting.

Harrison Shimens is a writer and teacher living in Ottawa, Canada. His horror is deeply influenced by the land he has inhabited: the metropolises of South Korea, the seaside of Newfoundland, and southern Ontario farmland. He enjoys video games, traveling, and has an unhealthy penchant for disgustingly sweet treats. His work can be found in Engen Books' *Sea Stories From the Rock* anthology, Scare Streets' *Night Terrors Vol. 21*, and in an upcoming anthology by Black Ink Press.

WINTER'S BITE

Robin Knabel

The cold bit straight through my skin. I feared if I touched my face, I'd find pieces missing–carved off by knife-like wind shears. My body trembled in the driver's seat of the wagon, but it was more than just the chill in the air. The town of Toffet lay just ahead. I'd grown up hearing horrible stories about the place—tales of slain livestock and folks gone missing. I questioned how much was true, but I wasn't eager to get stranded in these parts. I urged the horses to fight the cold, but they slowed down more with every mile.

Rubbing dry eyes, I leaned forward and squinted through the veil of swirling snowflakes. I could just make out a thin wisp of smoke, snaking its way out of a chimney, staining the sky as if the unforgiving wind froze it in place.

"Hot damn."

Pulling the reins with as much strength as my frozen fingers could muster, the horses stopped. Their warm breath steamed out of ice-crusted nostrils. Easing down off my perch, I tied them onto a fence beside the road, its rails buried deep within a frozen cast of ice.

At least they've learned to obey me.

I bought the two nags from a farmer a handful of days ago. Cost me my best hunting knife, too. A small price to pay to pass through the foothills before snowfall. In my haste, I'd forgotten to pack the saddles or spare blankets in the wagon. Without my hunting blade, I'd been subsisting on the jerky and hardtack stashed in my knapsack. The storm I aimed to avoid? Damn thing landed right on top of me. My only hope was to get to Eraway, regroup, and make plans to get as far from these Podunk towns as possible.

The last of my kindling was spent pitching camp last night. I'd been crafting a desperate plan to bust up my wagon for spare wood. It melted away as I set my sights on the small cabin, despite my vague fears about Toffet.

There was no road fit for travel up the steep, snow-covered hill, not even a small path. Pulling my hat down over my eyes and wrapping my arms around my torso, I trudged upward through the heavy, deep snow. My thinning wool coat offered little protection. By the time I'd reached the front porch, I'd forgotten how cold my feet were. Hell, I couldn't even feel them anymore.

I rapped frozen knuckles against the door. Small rivulets of blood filled the wrinkles on the back of my hand as dry, papery skin split open. I waited a moment, then knocked again. My body vibrated with the cold and the anticipation of being this close to taking shelter from the harsh elements. The smell of simmering meat wafted to my nose through a small gap around the door. I could almost taste it. I knocked again, with more urgency, receiving a splinter for my troubles.

Where are you? There had to be someone home. Who would leave a meal cooking and head out, especially in this weather? Growing impatient, I tried to open the door, to no avail. I walked around the back, determined to find another entrance.

As I rounded the back, I spied a peculiar tree in the distance. Its silhouette reminded me of a "sweets tree" when I was a kid. Mother draped sugary treats and fruits along the branches of a small tree in our yard every spring, low enough so my brothers and I could reach them. We'd gorge ourselves until we had stomachaches.

This tree was massive, though. It stood at least thirty feet high, and its branches were strewn with a bounty, like none I'd ever seen. Long, spindly casings swayed from its limbs in the gusty wind. The ropes holding them creaked and cracked from the strain, like the moorings on a boat. I wondered if the treasures strung up on those sturdy branches held animals, tied safely away from wandering creatures who could jump and catch their teeth in them. Or starving men, such as myself. The thought made my stomach growl.

Mesmerized by the impressive collection, and my hunger, I lurched toward the tree. As I drew closer, I was awestruck at the idea of so much. I fumbled in my pocket for a small knife, struggling with the loss of sensation in my fingers. Surely the proprietor of this haul could spare just one, just one for a man so close to starvation. I reached up, barely touching the bottom of one of the loads to steady it, and reared the knife back to strike.

"What'cha doin' with that knife, eh?"

I nearly jumped out of my skin, the sudden jolt causing me to drop the knife in the snow. I spun around, ready for a fight, but standing before me was a young woman, the top of her head just reaching my elbow. She aimed her pointed chin at me as her eyes measured up the would-be thief before her. Steamy breath escaped her taut lips, and I envied the pink of her warm cheeks.

"Sorry, Ma'am," I managed, my tongue numb and clumsy from the frigid air. "I knocked, but no one answered. I came 'round in search of another door, but I guess I got distracted by…" I waved my hand in the direction of the great tree.

"I see." She edged closer, placing a small hand around my upper arm, squeezing once. "Come with me," she said, then turned toward the cabin. I followed without question, enticed like a moth to the flame of a warm fire.

I followed her through a small door on the back of the cabin. Despite the sparse furniture, the interior was as cozy as I'd imagined. A wooden table with two chairs sat beneath a small window, the view of the bountiful tree fading as darkness fell. A fire roared with life, a cast-iron bowl hanging inside the hearth. My skin flinched and twitched as the heat awoke nerves from their hibernation, bringing a blend of relief and pain. She pointed to a chair at the table, and I obeyed.

"Where are you from?" she asked, pulling a stained apron over her blue dress. "I don't get many visitors, especially this time of year. Are you lost?" She turned away toward a counter, picked up a knife, and began chopping potatoes and carrots, angling her right ear in my direction.

"Aren't you scared–living out here in the middle of nowhere?" I asked, my eyes taking her in for the first time in the light of the fire. She was diminutive, but strong muscles in her forearms rolled against each other as she chopped the hard vegetables. With each push of the blade, her body wriggled beneath her simple dress.

"Why should I be?"

"I heard stories about this town, about a horned demon with legs like a goat who wanders the land feasting on livestock and weary travelers." I flexed my chest and arms, then leaned back in the chair. "Stories like that are for kids, though, I guess."

"You didn't answer my question," she said, still focused on her task.

"Nowhere special. I'm headed to Eraway, just a few towns over. Was hoping to avoid the storm's all. Used up all my rations just getting this far. Me and the horses were about starved."

30

The horses! I jumped up from the table. "Pardon, Ma'am, but my team's down by the road. Is there some place I can put them for a bit? I didn't see a way up here to bring the wagon, but maybe I could unhitch'em and bring'em up?"

"Sit," she ordered, her mouth rigid. "They're being handled. You're not the first to wander this way, aye." She carried the chopped vegetables to the fire, dumped them in the hanging pot, and grabbed a long spoon.

Handled?

"Oh, did your husband...?" I asked, shifting in my seat, wondering what kind of man I might have to face.

"Dinner will be ready soon," she answered, as if she'd never heard my question. "I suggest you remove your outer clothes and drape them over that rod near the fire. They'll dry soon enough, I s'pose."

Her voice was friendly, but her face was a shield. I couldn't tell if my gooseflesh came from the change in my conditions or my growing unease. *I hope the horses aren't hanging in that damn tree.*

"I appreciate that," I said, as I draped my damp shirt, trousers, and socks over the rod as she'd suggested. Despite our proximity, she didn't flinch or make eye contact. "Name's Jobie," I offered, sitting back at the table in my long johns. "Might I be so bold as to ask yours?"

The woman stood at the hearth facing the fire, stirring the contents of the large pot. She was speaking, but it was too soft to understand. It sounded like she was singing a song or reciting something. Maybe going over the recipe.

"I'm sorry, did you say something?" I asked.

The chanting continued until she pulled a cache of herbs from her apron pocket and tossed it into the pot. "My name is Elline, but you will refer to me as Miss Dickens." She turned to accept my nod of acknowledgement before returning to the stew.

31

Miss? I wonder who's tending the horses.

"It's ready," she said. My hunger pushed away any lingering questions.

WE SAT ACROSS FROM EACH OTHER AT THE TABLE, WITH THE sounds of slurping mouths and metal spoons clanking against bowls taking the place of conversation. Outside, the wind howled. It sounded like an injured beast.

"Thank you again, Ell... Miss Dickens, for your hospitality," I offered, setting the empty bowl down on the table. I felt groggy with relief, but the fear that she would send me back out into that cold wind hovered. And the question reemerged. *Where are the horses?*

Before I could ask, Elline stood and glided across the room, stopping beside a cot. It was draped with a thick brown blanket whose edges skimmed the floor. "You can sleep here," she said.

The temptation of a night's rest banished my questions to the shadows. I drifted over and collapsed onto the firm bed, pulling both sides of the blanket up and around myself.

Elline tossed a new log onto the fire. It hissed and spat, succumbing to the hungry flames. Dusting off her hands, she sat in a chair by the hearth. I saw her deftly thread a long needle with what looked like wire. I wanted to keep watching, but my eyelids felt as heavy as the cast iron pot in the fireplace.

I DREAMT OF THE TIME MY BROTHER AND I TOOK OUR UNCLE'S dinghy without permission. A squall rose out of nowhere, rain and wind pommeling our small, rickety boat. The craft rocked to and fro as we braced ourselves, huddled together against the bow. The waves were fierce, and I feared we wouldn't survive the night as we were tossed around in the darkness.

I woke in the pitch black. Bundled tightly in the blanket, though no longer lying on the cot. My body was upright, yet slumped, collapsed onto itself. Flexing my legs, I tried stretching to my full height, but met resistance. The dark enclosure had no give, and no amount of fidgeting or pushing provided any extra space around me. My breathing quickened as I began to panic. I managed to slide my hand up, thankful I could create a slight gap between the covering and my face. I felt myself gently swaying. Above me, the familiar sound of creaking ropes sung a sickening lullaby as I rocked.

I'm hanging in the tree.

I flailed about in my tight confines, awash with fright.

Worn out, I regained my senses enough to wonder if I could rub the rope back and forth on the branch until one or the other split in two. It was the hopeful thought of a child, but that didn't stop me. I pushed away the memory of the other cocoons hanging on the sturdy branches, rocking myself forward and back, forward and back, until I could no longer move.

The effort exhausted me, and I slouched defeated in my trap. A soft whine escaped my lips.

The frigid temperature acted next, as icy fingers wove their way inside, curling around my limbs. Tears froze halfway down my cheeks.

"*Tsk tsk tsk.* I didn't think a big man like you would crumble so easily."

"Let me out of here!" I screamed.

"Now, now. Settle yourself," Elline cooed. "I wasn't expecting you to wake so soon. I must have miscalculated the herbs this time. No matter," she sighed. "You've been prepared. I will offer you this warning, though—struggling won't do any good. Some others already learned that the hard way."

"What do you mean?" I begged, trying to turn my body to follow her voice. "Why am I here? What do you want from me?"

"Just close your eyes, let winter's grasp take you. An eternal frozen slumber is the best way. Otherwise, it will be a most painful experience if you're awake when he arrives. For that, I do apologize."

I could hear her chanting. Over and over, she repeated foreign, unnatural words. Her urgency grew with each utterance. A sudden, strong wind swirled around me, and the tree branch began to tremble. My casing jerked from side to side, and nausea enveloped me.

A deafening thunder roared, followed by screams reminiscent of frightened horses. I was struck dumb with terror. My bladder released and soaked my folded legs. I felt myself being lowered, as if the tree itself bowed down. Then silence descended, and I strained to listen.

I heard a growl, a low rumble like a wagon wheel traveling a rocky path. Snow crunched around me, and a snorting, hot breath warmed my neck through the barrier. I felt something sharp trace a line down my spine. I wished I hadn't woken.

It dragged along my cocoon, as if in search of a weakness in the material, until a claw pierced the thick sheath in the fabric I held away from my face. Beams of moonlight crept inside. A shadow passed over. A chill ran the length of my body as I looked at the hulking beast standing over me. Two curved horns sprouted from its head. Deep eyes burned fire red. A mouth elongated into a robust snout covered in thick silver fur. Drool pooled around sharp, glistening teeth. It exhaled into my face, and I choked on the pungent odor of burnt carcasses. I prayed for winter to take me, to freeze me on the spot and save me from the horrid beast.

Then, a creaking noise came from above. I felt the tree, dripping with sweetmeats, moving to stand upright once more.

For an instant, I thought I would be out of reach. Instead, with lightning speed, the beast sliced through me and pulled me to the ground. It tossed and tore at my body, and the chill descended over me once more. The demon rifled through my gut, my insides spilling out and melting through the thick snow. Miss Elline Dickens smiled affectionately at the monster.

"You never can resist the fresh ones, can you, my pet?"

Robin Knabel's short fiction has appeared in *The Raven Review*, *Hope Screams Eternal*, *Autumn Noir*, *Summer Bludgeon*, and has placed in the Writer's Digest Your Story Contest and in both the NYC Midnight Short Story & Microfiction Challenges. Her upcoming work will appear in the anthology *Darkness 101: Lessons Were Learned.* She's currently working on publishing a novella and her own collection of horror short stories. When not writing or editing, she can be found taking photos, sipping coffee, or being weighed down by a cat (or two) on her couch. www.robinknabel.com

TIME TRAVELER'S LAMENT

Emma E. Murray

It never snows when I travel back
though the air stings my lungs, just a couple degrees from
freezing.

She asks me why I go back so often
knowing I can't change a thing.
I only shrug her away or subdue her with kisses.
Nothing like ours, secret and terrible,
hidden away from your father,
full of shame.
Her family doesn't talk about women like they're wicked,
throbbing inside with poison nettles
in need of pruning, shearing, cauterizing
so nothing else can grow.

I go to the woods and watch you through barren limbs,
Hidden from sight because I'm not allowed to be seen.
I watch you walk to the tree we first kissed under.
Watch you hang

the rope.
Your knots are always perfect, like your mother's knitting.
Your body drops
with my stomach.
Biting winds rip through your thin sweater as you writhe
then dangle.
I hate myself for being protected by the bubble
that keeps our timelines from
tangling.

Why didn't you tell me?
I would've been there with you.
To stop you.
Take you away.
You couldn't see the future ahead of us.
Could you have meant to wander away alone on purpose?
To die in private, like an old dog.

If it was love, why couldn't you tell me?

Three days later it snowed, but you'd already been found and cut
down.
I never go back to that time.
Only to the place where I can torture myself
and keep you company
on the longest night of the year.

Emma E. Murray writes horror and dark speculative fiction. Her stories have appeared/are forthcoming in anthologies like *What One Wouldn't Do* and *Obsolescence*, as well as magazines such as *Vastarien*, *Pyre,* and *If There's Anyone Left*. When she's not writing, she loves playing pretend with her daughter, hiking, and being an obnoxious bard in D&D. EmmaEMurray.com

THE WINTERCLAUS TREE

Richard Lau

M y! What a nice ornament you have selected! I do carry a good assortment in my store, don't I? 'Tis the season, as they say, but I carry tree ornaments all year round. But with a store called "Emporium of Hang-ups" you'd expect that, wouldn't you?

Of course, I sell a lot more ornaments at this time of year with Christmas approaching. Plus, some of the braver folks have been buying them for the Winterclaus Tree.

What? You haven't heard of our Winterclaus Tree? I didn't take you for locals, but one shouldn't make assumptions these days. Still, we don't get many visitors way up here in the mountains.

The Winterclaus Tree is about five miles to the north of here in a small clearing. It's hard to find unless you know exactly where it is and can spot the unpaved road to it. You won't see any road signs or line of cars. It's not exactly a tourist destination. If you're really interested in seeing it, you can just follow one of the emergency vehicles heading out there. Heh. Sorry. Inside joke.

Ah! I've whetted your curiosity? Well, perhaps I said too much already. The Winterclaus Tree is one of our local secrets. Some residents won't even admit they know about it, but everyone here does.

But I'm the chatty, friendly type, and a good story is a good story, and the story of the Winterclaus Tree is certainly unusual, if not unique.

I'll relate some details to you, if you have the time and the interest, but just remember: you didn't hear it from me.

Deal? I'll even give you 10 percent off on the beautiful ornament you selected just to seal our little secret.

Now, where was I? Oh yes, the illustrious history of our Winterclaus Tree.

Long ago, when our village was even smaller than it is now, there was a wealthy man named Samuel Winterclaus. He was our resident Santa Claus. He kept his house decorated all year long, not out of laziness, but with the full, sincere spirit of Christmas.

People thought he was a little eccentric, but what harm was there? And aren't we all a little odd with our obsessions and hobbies? Especially way out here in the wilderness. If one isn't odd when one comes out here, a season or two will take care of that!

His jolliness and kind attitude were contagious, which helped many of the other villagers through difficult times. Even today, over half of our residents claim him as "family," despite the fact that it turned out he didn't have any close relatives nearby or otherwise.

When he died, he left instructions with his attorney for a tree to be brought over from his ancestral grounds in his home country. The name of the actual place is long forgotten.

Anyway, everyone in the community looked forward to the arrival of the tree, like a matter of civic pride for a village whose only bragging rights were to a small pond that froze over every winter. Everyone had expected something really impressive, like a giant sequoia or something. Just look at the sky-scraping trees around us! As I said, Winterclaus had been a very rich man. While he hadn't been one to boast, he'd always been generous, especially regarding the village and its residents.

So, everyone was surprised and disappointed by the runt of wood that arrived. While not a sapling, it was hardly more than five feet in height. The trunk was about as thick as my upper arm, and it was the damnedest oddest thing you've ever seen. It had the shape of a Douglas Fir, but instead of needles and cones, it was lush with big, elephant-ear leaves and white ping-pong-ball-sized fruit that sported a black dot, giving it the appearance of being covered with eyeballs.

Re-planting it hardly seemed worth the wait and all the trouble. The tree looked like something freakish from a tropical forest, and everyone doubted it would last its first winter. But it did.

Even after all these years, the tree barely tops seven feet tall, but it is the perfect height for decorating. But I'll get to that in a moment.

Winterclaus was buried in the clearing, and the tree planted over his body as a living memorial. He had donated all of his land to the village's public trust, with the stipulation that every winter solstice, the tree be decorated for Christmas. However, he also issued a caution along with his generosity: "Those who offend the tree by attempting to decorate it with inadequate or insincere spirit would face appropriate consequences."

Now, if there was a man in the village that was the polar opposite of Winterclaus, that man was Merle Hartoog. He couldn't be more stuck on himself than if he was a jar of peanut butter wrapped in duct tape.

At the time of Winterclaus' burial, Hartoog was the village mayor. Not because of popularity, but due to his oversized ambition and ego to cheat his way into the office. Most folks couldn't wait until his term was over, and hopefully, he would move onward, upward, and outward. In other words, out of our simple village and into a city that better matched his—how would you say it?—"sophistication."

For the tree's first decorating ceremony, Mayor Hartoog selected himself to be the first to decorate it, giving himself the honor of placing a gaudy plastic star topper on the tree. No junk like that here, I assure you!

Anyway, as the mayor approached the tree, he paused to bask at being the center of attention once again and turned to wave to the crowd.

At the same moment, a sweet six-year-old named Rebecca Siler, too young to know or care about political propriety, ran up to the tree, attempting to place one of her tiny rag dolls on its branches. The mayor quickly rushed over, almost flying over the snow on the ground, to sweep her up and put her behind him. "Mayors first, young lady," he chortled.

Then Hartoog leaned upwards to place his offering on top of the five-foot tree. Those who were there swear the tree's top leaned away, like a barmaid refusing the unwanted attentions of an amorous drunk.

Hartoog, not to be denied, reached into the foliage with his other hand to pull the tree's tip toward him.

There was a loud snap, and everyone assumed that the mayor, in his enthusiasm and determination, had broken off the top of the frail-looking tree.

But then the mayor screamed. He pulled out his arm, the end of it a mere stump, gushing like a water sprinkler pumping licorice-red liquid.

Hartoog was once again the center of attention as he ran to his people, screaming for a doctor and cursing the tree before passing out. It took a few seconds for those close by to the mayor to realize what happened, and word quickly spread through the crowd.

When the gathered villagers looked at the tree, it was proudly wearing Rebecca's doll as a crown.

Little Tommy Hickmon, who even now as an old man is known to tell a tall tale or two, said afterwards that while everyone was watching the mayor, Rebecca figured it was her turn. He swears to this day that he saw the tree bow its tip like a friendly horse, allowing Rebecca to place her doll at its very top.

Winterclaus' warning blew through everyone's mind like a chilling wind. Every generation hears about Winterclaus, his warning, his tree, Rebecca, and old Hartoog and his stump.

Later, someone found the mayor's glove spat out at the base of the tree. The glove was wrinkled and tattered, as if the tree had chewed it. It was still soaked with blood, but otherwise empty. His hand was never found.

Now, I can see the look of horror on your face. And I'm sure some big city folks would have immediately attacked the tree with saws and axes and torches.

But we here in this village are a different lot. Besides, not many people liked Hartoog, and many thought he had finally gotten what he deserved, especially after his treatment of Rebecca.

Our isolation in these mountains has left us very accepting of the joyful and horrible aspects of Nature. Two sides of the same coin, as it were. Can't have one without the other.

And in our respect and gratitude to Winterclaus, we've always accepted his tree for what it is, what it stands for, and cherish our tradition. The Winterclaus Tree gives our village a little extra bit of character, something we can call our own.

And the children, bless 'em. The sincere and the innocent decorate the tree without mishap. Those with doubts know they should decline. And I think they all grow up to be better adults because of it.

But even after all these years, at least two or three times a solstice, some fool gets the idea to test the tree. This time of year, there's often an uptick of wood-chopping mishaps, hands getting mangled in animal traps, or losing fingers to frostbite. No one looks into these "accidents" because, really, it ain't nobody's business.

I've taken up enough of your time with my little tale. I'm sure you have some place to go. Our humble little village is never a destination, just a short travel break or overnight stay on the way to somewhere more interesting and exciting. Someplace that offers more than a festive winter tree.

The other villagers always say I talk more than I should. Part of being a lonely old shopkeeper, I suppose. Everyone here knows everything, so there's rarely much to say.

So, when an outsider like yourself shows up, well, forgive me for being gabby.

Would you like your ornament gift-wrapped?

I'm afraid I might do a clumsy job.

Normally, it's tough enough to wrap fragile and round objects. However, with all these years of selling ornaments, I *had* gotten quite good at wrapping the little rascals.

But now, you see, I'm still getting used to having only two fingers on my right hand. The others got caught in a car door a couple of weeks ago.

———

Richard Lau is an award-winning writer who has been published in magazines, newspapers, anthologies, the high-tech industry, and online. He thanks Barbara, a reader for all seasons.

THE ROPE MAKER

Riv Rains

Her shadow was twisted.

Against the wall, it hung contorted. That wasn't the winter moon's fault. It rose full and steady, but that shadow... it was different. Ever since she'd crossed his grave. The Rope Maker's. Under the shivering willow tree.

Clank-clank.

The sense of his rattle and crank had followed her all afternoon. The whir of gears, the shush of the spools—a never-ending rhythm at odds with her heartbeat.

Impossible.

She'd gone about her day, documenting the old Ropery, collecting the memories of a place lost to time. Red brick and crumbling mortar, an avenue of musty, cold arches running for a third of a mile down the narrow ropewalk. At one end, timber stocks, gears, hooks—the fixings of the trade wilful in their silence—fibres of the last rope still clinging to their carcasses. At the other, shrunk by distance, the matching set, shafts of feeble dust motes weaving where men once withered.

Her shadow had grown thicker every step.

Normally, Razi loved her job. The silence of old structures like an eternal yawn. They hushed your chaos and parted your lips in reverence. She captured those moments for the new vintage market. The creep of ivy across a threshold, the rust mudding a lever shut.

Razi had a story to write. Chilled to bone or not, she'd wound on, the fall of her passage echoing through the long, narrow structure, feet scuffing on time's ridges, stone worn to channels by the artists themselves.

The footsteps of her shadow.

Refusing to tremble, she'd explored, forming history's decay into words, armed with a camera, notebook, and a pencil fumbled by frozen fingers. The assignment should have been a dream, tied to the banks of a lazy river—each bite of lunch soaked by a struggling sun—but as her day retreated, chill climbing the air, the rattle and bind seemed caught at the back of her throat.

Ludicrous, of course.

Unless it wasn't.

ALONE WITH THE NIGHT, RAZI WAS PLAGUED BY NIGHTMARES; her sleep scythed away by gnarled leather hands weaving yarn through her ribs. She hung shaking in the second-floor window of a clucking lady's bosomy B&B, with nothing to fear except her shadow tightening in turns. Since the sun had fallen, a whispered count came brushing against the back of her neck, the warmth within her calling out to the frigid night, and an incessant clanging of gears churned her soul from inside out.

She'd be butter soon, if they didn't stop.

Huddled on the windowsill, cold sweat icing her skin, Razi tried to keep the clatter from reaching her teeth.

Clank-clank.

The visage outside hung in greys, a painting no camera would do justice. By design, hers was the closest B&B to the ruins. Languishing fields surrounded it, dormant grasses washed into browns by moonlight. Along the river, frost-cold branches cracked their knuckles in a blued breeze.

A hushed evening.

Razi tucked herself behind the warped window frame, craning to watch as an owl vanished beyond the corner of the building, its bone-bright arc swallowed by the deeper shadows of russet arches. The Ropery.

His Ropery.

Clank-clank.

Her body reeled back, eyes forced wide by the leather and spin waiting behind them. Panting, she focused on the river. A silver ribbon drawn through the night, water rippling where willow canes rinsed their fingers.

His willow.

Razi blinked cogs; spun fibres scratching at her eyes.

What was going on? Most places she went didn't want to wake, or didn't need to—at least not to live again in her stories. They'd done so much in their time, known so many hands. It was their right to rest.

If only tonight, she could find some rest of her own.

Clank-clank.

She hadn't meant to disturb him, hadn't noticed his tired grave marker until already squatted upon him. There was little choice once she'd seen—leap up, pants and pee clinging in spirals to her bare thighs as she fled. She'd crashed to a stop on the other side of his skeletal canopy, the bared willow swinging.

She'd never peed on a grave before. At least, not to her knowledge.

Clank-clank.

Shadows tightened over her chest.

He was down there.

The Rope Maker. Shallow, in the riverbank.

Clank-clank.

Clank-clank.

HER FIRST STEP WAS COLD AS FROST. THE SHOCK OF IT SIZZLING a warning through her veins. Why didn't she remember heading into the night? No phone. No torch. Why hadn't she chosen to dress? Razi caught at the breast of her thin linen nightgown and let its softness coarsen her fear.

Why go out there at all?

Common sense turned her chin, the warm windowed embrasure she'd left behind, concealing the comforting arms of living folk. She couldn't relent.

It was him.

His whistling in her ears, the roll and turn of coarse fibres hushing her, tormenting her shadow—his shadow—pressing it back against her senses as she wavered.

Razi fought. The weapons of winter's darkness were cruel against her feet. Bare branches and brambles, tearing at skin and fabric, slicing frozen shin and thigh until she became a wild thing. Twigs in hair, sobs as song, moonbeams lodged in her teeth.

His shadow grinned.

He welcomed her plunge from grace, pushed her on with a cluck of his lip, his caressing, coaxing palms upon her skin, turning her attentions, winding her spirit with his fingers. He drew her as his rope-topper, urging steps becoming her pulse, her heart just a burr against his pull.

She went to him.

Unwillingly at first—the backs of her toes scraping grooves in the frosted leaf litter, mouth gasping, salt trails glittering in the light—then more quietly. He became firmer as she neared, her spine steady in his vice, strands bound so tight she could not bend, not turn, nor unravel within that grip. All the while, his shadowed hand rode in the back of her throat, stroking her screams, tuning each rasp to his hawser.

He was crooning.

Beneath frozen soil.

An old man's murmur, a lilting melody, called back from her purpled lips. Its pieces trapped as whispers all this time, in the pulley well, the horse halter, the church bell ringers, the butcher string on your shelf. His hums seeped from the hardened ground where rope lay rotting, each coil drawing her along, pared to the breathy whistles as he worked.

She chased his echo against the dark, through the Ropery until she reached his willow. Its drape a shivered caress, shredding her soul under the knowing eyes of the moon. Beneath that naked canopy, she twisted her toes into her own bitter stains.

He was there.

In silence thicker than ice, a cloying, stagnant thing that pounded at her head and crushed her pulse. He released her fetters, unspooling her like a dropped weave, casting her slithering to the ground. Her fingers clawed in frigid soil at his request.

Scraping.

Twists of damp ripped from her bitten lips as she worked, embedding him beneath her nails, crawling into the wintered earth—on top of him—hungry. She couldn't name her inhuman sounds, the guttural urges coaxed by his whistles. He had bound her will from reach, mastering her as easily as any braid, his walk down the lines now smooth, shadowy feet padding the arches again, shaping her as she deepened the night.

Her knuckles clanked against his.

She scooped at him, baring snowy remains worms had freed of flesh, scrambling to clutch him to her chest, to warm him as cascades and shards between her breasts. Grunts of glee choking out as his clotted earth slid cold across her thighs—against the sweated flesh beneath her linen. She would awaken him! Smoulder him back to life! Revive him with her essence, draw him to the heat of her blooded-heart and let it twist to his appetite.

She scavenged.

Every piece. Until they lay scattered, thirsty, and woken, a muddle of decay, her body cast back among his, sprawled with linen rucked past her hips, remains chattering bone to bone.

Nimbly, his leathered hands shivered through her, snipping her threads, releasing her windings, soaking her blood, bile, and sap into his grave dirt—bathing in her once more—burning off his dank of death.

She convulsed.

He'd unwound her to re-wind himself.

She was the ragged, spent ends of a rope, discarded beneath his canopy, cold melodious laughter for anaesthetic. But he'd made her thankful.

Until he let go.

Her wretched screams reached for the Ropery, the willow, and the owl. The lift of her ribcage as he clattered into being hung like a howl on the moon. Razi crumpled. Mere snips of breath left to her, sacrificial pieces dropped from an artist's deft fingers.

The wastage.

She lay, a weeping bruise upon the earth, blue as ice, listening to the clank-clank of the willow canes, The Rope Maker walking, leaving, whistling.

Her soul in his coils.

Riv Rains is a collection of rusting gears lubricated exclusively by chocolate. Bookgeek, author, and conjurer of creative daemons, she'd have a lot more time if she wasn't also captain and chief to two kids, four boats, and one husband. Born amid the sticks of rural Australia, she finds words in the magick of sunsets and river swells, chassis and unsuspecting rib cages. Riv welcomes you to seek out the spawn of her tumultuous mind at rivrains.com or on social media @rivrains and hopes to reach you through the gaps of many more heartfelt pages.

BLEAK WINTER

Dawn DeBraal

January 7, 1848

Clem hasn't come back from hunting. He left two days ago, and I am afraid something has happened to him. However, he left me a recent kill buried in the snow behind the cabin. I am grateful that there is plenty of snow to melt, and that I can breastfeed Jack. I am scared of being alone here and snowed in. The wind whistles and the big tree in front of the cabin rattles in protest.

When Clem left, he took the horse. We have no nearby neighbors. I have only Jack. There is wood that's split and stacked outside, so we'll keep warm. I hope it's enough. When Jack is asleep, I bring some to the cabin. Oh, Clem, my darling. Where are you? Hurry home. I am afraid you've had an accident. I can not take Jack out in this weather to search for you. I can not make it to the next settlement miles away carrying an infant in this cold weather.

JANUARY 9, 1848

There is still no sign of Clem. If he is injured, I pray he made it to the Miller's or some other cabin. Jack slept while I hauled extra wood to the door, trying to build a wall to prevent drifting. It's been snowing non-stop since yesterday. It's all I can do to keep the porch free of it. The wind drifts the snow up the side of the house, causing the door to be blocked shut. When Clem returns, I am going to tell him to change the swing of the door. A drift could keep us shut in here. I wish the window we ordered from Kansas City would have come before the snow. At least we would have a window to climb out of if the door is snowed closed. I think Jack feels my restlessness. He seems easily agitated. I hear the snapping of the oak in front and I realize how cold it is outside, grateful the fireplace keeps us warm.

JANUARY 10, 1848

I took the hatchet out and chopped at the frozen meat in the snow. I still have potatoes and carrots stored in the root cellar. I made it out to the locker but had to shovel snow and chip at the ice to get to the vegetables. I found frost on some baskets near the door, and dragged them away from the opening, selecting some of the frozen vegetables to bring in. I do not want rot to take hold once things start to thaw.

JANUARY 28, 1848.

Wolves were outside our door last night. I loaded the gun with the few shells we have. I see they tried eating the frozen meat buried in the snow. I am angry, but I also feel sorry for them. Like me, they are stuck with the relentless cold weather and deep snow. Clem, oh, my dear, where are you? I pray that you stay safe with a neighbor and that things are alright. The meat you left might not last much longer now that the wolves have found it. I try to put some firewood over the carcass to keep them from taking our food. I stacked the wood high, so it will take time to get at it, but at least it will be there when I need it. I pray every night for your return. Jack feels your absence and is fussy. I will get him outside when the weather is better.

FEBRUARY 11, 1848

I fear Clem is dead. He would have found a way home if he were alive or sent a neighbor to let us know. When will this snow stop? I wonder if there are others out there going through the same thing? If I were by myself, I would travel to the Miller's. I am going stir crazy sitting here thinking the worst. When I went out to the larder, I saw the wolves had knocked some of the wood pile over. Lucky, they did not get to the frozen meat. I chipped away with the hatchet to take some shavings of venison. I will make soup tonight. Opening the root cellar, I found a rat eating my vegetables. Screaming, I took the shovel, struck at it, and cut its head off. It's survival of the fittest as a mother to an infant. I will survive this. I threw the body out and took some vegetables inside.

FEBRUARY 13, 1848

The rat carcass is gone. I imagine the wolves got it last night. Now I am angry with myself. I should have cleaned it and buried it under the woodpile. I don't know how desperate one must be to eat a rat, but what Clem left behind is almost gone. He is dead. I know this and feel it in my heart. I chopped at some branches that fell from the large oak to use as kindling. I am so bored I could scream.

FEBRUARY 28, 1848

A branch laden with snow on the huge oak crashed down and crushed the porch. I panicked when I realized I could not open the door. Damn you, Clem, why did you install a door that opens out? I paced the floor in a panic until I spied the hatchet. I went to the bedroom and started chopping at the logs. I swung wildly, watching wood chips fly away, and then fell exhausted. It will take me a great deal of time, but I will keep at it until I put a hole in the wall to get out. Then I must find a way to remove the branch in front of the door. I remember telling Clem to build the cabin back from that tree. He said it was perfect where it was, it would cool the house in the summer. I should have put my foot down. It will take me days to carve out a new opening. I have only a bit of food and a bucket of snow melt.

MARCH 3, 1848

I reached daylight today through the thick logs of the cabin. I am making progress. I hope I have enough chipped away to squeeze through the opening soon. Then I will tackle the branch barring the door. My arms and back ache. I have taken to wearing Clem's pants and shirt. They are much warmer than a dress. Jack feels my relief and has been less fussy. Poor baby has to listen to the hatchet against wood all day.

MARCH 4, 1848

I got through the opening! The wind whistled through the hole in the back, but I stuffed some clothing and old blankets in the opening. Once outside, I saw the oak branch that bars the door. It's so large, and together with a good portion of the porch roof that it crushed when it fell, it has us blocked in. At first, I chopped in the middle to chip away at it, but I feared it would all come down on me. I couldn't risk the tree branch falling on me, leaving Jack alone–a thought I can't bear.

I will have to use the new opening instead. At least I can get in and out of the cabin now, and there is no large oak to stop me. Earlier, I grabbed wood, vegetables, and a bucket of fresh snow and shoved it through the opening.

I'm going to need a door for this new doorway. Earlier, I grabbed a saw from the lean-to. Sawing the wood is easier to manage than hacking at the logs. I'm using the wood that Clem had stored in the lean-to to fashion a door of sorts. We were going to build Jack a bedroom, but that isn't going to happen. I refuse to live here. I am moving to a city and will never live in the wilderness again.

APRIL 1, 1848

So here I am on the day of Fool's, trying to survive. At least the snow is starting to melt. It gives me hope that I can tie Jack on my back and walk to the Miller's. I am sure I know where their house is. How I wished someone would come out here and rescue us. I am so exhausted. When I feel myself losing touch with reality, Jack pulls me back. Oh, Clem, you have missed so much of your boy. He is crawling now and getting into everything. I've torn apart one of my heavy dresses to make him some new clothes. I am not a seamstress by any measure, but I am proud of my work.

APRIL 15, 1848

I walked miles from the cabin with Jack tied to my body. It took several hours, but we made it to the Miller's! Ever Miller says he'll return to the house with his mules when the snow melts. He will help me move to the city. I am grateful for kind neighbors. I tell them about the branch falling on the front door and the days of chopping at the logs with the hatchet. Penelope hugs me, telling me she is proud of what I've done. We wait out the weather.

MAY 1, 1848

Tomorrow we head to the cabin to pick up my things. I am eager to leave the area. Before I left to walk to the Miller's, I wrote a letter and left it at the cabin for Clem, just in case he is still alive and comes home. I told Mr. Miller he could have all the vegetables from the root cellar. I don't want to go back, but there are things I can't bear to leave behind.

MAY 2, 1848

I can hardly write this entry. I have given my son Jack over to the Miller's. They don't know it yet. They say they understand, but I don't think they do. I will be arrested if I go to the city.

When we went back to the cabin, Mr. Miller loaded up

vegetables from the root cellar into the back of his wagon while I grabbed the few precious things I needed. I saw the note still on the table for Clem where I'd left it, letting him know to contact the Miller's, that they would know where I am.

I took one last look around the cabin and went outside for the last time. When we were getting ready to leave, I noticed the woodpile and spied a piece of plaid material. I went over and scraped at the material with my foot. Curious, I started to remove the wood and screamed when I found a rotting hand.

Mr. Miller moved me aside and began throwing the wood.

"Clem!" I screamed. He had not abandoned me, but was buried under the woodpile all winter.

When Mr. Miller dug the body out, there was a bullet hole in Clem's forehead, and much of his torso and thighs were missing.

I don't remember shooting Clem or burying him under the woodpile. After much thought, I remember how we first ate Daisy, our horse. When we ran out of meat, I thought Clem went hunting. The buried carcass was not a deer, as I had convinced myself, but my husband. He didn't abandon us, but fed us through the winter.

I am going to cut my wrists. I can't live with the guilt and the shame. A mother will never let her baby starve to death, no matter what. Jack depended on me to provide milk. I did what I had to do to keep my son alive.

God, forgive me.

Sarah Wainwright

Dawn DeBraal lives in rural Wisconsin with her husband, Red, two rescue dogs, and a stray cat. She has published over 500 stories, poems, and drabbles in several online magazines and anthologies.

IT ONLY CAME WITH THE SNOW

RJ Fuller

I
t only came with the snow. This... thing, this entity which could not be named, it only came with the snow.

Some say it was a long-forgotten god, an angry and resentful Old Testament kind of god bound to the Earth and its people. A god with wrath and vengeance in its heart.

Others say it was the tree that carried the evil. An apple tree, borne of a seed no bigger than a tick, was planted on the hilltop just days before a raging battle of the country's great war. It soaked up the blood of the town's fathers and brothers, drinking in their anger and hatred, then sprouted and grew into something unnatural. A tree that in the dead of winter, when it was barren of life and fruit, demanded there be blood to keep it alive, in a vicious cycle of greed and fear.

I believe it was the snow.

We had an unnatural snow.

It came only one day a year, always in the first week of December. The exact day varied, though nobody knew why. But we all knew it was coming. And with it, death.

The snow fell on December third this year. The day before

the snow, a familiar hush had fallen over the town. Gone were the neighborly waves hello. Gone was the chitter of local chatter. People tugged their heavy coats close to their chests and glanced at the sky with trepidation, shivering despite wool and fur.

The shops along main street closed by six that evening. By half past, the streets emptied, the residents having holed up in their homes with the drapes snapped shut.

Our home was no different.

Mother made a hearty beef stew with vegetables for dinner. However, the warmth of the kitchen and familiar smell of her best dish lacked the usual lively banter between my sister and myself. We slathered fresh butter on warm bread in silence, while Mom and Dad watched us. Mom chewed her lip. Dad fidgeted with his fork.

After dinner, my sister took her evening bath while I sat between my trembling parents and watched some bland sitcom on television. The sound of the T.V. grated, rather than comforted.

But it was normal.

When my sister finished, I took my evening bath. I lay in the tub until the water turned frigid and the skin on my fingers and toes shriveled like an old man's. When I returned to the living room, my sister was seated between my parents on the sofa. Her blank stare at the television screen seemed to echo my own hollow soul.

By ten o'clock, we were in bed. Though we were far too old to sleep in their bed, my parents pulled us into their room to sleep, curled up on either side of us. We didn't protest. We didn't sleep, either. My father's hand trembled on my shoulder all night. My mother silently wept. My sister lay facing me, her bottom lip quivering. Occasionally, a stray tear fell from her closed eyes, but she, who was normally prone to teen-girl hysterics, remained still and silent.

We were out of bed by dawn. My sister and I trudged to our rooms to get ready for the day. The smell of pancakes drowning in hot, sticky syrup wafted up the stairs as I dressed. I squelched the nausea.

We exited our rooms nearly simultaneously, then descended the stairs in silence, my sister leading the way. Father sat in his chair watching us, his morning paper missing. Mother stood behind the dining room table wringing her hands. She'd laid out a spread: bacon and eggs, freshly squeezed juice, pancakes. My sister looked at our mother, looked at the food, looked at my mother again, then turned away and shrugged into her heavy winter boots and coat.

Our mother opened her mouth as if to say something, then quickly slapped her hand across it to cover it up. I gave her an apologetic smile, then stuffed myself into my own winter boots and oversized coat.

Mom and Dad didn't move.

My sister opened the door.

A cold rush of wind blew in, as if it had been waiting at the threshold all night for us to let it in. More likely, it had been waiting for us to come out.

My sister took the first step. She hovered on the threshold for a moment, her body rigid, caught between warm and cold, safety and fear; balancing like a girl on an invisible tightrope. As if it sensed her trepidation, the snow sunk beneath her boot, pulling her forward and forcing her away from the comfort and security of our home.

She didn't so much as gasp.

I hesitated only a second longer. The warmth of the kitchen beckoned me back inside as I faced the biting wind and drifts of untouched snow before us. I nearly turned away from the cold sting of morning, wanting desperately to run back into my mother's arms and forget the rest of the world. But that wasn't an option. The wind reminded me of that, as it blew into the house once again and turned around and shoved me out the door.

I fell forward. My boots sank in the powdery snow. My sister grabbed my hand and steadied me before I could fall, but I shivered against the cold.

The door slammed shut behind us. We didn't look back. Our eyes remained steadfastly forward, glued to the blanket of white that had overtaken our colorful world.

The walk was slow and arduous, each step an effort of Everest proportions. The further we walked, the deeper the snow became, until my legs could barely push forward. Only the wind kept me going. The burning, biting wind seemed to reach into my chest and squeeze its skeletal hand around my lungs and drag me forward.

It wasn't long before we saw other prints in the snow, the heavy footprints of the other children. It should have been a consolation seeing their footprints, but it only made the sky seem even grayer and heavier.

My sister clutched my hand so tight, I bit a gloved finger on my free hand to keep from crying out. The closer we came to it, the harder she squeezed, until finally it was within our sight.

The tree sat on an empty hill at the edge of town. Its black branches stretched out over the field of untouched white, like some sullen and macabre snow globe. A circle of children had already formed around the base of the hill. My sister and I walked up and took our places with them.

A few stragglers quickly claimed their spots in the circle. I glanced around at the pink, weather-beaten faces of the other children. Every face belonged to someone I knew, went to school and church with.

My sister was on my left, still clutching my hand in hers. To my right was Bobby Billingsley. I couldn't say that Bobby was a friend. He'd once punched me in the face and stolen my lunch

money. But when he clasped his hand in mine, and I felt his
fingers quiver with a shake that had nothing to do with the cold,
that bloody nose didn't seem quite so important anymore.

I squeezed his hand, offering what little reassurance I could.

When all the children had joined hands, the air stirred. Snow
began to trickle off the tree limbs.

I held my breath.

The tree's great branches rocked. Its black and barren limbs
swayed over the blanket of white and steely gray backdrop.

Our circle inched forward.

One step.

Another.

The branches scraped at the sky, clawing blindly at the bitter
morning.

We took another step forward.

The branches creaked in anger until the bark twisted and
broke. It was as if the tree was angry at the ground for holding it
immobile. A long whip of a branch swung past, whistling angrily
in my ear. My breath caught in my chest. The great black
branches swooped over the crowd like a drowning man clawing
at the ocean.

A soft sound filled the snowy silence. The creaking and
splintering of wood pierced the biting wind. Snow fell over the
circle, marking each child as if it were a game:

Duck…

Duck…

Duck…

A scream shattered the circle. The branchy black fingers
swooped down and clawed at the crowd. I shut my eyes tight,
still clinging to my sister and Bobby Billingsley.

The screaming stopped as suddenly as it had begun.

The whistling of the branches and creaking of the wood
slowly ebbed until the tree was silent once more. My sister fell

to her knees, pulling me down with her. Somewhere, I heard a cry.

"Emily! It got Emily!"

My sister wrapped me in her arms and sobbed. Bobby Billingsley remained standing, still gripping my right hand, but I could feel his body shaking. I pulled him into our embrace.

It was midday by the time the children in the circle released our holds on each other. We all trudged away from the tree. I watched Bobby shuffle through the snow towards town, his back hunched and shaking, while my sister and I made our way home in silence.

Mother and Father were waiting at the door. They pulled us into their arms and wailed. My sister and I let them, but we had no more tears to give in return.

The next day, the snow was gone. Green grass swayed in the breeze on the hill with the tree, and apple blossoms danced on its lush branches.

RJ Fuller is a hard working mom who loves all things fantastical. She's a sucker for creepy tales and hard-boiled detective stories. When not creating worlds of her own, RJ can be found baking sweet desserts or hanging out with her kid and her dog.

THE LAST DANCE

Mia Dalia

"Dancing, huh? I wouldn't call it dancing."

"What would you call it?"

I looked at the twisted shapes before me.

"Writhing, maybe. Writhing in torment."

"That's dark, man."

"You asked."

I shrug. Simon shrugs right back at me.

We are in The Dancing Forest. Or, more specifically, Танцующий лес (that's Tantsuyushchiy les in romanized form, and I can only pronounce the second half), a pine forest on the Curonian Spit in Kaliningrad Oblast, Russia. In the middle of the winter.

That's probably where the dark imagery is coming from. No one should go visit remote Russian locations in the winter.

Being from Michigan, I thought I knew winter. I did *not* know winter. Nothing like this. Nothing like this forbidding, foreboding brutality of weather. It makes you feel like summers were only ever an illusion. Like winter is all there is. Like you'll never be warm again.

They call it the dead of winter for this reason, I believe. Absence of warmth equates itself to the absence of life. We shouldn't be here, I think, over and over again. But this was the plan. A carefully constructed and meticulously carried out one, at that.

We dreamed of this place. Ever since we found out about it. It sang a siren song to both of us, albeit on different frequencies.

Simon sees it as a nightmare come to life–a subject of his new documentary.

Me, I'm an arborist and a dendrologist, who minored in silvology. I have never encountered a single layperson who knew what all three of those words meant. Most don't know any and so I got used to immediately following it up with, 'trees, I study trees and forests.'

"Ah," most people say, "a tree hugger."

Sure, that's me, a tree hugger. I never met a tree I didn't like. Even these strange, bewildering pines before me. I'm mesmerized by them.

I only wish I could admire them and still have feeling in my extremities at the same time.

But no, Simon insisted we go in the winter. Flights will be cheaper, he said. The scenery will look starker. He's always thinking from behind his camera lens.

Right now, he's thrilled. Fully in his element. The camera is on, and he asks me to say a few words for posterity.

I don't love doing it, but I've gotten used to it over the years.

"Hello. My name is Evan Reid, and I study trees and forests. We are standing in the middle of the famous Dancing Forest of Russia. The pine trees around us have convoluted themselves into the whimsical shapes that most associate with dancing, hence the name. There is no other forest like that on Earth.

"There are other forests where trees are twisted and oddly shaped–most notably in Poland–but that's a different story altogether. In Poland they mangled the trees on purpose to produce unique furniture. Only WWII interfered with those plans, and so nothing ever came of it.

"There are also places known as drunken forests where trees, rotating out of their normal vertical alignment, seem like falling-over drunks. But, again, those are different. And are mostly present in the northern subarctic taiga…"

Simon is doing that thing with his hand, like I'm going too far into technicalities for the general audience.

"Point is, there is nothing in the world like these trees around us. Planted in the 1960s with the intention of stabilizing the sand dunes, some say the trees' dance follows the movement of the sands. But the real reason behind the shape of these trees is unknown. It's only speculation. Scientists suspect it might be the fault of a certain moth caterpillar that damages the trees' apical buds at an early age."

I sense myself beginning to veer off into too much science once again and course-correct. "But it is the locals who have the best tales."

Simon takes his cue, reverses the camera, and jumps in.

"Hi there. I'm Simon Wright, and I'm the fiction to Evan's facts. Or am I? We've been staying locally for the past week and gathering stories about this forest. Let me tell you… it's wild. It's really out there."

Simon grins. He loves this. Even his voice changes when he goes into this mode. He's a surprise-delighted kid and an intrepid adventurer in one. The guy holding back the curtain for you to take a peek at the mysteries of the world. This is why his programs do well–that genuine sense of excitement.

"According to one of the local legends, the trees were made to dance to prove the power of God. Or maybe the famous Russian witch, Baba Yaga, has enslaved these poor souls for eternity for some unforgiven trespasses. Or maybe the ghosts of

Nazi soldiers haunt this place. Believe it or not, there was a Nazi gliding school at this remote location before the trees were planted. Some locals say the forest is a place where positive and negative energies clash, and the force of that power has manipulated the trees into their shapes."

Simon pauses, his eyes shining with excitement.

"I'm vibing with that theory, personally. The idea that there are places in the world where the barrier between the two worlds is thin, permeable even–that's nothing new. In fact, dig around and you may find references to this exact idea throughout time and in many cultures and continents. Why not here? Look around." Simon slowly pans the camera away from him to do a 360 shot. "Why wouldn't it be here?"

He brings the camera back to himself. Beams his trademark grin. Then powers it off.

"What do you think?"

"It's good. Maybe throw in some local color, and you got it in the bag."

The local color is tougher, given that the color seems to have been bleached from this land due to a harsh climate and harsher living conditions. Western culture doesn't appear to have penetrated this place. The locals are not friendly. Too insular, too distrusting of foreigners.

Look at Curonian Spit on the map. This very location is surreal: a long narrow strip of land surrounded by the Baltic Sea. It looks like someone drew a line on a map by mistake, but no, it's a real place. It has changed hands throughout history but has long been firmly in Russian grasp. Politics and geography are never far apart.

We're staying in Rubachy. The name has something to do with fishes. It's a small rural settlement with almost nothing of note but an old church revamped from Lutheran to Russian Orthodox some time ago.

Our accommodations are at the Altrimo hotel, the only local place available. Three well-earned stars, it's a small oasis of modernity, surprisingly charming and bright. They speak English there too, however stiltedly. Plus, there's free Wi-Fi. It's surprising how expensive it is, given that there are no other options. The deal on the flights more than offset the hotel costs. Simon's good about things like that, having worked for so long on a shoestring budget.

When we left the hotel this morning, I bundled up in an Arctic-rated parka, warm hat, gloves, socks, everything. Layers upon layers of thermals and wool, and yet I feel the warmth leaching out of me on a bone-deep level. Strangely enough, I'm starting to blame it on the forest, on these twisted trees.

I don't want to buy into Simon's supernatural bullshit. Hell, Simon doesn't even buy into most of it; it's just what sells. But when I look around, I can imagine with an alarming ease that we are in a different world. An infinitely stranger and more dangerous world than the one we left behind just this morning.

When I first started researching this place, I looked at some images from the summer. It was sunny, bright, lively. It looked like a remote beach resort. The winter has stolen all of that color and liveliness and put on a stark monochromatic scenery in its stead. The ground is white with snow, and the trees appear as black silhouettes against the milky white sky.

The change of seasons here must be serious business–like going from a technicolor movie to a black-and-white one. The brightness of our parkas, our very presence here, feels like a violation upon this land.

"Can we go?" I ask my friend.

"Getting freaked out?" Simon wiggles his eyebrows at me comically.

"Nah, just… hungry," I lie.

It is much darker in the forest than it is outside of it. The dancing trees are doing a terrific job of keeping the sunlight away from reaching the mossy ground. In person, it looks almost nothing like it does in the pictures. The atmosphere here is thick enough to cut with a knife. Oppressing. Gloomy.

Simon hands me his camera and starts to climb one of the trees clumsily in his gloves and winter boots.

"What are you doing, man?"

"The locals have this theory that climbing a tree can make a wish come true or add a year to your life."

The tree Simon is climbing features an almost perfect external ring not too far from its base. Not at all the sort of tree rings I'm used to studying.

I take my gloves off and snap some pictures of Simon, then immediately put them back on. Simon has adapted for this, of course, by cutting off the tops from the fingers of his gloves. I don't know how he even has enough feeling in his fingertips to press the camera buttons.

He completes his climb and jumps down.

"Did you do a wish or a year?"

"Not telling," he grins, like a kid.

"I don't think it's like a birthday wish and you gotta keep it a secret or it doesn't come true."

Simon shrugs. "You never know."

He takes off his gloves and puts his fingers in his mouth.

"What happened? Are you ok?"

Simon takes his fingers out and shows me. The tips, left unprotected by his gloves, are riddled with tiny bloody cuts.

"The bark got me," he says. "Sharp. Didn't even feel it happen."

"I wonder if the car has a first aid kit."

"I'm surprised that thing has all four wheels."

It's true. Our rental is cheap and runs, albeit begrudgingly,

70

but it features nothing but the basics. It's a jalopy without even properly working heat.

"We'll fix you up at the hotel."

"Don't fuss, man. It's fine. I'll be playing piano in no time." Simon does a shuffle that has nothing to do with piano playing, not that he even knows how to play one. He takes the camera back from me.

"Can we head back now?"

"Sure, sure, you big baby. I told you to bring snacks."

I did bring snacks–everything I could sneak out from the modest free breakfast buffet–but I ate them all. I'm not sure how long we've been here. Time seems to work differently in this place.

"Do you remember where we parked?"

"Sure I do."

Simon prides himself on his innate navigational abilities, his internal Ariadne's string. No small feat in this day and age of GPS apps. He seldom gets us lost, and so I follow him with reasonable confidence as he traces our steps back to the car.

We walk fast, and I'm starting to warm up. The trees observe our passage in silence. There's nothing here to concentrate on but putting one foot in front of the other. My mind, unchained from focus, unwound from the weight of responsibility, eases itself into a trip down memory lane.

MY FATHER'S MID-LIFE CRISIS ARRIVED RIGHT ON TIME, JUST AS he turned forty-five. He left my mom, quit his insurance office job, and ended up working for a forestry department and living with a much-younger woman named Gaia. Though I snuck a look at her driver's license once and, sure enough, it was Gayle.

Gayle/Gaia was perfectly nice. It made it impossible to hate her, but I could never bring myself to like her either. She had a curious effect on my father, though, mellowing him out into a barely recognizable version of himself. During my mandatory weekend visits, I'd look at the happy bearded man across the table from me as we gathered over yet another variation of bland grains and rubbery tofu and wonder, "Who is that man?"

The man my father became in the second act of his life loved trees. He taught me to love them, too. It was the only thing we had ever wholeheartedly agreed on.

When a heart attack carried him off into an early grave, I wept into Gaia's patchouli-scented shoulder with a force of emotion I didn't expect of myself. And then I went back to school and changed my I-don't-know-what-I-want-to-do-with-my-life English major to forestry.

School was also where I met Simon.

A most inauspicious of meetings, really: I puked on the guy during a party at a fraternity neither of us ended up joining. He found it hilarious. We've been best friends ever since.

Unlike me, Simon always knew what he wanted to do with his life. He loved movies, with a sort of deep, steady love that precludes a person from considering any other choices. He veered into documentaries later, seemingly as a direct response to the rising prevalence of CGI in cinema. He said he wanted to deal with what was real. Or surreal, if possible.

It wasn't an easy field to break into, but eventually, Simon blew up on YouTube. Something about the locations and the stories he picked, and his inimitable brand of enthusiastic presentation, resonated with the audiences.

Unlike many college friends, we didn't drift apart after graduation. We made a concerted effort to stay in each other's lives until it was no longer an effort, but a second nature. Throughout all the changes in our personal lives and our careers, we remained one another's constant. I, for one, drew a great degree of comfort from it. I think Simon did, too.

This trip was our annual thing. Every year, we picked a location from our beloved Atlas Obscura and went there. Most of the time, it was a blast. One time we almost got kidnapped. Another time, Simon got bit by a snake and had to be airlifted out. It wasn't always perfect, but it was always an adventure. And we always thought it was worth it.

THIS TRIP, TRYING AS IT'S BEEN AT TIMES, REALLY IS THE perfect combination of our fields of interest. You can't love art and not go to museums. You can't love trees and not come here. And Simon has focused on the darker side of folklore lately, so the myths and legends surrounding this forest are right up his alley.

"We should be there by now," Simon's voice breaks through my thoughts. "I don't get it."

He spins around. It's trees every which way.

"Did the great Simon Wright get us lost?" I joke. "Is he losing his touch?"

My friend seems frustrated. He pulls up the sleeve of his parka and checks his watch. It's a military-style watch-compass combo he never leaves home without.

Simon taps the watch face with a blood-encrusted fingertip. "It's like it's off somehow. Like it doesn't register north."

"How's that possible?"

"I don't know," he shrugs. "I mean, there are places on Earth that can mess with the natural magnetic fields. That would do it."

"Here?" I gesture around us.

"It's like I said earlier: why not here? Here's as good as any place. Better than most."

Simon's frustration always rides in tandem with anger. I

don't want to rile him up, but I'm feeling pangs of something that isn't hunger emerge, something more akin to panic.

Should I panic? I try to have a logical conversation with myself the way a therapist once taught me. I had vicious panic attacks as a kid. Anxiety too. I've mellowed out a lot over the years. Logic always helps.

So, let's see: logically, who knows we are here? I told my mom and some of my colleagues where I was going. Simon told his landlord, whom he's friends with, and Lucy, his on-again-off-again girlfriend. I wonder if he told any of his fans and online followers, but I want to give him a minute to cool off and/or figure out where we are before I ask.

People at the hotel in Atrimo know where we went. At least, I think they do. The language barrier is significant. Simon tried to learn some Russian in the months preceding our trip, but outside of a few mangled basics like food or bathroom, no one here seems to understand him.

I tried too, for about five minutes. I found the language to be more impenetrable than any forest I had ever seen, thickly treed with harsh guttural consonants and axe-hewn vowels. My Russian extends to *les* (forest) and *spasibo* (thank you).

So, between us and a hotel clerk who helped us arrange the car rental, we could be anywhere as far as they know. I take a deep sigh, trying to steady myself. Surely, we managed to convey to the hotel people that we were going to look at the dancing trees.

Eventually, my mom would start calling around too. Maybe even Lucy, despite her notoriously laissez-faire approach to life. But it wouldn't matter. By then we'd be stalagmites. Russian winters don't treat their wanderers kindly.

Don't panic, don't panic, don't panic. I can no longer tell if the internal pressure building or the weather is what's making me shake. I suppose it doesn't matter.

"Let's try again," I tell Simon. And we do. We try to remember every tree shape in our path. We walk for what feels like hours. My feet feel like foreign objects, weights I'm stuck dragging around in my boots. Though my heart is the heaviest of all.

After a while, the trees blend together; their distinct shapes no longer singular. It's almost as if they are all caught in a dance. Winter dervishes. I think I can hear their music, but it's only the wind. Isn't it?

We sit down to rest and doze off almost immediately. Simon shakes me awake, screams at me that we can't sleep. That sleep is death.

We trudge on. I have no sense of direction. Neither does Simon. Whatever bleak watery sunlight that could push through before is nearly gone now. Nights come early here.

We came here. We shouldn't have come here. My mind is spinning.

We've done so many strange, wild, and crazy trips over the years. We've flirted with danger plenty and always got away relatively unscathed. Did we finally push it too far? Do we finally lose this Russian Roulette of adventure here, in the country of its namesake?

I think the trees are closing in on us. I think they are mocking our hubris, laughing at us. They are so young in the arboreal sense. They've only been here since the 1960s. And yet they feel eternal.

Makes me think that maybe there is a world where all the trees look just like it. A world where people don't belong. Maybe we have somehow crossed into that world. Maybe the locals were right when they said this place was a border of mingling energies.

I want to share this with Simon, but I can't bring myself to. My friend is crying angry, ugly tears. He's trying to hide them, but the tears are frozen tracks on his cheeks. I put a hand on his shoulder, and he shrugs it off.

"It's here somewhere. We're not lost. We can't be lost."

But we can, I want to tell him. For the majority of human existence, people were lost. They were small, and the world was vast, and it was easy, too easy, to go off a beaten path and just disappear. They looked at the stars to orient themselves. They learned what they could and wrote *Here Be Dragons* on their maps for the rest.

Modern civilization made huge strides. We've mapped out our entire planet, created sophisticated navigational systems and tools. It wore away at our natural ability to orient ourselves in the world. When those systems and tools fail, we're thrown right back to being small and scared and lost. Only now an annoying voice chants, 'recalculating, recalculating, recalculating.'

The trees, these trees, will never be lost. They are exactly where they are supposed to be. It is only us–driven by this mad, unrelenting wanderlust–who are out of place.

I trip and fall and find no strength, no will to get up. Simon tries dragging me, then gives up and plops down next to me.

It's dark now. The wind has blown straight through to our bones. We are beyond tired, long past exhausted. I feel like we have circumnavigated this entire forest and yet, in some ways, it seems like we've been merely walking the same patch in circles.

The trees lean down to us. Whisper to us. I can't understand a word. But I listen, I listen.

I read that dying from exposure isn't the worst way to go. That you get into a sort of delirium at the end, warming right up before slipping away. Some trick of blood circulation. So that's something to look forward to, I suppose. One last moment of warmth.

I tell this to Simon, already half asleep. I want to keep him awake. I don't care if it's selfish. I don't want to be left alone here.

He mumbles something back, barely coherent.

I talk to him about a book we both read recently. A true-life expedition, a search for a mythical land. Simon's favorite kind, while I tend to go for biographies and sci-fi.

I talk and talk into the scarf I have wrapped around my face, moistening it with my breath. Soon this moisture will turn into ice, I think. Soon, everything will turn into ice.

I look away for a moment. When I turn back, his eyes are closed. I shake him. "Simon. Simon."

There's no response.

"Simon. The tree… what did you wish for? Simon. WHAT DID YOU WISH FOR?"

There's only silence.

The trees must prefer it that way.

I lie back. The dancing trees look even taller, even more inexplicable from this vantage. There is nothing left for me to do–it's a strangely comforting notion.

I close my eyes and experience something like a brief waking dream. I am conscious enough to know I'm dreaming, but helpless, a mere observer.

I see Simon lifted by the branches, stripped of his clothes, and remade into a dancing tree. I hear his bones scream in protestation, but the process is mercifully brief, and soon he is an arboreal being. The bark covers him, starting from the toes. His face is last, and I get one final look at my friend. From what I can tell, he looks peaceful enough. Maybe it's the shock. Maybe it's his wish coming true. Or some sort of evil genie's twisted interpretation of a wish, anyway.

The sky above me looks black. There are no stars. No moon. Only the trees. Only the trees. I'm next. A lunatic's idea of irony–an impossibly appropriate fate for a man who studied and loved trees for so much of his life.

I was never much of a dancer. Two left feet and all that. I suppose that's all about to change. I don't close my eyes because I want to see. Eventually, contorting like circus performers, the branches reach for me…

Mia Dalia is an author, a lifelong reader, and a longtime reviewer of all things fantastic, thrilling, scary, and strange. Her short fiction has been published by Night Terror Novels, 50 word stories, *Flash Fiction* Magazine, *Pyre Magazine*, *Tales from the Moonlit Path*, Sunbury Press, and HellBound Press. Her fiction will be featured in the upcoming anthologies by Black Ink Fiction, Dragon Roost Press, Unsettling Reads, WMB anthology of Lunar Horror, Phobica Books, Wandering Wave Press, Off-Topic Publishing, and *Dracula Beyond Stoker* Magazine. Mia's Noir tales have been featured by *Mystery Magazine* and *Bang! Noir Anthology* from Headshot Press. Her debut novel, *Estate State*, is tentatively set for 2023 release.

COMPOSITION IN BLACK AND WHITE

Buzz Dixon

They just finished burying the little girl when the invader appeared.

They buried her under a rocky overhang on the mountainside where there were few pines. The day was overcast, so the dark barren trees stood out in stark relief to the endless snow and cloudy sky.

The ground proved too frozen to dig, of course, but they could pull loose smaller stones and stack them in a cairn around the three-year-old's cold, cold body.

In the spring, vermin and scavengers would inevitably find her, but she was already beyond caring. And by then her clan would doubtlessly have other, more pressing issues to deal with.

Her father put the last stone in place and mumbled a short, perfunctory prayer. When the small family group opened their eyes, her ten-year-old brother saw the invader just standing there, twenty paces away.

It stood as an obscene parody of a human being: A series of black spheres joined together to form feet/legs/torso/head/arms/hands/fingers.

It reminded the grandmother of a wooden bead doll her grandmother made for her as a child, but the invader stood nearly two heads taller than the father.

For a moment the family froze, the invader making no move.

The twelve-year-old boy remembered stories, that if you saw an invader and just walked away slowly, it wouldn't follow or attack you. His parents and grandmother told him that was just a lie, though, to fool good people and get them killed.

Still, his father hesitated, wondering if maybe the invader didn't see them in their white camouflage capes and cowls.

The grandmother harbored no reservations: "Kill it!" She shoved her son in the invader's direction. "Kill it! They ain't immortal! They ain't invulnerable! Kill it!"

His decision made for him, the father unslung his crossbow, an old hunting rifle stock now outfitted with a strong metal leaf spring taken off an even older vehicle. He put his foot in the stirrup, slipped the steel bowstring over the hooks on his belt, straightened up, cocked the weapon, and dropped a bolt in place.

As always, his aim proved straight and true: the bolt struck the invader square in the chest.

And bounced off.

The father tossed the crossbow aside, drew his hatchet, and ran headlong at the invader, screaming obscenities at the top of his lungs.

His youngest son instantly drew his hatchet and followed his father, echoing his profane scream, and the older boy, not wanting to be shamed by his younger sibling, followed a split second later.

The invader did not retreat from their attack but did attempt to block their blows.

"Git the rope!" the old woman shouted, shoving her son's mate into action.

The younger woman snapped from her daze of mourning and yanked loose a long hemp rope she and the older woman had braided from plants they found growing wild.

The invader continued parrying the father and sons, easily blocking their blows with lightning fast speed.

The mother threw a noose around the invader's neck—or rather, that junction between its upper torso sphere and its smaller head—then tossed the rest of the coil over a tree branch.

She and the grandmother grabbed the rope and pulled hard, but the invader weighed too much for them to lift.

"Boys! Help!" the grandmother shouted, and her two grandsons reluctantly broke off their attack and ran to help their mother and grandmother.

Even they weren't enough to lift the invader. The father, knowing they needed his help, decided the situation appeared serious enough to spend a bullet on.

He pulled out the ancient revolver, inherited from his father's father, and fired at the invader's head.

The cartridge—a handmade reload with crudely mixed gunpowder instead of real cordite—fizzled. It made a vulgar, almost comical sound as a small but dense cloud of smoke spewed out between the cylinder and the barrel.

The father cursed and tried to cock the hammer back, but the cylinder wouldn't turn.

Realizing the bullet sat jammed between barrel and cylinder, he almost tossed the weapon aside. Then he saw the invader turn, grab the rope, and slowly start pulling his family up off their feet.

Yanking a knife from his belt, the father wedged it between the revolver's cylinder and barrel, pushing the bullet forward until he could swing the cylinder free.

Using the ramrod from his cleaning kit, he knocked the bullet out of the barrel and repositioned the cylinder.

Praying the next cartridge wouldn't be a dud, he aimed at the back of the invader's head, squeezed the trigger, and fired.

This time, he enjoyed a satisfying *crack!* and felt the gun jump in his hand like a freshly caught catfish.

The bullet slammed into the back of the invader's head and ricocheted off, but the impact did its job.

The invader's head pitched forward. It sagged to its knees, arms dangling limply by its sides.

The father ran to his family, and together they hauled the invader up until its feet cleared the ground.

While it dangled, they screamed and cursed at it. They hit it with hatchets and broken branches. The women spit on it as the father and boys urinated on the invader's legs.

"Let's build a fire and burn it!" the old woman said, but the father shook his head.

"No. These things are always in touch with one another. While we're wasting time gathering firewood and kindling, they'll be sending reinforcements. No, we gotta git moving. North. Deeper into the mountains. Try to find some of our clan."

The grandmother looked disappointed at not burning the invader, but the father was the official leader of the group. If he made a decision, none of them should disagree.

She abided by his decision, but as their tiny clan gathered up their belongings, she noticed the older boy looking queasy.

"Feel sick," the boy said.

"Don't feel sick over the likes of *them*," the grandmother said, spitting in the invader's direction.

To cheer them up as they headed north, she told her grandsons the story of their people, how long ago they had sailed across the stormy sea to arrive in this great and blessed land, how they carved first their homes and then a nation from the wilderness, driving off the savage natives who wanted nothing more than to kill and rape, how they fought a noble war against those who would destroy that nation, how they lost but how they never forgot, never forgave, and how they tried living peacefully with the inferior races around them.

And how those races demanded more and more from their clans, demanding to be treated as equals, as…as *human beings* instead of the savage animals they were.

And how they fought another war to throw off those evil tyrants, but those tyrants were cowards who never fought fair, and they used machines and chemicals and disease and they wiped out most of the clans.

And the clans that survived now hid in the wilderness, living like the ancient savages once lived, biding their time, waiting for the invaders to grow lax and lazy and inattentive…

And then they would rise up yet again.

And this time, they would win.

And make their enemies kneel.

Make 'em crawl.

Make 'em beg.

Make 'em know their place.

The invader waited until they were two kilometers away, then used its laser to cut the rope.

It dropped to the ground with panther-like grace and immediately began moving off in the opposite direction of the departing clan.

It ran faster than the fastest deer—well over 50 kilometers an hour—silently, nimbly leaping over boulders and fallen trees.

All that could be heard was the rush of air as it passed, the dull muffled tread of its feet on thick snow covered leaves.

The people who built it—people with names like DeShawn and Nia and Santiago and Maria and Rasul and Fatima and Kwan and Ha Eun—knew their history and were smart enough not to make the same mistake twice.

It took two generations for the second civil war to end, and while many of the losers submitted to reeducation camps, more retreated into the hills and swamps and wilderness.

No matter.

The victors built the robots to seek out the fugitive clans (they used "clans" completely without irony).

They programmed the robots with three sets of possible responses:

Should a clan or an individual approach peacefully and attempt to communicate, the robot would provide whatever aid or assistance it could, bringing in drones with food and medical supplies if needed. (This option was never exercised.)

Should a clan or individual ignore the robot or move away from it, the robot was not to follow. (This happened occasionally.)

Should a clan or individual attack the robot, the robot would offer token resistance as long as the attack continued.

Token resistance until the miniature nuclear reactor in its torso was unshielded.

The robot's vital circuitry nestled in its own radiation shielding, but thin sheets of carbon nanotube grids composed the rest of its body, rendering it completely and totally impervious to any sort of attack the clans could launch against it.

Impervious to attack… but transparent to gamma radiation.

The longer and more closely a clan or individual attacked a robot, the longer and greater their exposure to gamma radiation from the unshielded mini-reactor would be.

Had the robot been capable of wondering about such things (it wasn't), it might have speculated on which of the five clan members would die first, and how soon.

The children? The old woman? Certainly the man would die before the young woman simply from the length of exposure.

And when?

As early as three days, as long as two weeks.

None of that concerned the robot.

With its chest reactor re-shielded, it moved off in search of other clans.

Drones reported another small group a hundred kilometers to the south, and it headed in that direction.

Whether that group lived or died was entirely up to them.

Buzz Dixon writes oddball TV / movies / games / comics / novels, putting words in the mouths of Superman, Batman, Conan, Optimus Prime, The Teenage Mutant Ninja Turtles, Scrooge McDuck, Bugs Bunny, plus more G.I. Joes and My Little Ponies than you can shake a stick at. His short fiction appears in Mike Shayne's *Mystery Magazine*, the *Pan Book Of Horror* stories, *National Lampoon*, *Analog*, and numerous original and "best of" anthologies.

PART 2

TUNNEL VISION

David A. Goodrum

David A. Goodrum is a photographer/writer living in Corvallis, Oregon. His photos have graced the covers of *Cirque Journal*, *Willows Wept Review*, *Blue Mesa Review*, *Ilanot Review*, *Red Rock Review*, *The Moving Force Journal*, and appeared in many others. His poems have been published in *The Inflectionist Review*, *The San Antonio Review*, *Spillway*, *Star 82 Review*, among others. www.davidgoodrum.com.

BITTER WATER

Simone le Roux

"Perhaps I should check ahead while you pack up," Greta said, pacing somewhere behind me.

"I'll only be a minute. The water-skin is almost full."

The wheels of Greta's mind seemed to be spinning too fast. She would not be placated. "I don't think we'll need full ones," she said. The next village isn't half a day's walk."

"Then there's no rush," I watched the bubbles rise from the filling skin. My shoulders were tight, as though her tension was my burden to bear.

My sister was skilled at many things. She could whip a crowd into a fearful frenzy, then assuage their worries with clever promises. She always navigated us to the next village, as if by magic. She had a knack for finding the best spots for our donkey, Beatrice, to graze, even with frost coating the ground.

What she was not skilled at was patience.

"It'll be dark in half a day, Johan," she said, pausing her pacing.

I suppressed a shudder that had nothing to do with the cold. I was all too aware of the trees at my back. "We'll make it," I said, quietly.

"Besides," she went on, as though her sombre reminder had never happened, "it's harder to get a crowd together after dark."

I closed off the last water-skin and secured it to Beatrice. She nosed agreeably at my shoulder while I worked, unfazed by my sister's nervous energy. After staring into the slush-lined river for so long, I felt blinded in the gloom of the forest. I could hear Greta's sighs well enough, though.

I tried again to assure her. "You always find a way," I said. "You like some mystery about us, don't you?"

The outline of Greta shrugged. "Business was bad in the last town. This one must go well."

"We could still take the longer route around the forest and arrive in the morning," I said. I tried to keep my voice casual, but it was edged with a plea.

"No. If we're coming out of *this* forest, it might make us seem especially miraculous."

Greta always had a reason. I finished tying off everything on Beatrice's back and scratched through my mind for more excuses to stay under the open sky. "And you're not worried the rumours about the forest are true?"

Greta scoffed. "I'm not going to listen to rumours from the people who believed our potions cured Rinderpest, of all things."

"I think you've got something special with this last batch," I said, changing the subject. For emphasis, I shouldered my pack. It clinked with stoppered bottles. "It smells… medicinal."

I pulled gently at Beatrice's rope and led her towards the path. Greta's face, finally clear to me as my eyes adjusted to the dimmer light, had relaxed. "You think so? I've never seen that plant before, but I thought it smelled nice."

"You were right," I said, knowing how much Greta liked to hear that. It was all I could give her. I could only feign so much enthusiasm telling her that, yes, people would be sure to believe this concoction cured the plague or gout or dropsy or whatever was causing them the most despair. I could only muster so much confidence that we'd be able to leave with someone's prized possessions in exchange for lies as flowery as the murky water they thought was their salvation.

What I had said was enough for Greta, though, and we walked on in silence: a brother and sister wandering into the forest to search for their next meal. Again. I could almost see the bread crumb trail behind us. As the bare branches blotted out the sky, I gave in to another shudder that had been crouched at the base of my spine. Greta didn't notice.

―――――――

"WITH YOUR FACE LIKE THAT, I THINK I SHOULD PLAY THE CURED one this time," Greta said. The lilt in her voice told me she was teasing, but there was an edge there that gave me pause.

"What do you mean?" I broke away from my examination of the trees to our left. Their knobbly branches were unfamiliar: they looked like knuckles on a too-long finger.

"You look so melancholic. No one would ever believe you've been cured of anything."

I tried to push a smile into the corners of my mouth, but it didn't work. Instead, I gave as much of a light-hearted shrug as I could. "It's the forest. You know." And that was true. She knew I hated to travel through the forest. It gave me nightmares of being lost and starved and cold, of being covered in soot and—other visions I'd made myself lose. They crouched at the edges of my mind and inched ever closer whenever I found myself in a forest.

Greta worried at her lip with her fingers before saying, "But you've been like this for weeks, Johan. Since Ulm at least."

I had tried to forget Ulm the same way I forgot so many

things in our life, and I thought I'd succeeded. The image of Greta kicking at an elderly woman who clung to her skirts haunted me. Of course, sometimes we had to flee villages when people realised our treachery, but that hadn't been the problem there. We'd run out of stock, and that poor woman with her swollen hands…

I shoved the thought away, knowing Greta was watching my face.

She was right, though. Some part of me had known that I hadn't been't quite myself since Ulm. Laughter was fleeting, when it came at all. Smiles were only for the benefit of the people to whom we sold our wares. That day with the old woman in Ulm, I felt something small break inside my mind. My belief in order, in the reliability of the way of the world—in Greta—fractured. I wondered what had crept in through the cracks. What had yet to creep.

I couldn't talk to her about it. The quiet knowledge that my clever, practical sister could do nothing to help silenced me. No brilliant thing she could say would evaporate my doubts this time. I trusted her with my life, but not this sadness.

We picked our way through a particularly overrun part of the path, and I almost recoiled at the touch of the branches we had to squeeze past. Their bark rasped and caught against my clothes like small, clawed fingers. Even Beatrice skittered in her haste to be out of their reach.

Greta spoke into the silence, apparently more disturbed by me than by our unsettling surroundings. "Is it—did I do something wrong?"

Her uncertainty pained me. It was uncomfortable, like she was trying on a dress that was too small for her. I couldn't answer her, though. Not really. As much as I'd tried, I couldn't track the source of aching doubt that wove its way through my thoughts like a fog. This wasn't a problem that she could tackle.

"It's not you," I said. "It's just how I'm feeling now."

Greta reflected on this, but not for too long. "Is it what we do?" She gestured to my pack.

I sighed and rubbed the back of my neck. "It certainly doesn't help, Greta. But no, I don't think stopping would solve anything."

Greta nodded, as though she'd heard the answer she'd been searching for all along. "It's hard to be happy when you're starving," she said. "And you know…" She twisted one hand in the air, prompting me.

"If we don't take, we'll have nothing," I recited. I'd repeated the phrase so often over the years that it had lost all meaning, ground to a shard that was meant to cut off conversations Greta couldn't win.

"That old hag knew what she was talking about." Greta's voice had recovered its confidence now that she'd retreated into the familiar rhythm of a topic that didn't confound her. A topic that wasn't me.

"Until she didn't." I hated talking about *her* while we were in the woods, so like the ones she'd found us lost in. She felt close, like we would turn a corner to find her cottage in the clearing, unburnt. *What happened had to happen*, I reminded myself, *and what happened isn't worth remembering.*

"Have we gone in a circle?" Greta said suddenly, halting. Beatrice lumbered on a few steps before coming to a stop. We've passed this tree already. I'm sure of it."

I followed her gaze. The tree *did* look familiar, but it was hard to trust my eyes in the forest. They always played tricks on me. If we *had* passed this tree before, I don't know how I would have missed it. It stood out from the rest of the trees: more twisted, more knotted. The bulbous knobs at its roots would've seemed freshly sprouted, if not for the peeling bark, which stretched like dead skin across them.

"Our path has been quite straight," I said, though my voice pitched high as it left my mouth. "I don't think we've seen this one before."

Greta picked at her lip. "I'll mark it. Just to be sure."

She pulled a knife from her boot, and it took everything in my power to stop myself from grabbing her arm and yanking her back. I couldn't understand it, but every ounce of me wanted to keep her from plunging that knife into the bark of that odd tree.

As Greta lifted the blade, Beatrice, the most even-tempered beast ever to walk the earth, gave a loud bray, startling us both.

My eyes met Greta's. The knife shook violently in her hand.

"Maybe we ought to leave a trail of breadcrumbs instead," I said. Greta didn't laugh.

AFTER WALKING FOR A TIME, AN UNSETTLING REALISATION dawned on me. I hadn't noticed, but had sensed it all along. Who knows? Perhaps I would've grasped it sooner if I hadn't been so preoccupied. What finally alerted me was Beatrice's harsh breaths advancing into... the absolute silence.

There really was no other sound. Even for winter, the forest was unusually quiet. No birds or dripping water or scurrying creatures or sloughing snow. Only branches creaking in a breeze that I could not feel so quietly that I struggled to hear it over the blood rushing through my ears. I placed a hand on Beatrice, but I wasn't sure which of us I was trying to calm.

"We must almost be there by now," Greta piped up. "It's been about half a day and the path hasn't diverged."

I looked ahead into the darkening wood, unconvinced. If anything, it seemed the forest was growing denser the farther we walked. If Greta had noticed the odd emptiness of the forest, she hadn't said anything about it. Surely, she found the near-silent undulation of the trees odd? Perhaps it was best not to alarm her. The calmer she was, the better for me.

"If we don't find our way soon, we'll have to stop and rest," I said. "No sense wandering in the dark." Like Greta, I tried to sound brave, as though the idea of a night in the forest didn't fill me with a dread fueled by obscured memories.

"Soon," Greta promised. "Don't worry."

And then we saw that tree again.

Greta's hand flew to her mouth. My breathing became heavy, and panic unfurled through my chest. I knew it was the same tree. Each strange, bulbous knot in its branches had been carved into my memory after the last encounter.

"But we've been walking for *hours*," I whispered, as though reality would right itself at my factual statement.

With a sudden enraged cry, Greta plunged her knife into the base of the tree, attacking the only thing that seemed like a viable target in our incomprehensible surroundings.

I shouted too late. The knife sliced through the thin bark, and it parted like flesh. From underneath, dark sap splattered onto Greta's hands as though she had burst an infected boil. In the gathering dark, it looked like she had murdered someone.

Beatrice gave no warning. She dropped into a dead sprint and screamed the most human scream I'd ever heard leave an animal's mouth. I didn't know donkeys could make that sound or run that fast. I stood frozen. Greta knelt at the base of the tree, staring at her spattered hands in horror.

My mind spasmed. I'd seen this before. Seen her as a girl with bloody arms and hands.

We have to burn it, Han. We have to burn her body. People will know. I heard a younger Greta whisper urgently. *Help me lift her into the oven.*

Another flash of memory: Greta's twisted, furious face, older this time, as she kicked at the head of a different old woman, who clung to her in desperation. That rage.

As before—as always—I fell to my knees and covered my face with my hands. I couldn't look at her. I couldn't help her. I couldn't forget.

I CRAVED SOUND ALMOST AS MUCH AS I CRAVED WATER. Beatrice had fled with our water-skins tied to her broad back, leaving us only what was in our packs. Snow had not yet penetrated the canopy above, and the forest's coating of ice and dew only served as mockery. My throat burned after the effort of chasing Beatrice, and it was not soothed by my hysterical laughter when I realised that the only water we had was in our potions.

We walked on. Greta scraped at her hands with her nails. No amount of washing, whether rubbing with dirt or pouring on a carefully rationed dribble of potion, would dislodge the sap from her skin. It didn't stop her from trying, though.

"You're going to hurt yourself," I murmured, placing my hand over hers. The sap had hardened, shell-like, around her skin, and therefore, didn't stick to my hand at all. If I sounded calm, it was only because I was too tired to sound any more scared.

Greta nodded, clenching her caked fists. She needed to drink something soon.

"The potions should be harmless. They'll only taste bad. No sense us dying of thirst while our packs are bursting with good water." I sounded just like her. It seemed only one of us could be pale and lost at a time.

I reached into my pack for two of the bottles. Glass was expensive and hard to come by, but worth the price. If something came in a glass bottle, people believed it. We'd recently re-stocked and, by my calculation, could have enough bottles to last us several days if we were careful.

I passed a bottle to Greta and pulled at the precious wax seal of mine without a care for the cost. I knocked back the herbaceous mixture and finished it in two big gulps. It burned bitter on my tongue, but all my throat cared for was the sweet relief of water against it. I groaned.

"Give me another," Greta gasped. Her eyes were feverish and alive. I imagined her brain filling with water like a sponge.

"I think we should save—"

"Give it."

I obeyed.

In the gathering darkness, it didn't occur to us to stop and make camp. Why bother when we only wanted to leave? Broad daylight hadn't been any kinder to us in our search for a path that didn't lead us in circles. And there didn't appear to be any animals to harm us, either. There really was no reason to wait for morning. Without speaking, we agreed that the best way was out, and the only way out was forward.

In the dark and quiet, with the knuckled branches of the strange trees clutching at the sky above, my mind began to feel pliable, like softening clay. My thoughts were fluid; easy to shape, but hard to hold, like the steam of my breath. In a way, it was nice to have relief from the heavy feelings that had held me stiff and stupid for so long.

For the first time in a long time, questions began to form in my mind.

"When you give your speeches to the townsfolk, do you ever believe what you say? Even for a moment?" I asked Greta.

Greta, her own voice dreamlike and faraway, answered after a long pause. "I believe that they want to believe it, I think. They need to."

The words spiralled down my thoughts until they hit
something solid. "Do you do that to me? Say things you think I
need to believe?"

"Of course," Greta sighed. Her eyes were unfocused, and her
feet dragged. She reached out a hand to steady herself on a
donkey that wasn't there and stumbled before righting herself.
"Or else you'd never have come with me."

Something simmered in the pit of my stomach. I couldn't
place it. Curiosity? Dread? Both?

"What do you mean?" I whispered, feeling as though steam
would come spilling out of me instead of words.

"You know you're too soft, little Han. You need to be led, or
you'd never go anywhere, never get anything. You would have
died in Father's cabin if I hadn't pulled us from his breadcrumb
trail."

I held my breath as though that would still my thoughts long
enough for me to understand them. A rushing sound filled my
ears, and I didn't know whether it came from the rustling,
twisting branches above or from my own hot blood. "You said he
left us."

Greta gave a shrug. "If he'd had any sense, he would have.
He couldn't afford to feed us."

"He *loved* us," I said before the meaning of the words really
struck me. He hadn't left me at all. He hadn't abandoned me to
die. He'd searched for me.

"He loved *you*," Greta corrected. "The son. No one wants a
daughter. Not him, and certainly not that old crone." Revelations
were flowing from her lips like ink, staining everything I thought
I knew.

"We almost died, Greta. We were children." That last
sentiment echoed around my skull. We had been children *then*,
but had I ever really stopped? Was I not still meekly following
my big sister around the forest? Had I not followed her into this

one and ignored every part of my heart that begged me not to? Just as I'd run from Father, just as we'd burned—

"The old woman," I said. "She *wasn't* cruel to you, was she? The one who found us when we were lost." My voice emerged clear and direct for once. I couldn't remember ever speaking to Greta like this.

In my mind, a cottage loomed, large yet cheerful. A wrinkled smile shone down. I tasted sugar on my tongue.

Greta gave a long, weary sigh and swiped at the hair hanging in her face. "The chores she made me do, Han, all while you just sat and ate her breads and sweets. If that's not cruel, I don't know what is."

My skin felt like it was on fire. Knowledge burned through my veins. Perhaps it had always been there, smouldering, waiting. Perhaps the fog that had crowded and confused my brain for so long had been the smoke of a dormant rage. Seeing Greta in Ulm kicking that woman, recognising the contempt that fuelled her heart, had given air to a fire waiting to flare to life.

"She was blind, and I was six years old. You said she beat you. You've complained about your aches for *years*."

Greta laughed then. She *laughed*. "She couldn't hit the broad side of a building if she tried. But you never would have helped me if I hadn't said that."

The sap on Greta's hands glistened in the moonlight, and it might as well have been the blood of that kind woman. I could smell the cottage, the brightly painted one, burning, always burning in my dreams. The trees surrounding us undulated, as if lit by the flames only I could see.

And then the tree came into view again.

Torn tree-flesh seemed to pulse around Greta's knife, still buried to the hilt. The tree's sap crystalised into tiny, amber jewels that glinted in the moonlight like embers.

Greta stumbled and didn't catch herself this time. She went

sprawling into the dead dirt and leaves. I waited for her by the tree, the dutiful brother who couldn't bear to be alone. I chanced a glance at the knife again. It looked like it was on fire. Just like me.

"I've only ever tried to keep you close, Han," Greta said. She was trying to pick herself up, but her movements were jerky. She looked like a puppet with cut strings, like a fabulous machination that had lost important joints. "Keep you with me."

The knife was in my hand, though I didn't remember pulling it from the tree. Its blade was clear of any sap, as if the tree had been holding it for me, waiting. The creak of its branches assured me this was so.

I squeezed the hilt until my hand ached.

"You were the only person who loved me." She scrambled in the dirt, this spiteful, selfish creature, unable to bear loneliness, even at the expense of her stupid brother.

"You don't love me, do you?" I asked.

She tried to move towards me again, to stand, but her skirts were snarled on a root. It looked like an old, arthritic hand in the dancing light. Clenching and pulling. Holding her there.

The trees around me groaned with a keening animal sound that shuddered out of my throat. I couldn't tell whether my pain resonated with them or if their twisting strangeness had spurred a similar strangeness hidden in me all along.

Greta looked past me, to the dark forest. "Han. The trees... have you noticed the trees? That *sound*..."

Her eyes widened as they met mine. She at last saw what I saw, heard what I heard, knew what I knew. No more made-up tales about hateful fathers and evil witches. There was only the forest and the truth raging through me.

The moon shone high above us, illuminating the scene of a brother and sister lost in the woods once more. I dropped the heavy pack from my shoulders, heard the bottles shatter. Their contents soaked into the ground behind me as I started towards my sister. Her face contorted in horrible realisation, and I could see her mind working furiously to find the right words, the right lies. I did not give her the chance.

Simone le Roux is a third culture kid (still figuring out the culture part) who lives in Cape Town. Her work has been published in *Dark Hearts*, a Ghost Orchid Press Anthology and in Scott J. Moses's *What One Wouldn't Do* anthology.

THE RITE OF SPRING

Rose Strickman

T hrough the snow they come, heads bent against the bitter wind: men and women, old and young. They come out of their thatched houses, flow from their sparse towns, thread their way through barren fields, seeded only with frozen puddles that reflect the iron skies. A chill wind blows, whistling ice into their faces. Two men lead the procession, beating drums, their percussion interspersed with chanting. Behind them, more men carry banners, incongruously bright on this gray winter's day.

Behind the banners walk the Offerings.

The people must do this. If they do not, then spring will never come and all will perish. The Offerings know this. They walk—one man and one woman—with their heads held high. They walk with gold on their heads, silk on their bodies. They are two of the strongest, brightest and best among the people, their eyes clear, their shining hair tossing in the winter wind. They walk ahead of even the Chief and the High Priest, who follow with lowered heads. Today the Offerings are royalty.

Behind the Chief and the High Priest come the ranks of the

priests, all of them chanting in response to the leaders of the procession, their voices massed and sonorous. Behind the priests march the nobles and then the common people, men with their brothers, women leading their children by the hand, all of them dressed in their best. But they march silently, with grim faces. Winter is not over yet, and they have more icy work to do.

The procession passes through the barren, icy fields, through the frost-limned cow pastures and sheepfolds. Their beasts are thin after a winter of hunger and cold, and huddle together in miserable groups. The animals move aside slowly as the procession winds past, the drums beating, the priests chanting. Their eyes follow the humans, as though they understand the import of their strange parade.

The forest looms on the edge of the pastures, the trees a gray palisade. The procession enters without hesitation.

Here, an eerie silence reigns. The trees are iron pillars, the snow an unbroken marble floor. Most of the forest animals, winter-thin and wary, avoid the procession. A few ravens follow the people, hopping from branch to branch, shouting and jeering.

The people pay no attention. They go deep into the forest, breaking a path through the snow. Deeper they go, and deeper, into the silence of the winter wilderness, until they find The Tree. It sits in its hollow, all other trees held at bay by its great boughs, its grasping network of roots.

What kind of tree is it? Not even the High Priest can say. It is The Tree: huge, tall and wide, its odd-shaped leaves brilliant green even in winter. In this dead forest, it breathes vitality. The air is warmer here, with no snow to weigh down The Tree's branches or wet its roots. The Tree beats, thrumming the air, the living heart of the winter-dead forest. A low, awed murmur runs through the procession, and even the ravens fall silent.

Most of the people stop at the edge of the hollow to genuflect and murmur respectful ritual phrases to The Tree. The drummers stand aside, and the banner-bearers plant their burdens in the softened ground. The ordinary priests raise their arms in ritual praise, their music taking on a high-pitched, eerie tone. But even they halt at the edge of the hollow, not touching even The Tree's furthest roots. Only the Chief, the High Priest, and the Offerings dare to approach The Tree. They slip over its roots and edge near its vast, gnarled bole.

The air near the trunk is warmer than ever. The Tree breathes off the warmth of a thousand springs. Even the Offerings relax a little, enjoying the unaccustomed heat, so welcome after a long winter of cold and snow. The Chief leads the way, processing clockwise around The Tree. The Offerings follow him, the Chief Priest just behind. Three times they circle The Tree, then kneel at the little spring at its roots, at the crystal water burbling up. Bending low, the Offerings drink of the warm water before standing, turning to face the High Priest.

The High Priest steps up now, slightly unsteady on the knobby network of roots that hides the ground completely. Raising his hands, bracelets flashing red-gold, he sings out the final long chant. The ancient words acknowledge what they must do on this day and honor both the Offerings and The Tree. The chant tells of the gift the people must give to receive The Tree's gift in return. The people remain silent at the edge of the hollow, listening, and only when the Priest has finished do they bow.

Now the Offerings kneel once more: a young man and a young woman in their prime, their bodies strong, their minds bright. They are the best that the people can offer, and their eyes shine with both pride and fear.

The High Priest and the Chief bow low to the Offerings, acknowledging their sacrifice. Then the High Priest draws the knife.

The Offerings slump down as their blood gushes onto the exposed roots, and a long, low cry rises from the people: the ululation of mourning. The drums rumble in an expression of the people's grief.

The Tree drinks of the blood. The Chief and the High Priest watch the blood soak into the roots, absorbed by the wood. Tendrils emerge like fingers from the main network, wrapping around the Offerings' cooling bodies.

An uneasy murmur arises, and some gasp, as The Tree draws the bodies of the Offerings down into its roots, wrapping more tendrils around dead limbs. Bark and wood close over the corpses like water, subsuming their silken hair, consuming the succulent young flesh. Within minutes, the Offerings are gone, and only their crowns remain, glinting on the Tree's roots.

There comes a sound—not from the crowd, which has fallen silent–but from The Tree. A great sigh runs through its boughs, of satiation and satisfaction. Its branches shake, as though relaxing from some long-held burden. And a warm wind blows, sweeping down from the Tree's bright green crown.

The people cry out in wonder and delight as the first spring breeze wafts from The Tree, gentle as a kiss. A wave of warm air washes over them, emanating from The Tree. The snow melts beneath their feet, turning to slush. The other forest trees offer tender green buds, leaves unfurling before the people's eyes. Within the space of a dozen heartbeats, the snow disappears and the first flowers emerge from the wet ground. Snowdrops and crocuses peek from emerald moss. The air warms still more, and overhead the iron-gray winter clouds part and let through bursts of sunlight, turning the world to gold. The first songbirds flit from branch to branch and carol for joy. Even the ravens throw back their heads, calling out in surprise and pleasure.

The Chief and the High Priest genuflect to the Tree, followed at once by the priests and the people. Already, they are forgetting the horror of what they have witnessed today, what they did. Now there is only wonder and relief that the rite has worked again, and The Tree has cleared away winter and granted them spring. They will plant crops and harvest grain. Their cattle will provide milk and throw off calves. Their sheep will soon have lambs playing by their sides. The people will be fed another year, and their children will grow tall.

The Chief kneels before The Tree and collects the golden crowns of the Offerings to use again next year. Then, along with the High Priest, the Chief leads the people out of the hollow through the greening forest. Laughing and singing, dancing and skipping, they return to their towns and fields. The sweet scents of spring arise, and life unfurls in soft buds and leaves around them.

Left alone in its hollow, The Tree sucks the meat from the bones of the Offerings. Roots squeeze the flesh from their broken bodies into withered dryness, popping out their eyeballs, cracking their marrow-wet bones. Energy hums through it, from its crown to its roots. The strength of a thousand springs lies hoarded in its wood, in its sap, and it will drink a thousand more.

The Tree will devour spring even as it grants it, and every year the people will cede it still more power. They will never dare do otherwise. Never will they realize that they are sacrificing their own spring as they offer the blood of their sacrificial youths. Winter frightens them too much for them to fear The Tree.

A shiver of pleasure runs through The Tree's branches, and its roots extend an inch further, advancing beyond the hollow.

Rose Strickman is a fantasy, sci-fi and horror writer living in Seattle, Washington. Her work has appeared in anthologies such as *Sword and Sorceress 32, UnCommon Evil* and *Nightmare Fuel*, as well as several e-zines including *Luna Station Quarterly* and *Eternal Haunted Summer*. She has also self-published several novellas.

THE HANGING TREE

David C. Kopaska-Merkel

They say more than 40 black men
(not what they called them)
Were lynched, hanging from its stout branches
I believe it
The bare branches claw at the sky
Like the tree can't get its breath
The old oak looks dead, a tombstone
For the innocents
That's how it looks in December
Other trees are strung with lights
This one with ghosts
Struggling for their breath
In the cold white moonlight
I think I can hear their
Desperate sounds
January, February, tombstone corpse
But come March it's resurrected
Green leaves push out
Transform blackened limbs

Soon, catkins mantle the earth
Where contorted bodies fell
And left no impression
None at all.

———

David C. Kopaska-Merkel, a discerner of fossils, has been writing speculative poetry and fiction since the 1970s. He won the 2006 Rhysling award for best long poem (for a collaboration with Kendall Evans), and edits *Dreams & Nightmares* magazine (since 1986). He has edited *Star*line*, an issue of *Eye To The Telescope*, and several *Rhysling* anthologies, has served as SFPA president, and is an SFPA Grandmaster. His poems (more than 1200 of them) have been published in *Asimov's*, *Strange Horizons*, and more than 200 other venues. Some Disassembly Required, his latest collection of dark poetry, was published by Diminuendo Press in 2022. @DavidKMresists on CS.

THE WIDOW, THE WINDOW, AND THE WIND

Michael Gray Baughan

I da stands at her kitchen window with both hands around her favorite mug. Between sips of tea, something heavy thumps onto the roof. At that very same instant, as if summoned from the ether, a small hunched figure breaches the white expanse framed by the window and scurries with a gnomish hitch and hobble towards the henhouse. The broken and stilted way it moves strikes Ida as both oddly familiar and unspeakably wrong. Though barely seen, it radiates a feeling of dread so strong and palpable her heart hammers in her chest.

Decades of solitary homesteading have accustomed her to dispatching the occasional varmint, but at her age Ida is far less confident against a human interloper. And yet even that assumption slips into question as the thing lurches from pane to pane along the ancient glazing of the window's center rail. Fractals of frost and optical distortions in the old cylinder glass pucker and bloat the trespasser like something trapped in a malfunctioning lens. Ida shifts her weight and strains for a better vantage, but it too quickly escapes into the empire of nothingness beyond her narrow field of vision.

The wind moans and rattles the window. The numbers on the analog thermometer mounted outside the window are too hard to read. Whatever its true reckoning, it will be even colder out there in the snow and the wind. Ida considers bothering the sheriff, but when she picks up the old phone from its wall-mounted cradle, she gets no dial tone at all. Lines must be down again and, no wonder, they run straight through the woods. She never bothered with a cell phone. With no towers near enough, what would be the point?

One sad, slow breath is all it takes for Ida to decide. Like every day before, she will deal with what this day has delivered. Times are hard, and people are hungry. Best guess is that her chickens are what the stranger is after. If so, they will be easy prey, huddled together on their roost, sitting on their feet to stave off frostbite and uneager to move, even in defense. Ida feels much the same–but snowstorm or not–she will not stand idle and let some two-bit poacher pluck her hens like ripe melons from a carefully tended vine. She loads two more stout logs into the woodstove and puts her mug on top to keep it warm. She lifts her father's double-barreled L.C. Smith from its handmade rack and goes to the door for her heavy coat.

The wind immediately dusts a haze of snow crystals across her eyelashes, overlaying everything with an icy blue blur. The shotgun feels leaden in her hands, a tool of messy death with which she has never become friends. She readjusts her grip and braces the barrel in the crook of one elbow, as one might carry an injured dog or a pile of firewood. Advancing like this, each awkward stride drives another rail spike into her twice-broken hip.

She stops to listen halfway down the hill, but her flock is silent and unaware that anything is amiss. Squinting into the whiteout glare, she tries to spot the figure again but sees nothing in the line of pines that sway like spirit-drunk supplicants at a cult revival. The woods around her plot have been uncut for ages and effectively isolate her from anyone who might be of aid. When she looks down for a second to rest her watering eyes, she sees the blood. Dark red dots and dashes leave a Morse message for her in the snow. She feels on the cusp of understanding another meaning, but the sense of it passes too soon. Instead, she considers the possibility that the poacher is already injured, and thus liable to react unpredictably.

She turns back, her conviction wavering. Tainted by the blood in the snow, the usually quaint tableau of her farmhouse— single-story rancher with white scalloped shingles, tin roof of mossy green, ancient oak tree overarching, a question mark of wood smoke curling in the windswept sky—it all registers as somehow incorrect and unfamiliar. Like the spelling of a simple word gone suddenly suspicious.

She gets moving again to put the odd idea behind her, but the farther she gets from the house, the more she senses that something is off. For every step forward, she feels transported two steps back. The expanse of white quicksand grows ever more ominous with each effort she takes to lessen it. She doesn't know the term *dolly zoom*, but if shown the classic film effect, she would have marveled at its perfect depiction of what she is experiencing. The futility of her efforts is frustrating, but just before despair claims her, she crosses some invisible threshold, finally able to make some progress. The land flattens and the snow drifts harden in the lee of the chicken coop.

"Better come out of there and show yourself," she shouts from no more than ten feet away, but her words only sink into the muffling snow. Weeks often pass between instances of hearing her voice aloud, and she has forgotten how hollow and feeble it sounds outside her head. She has lived alone and managed well enough ever since Earl's accident–going on thirty years now. This is hardly her first armed search of the outbuildings. But if she has ever felt this frightened before, she cannot recall.

She gives the interloper ten more seconds to comply, and then she advances. As she passes through the door, she is ambushed by another surprise. Instead of molted feathers and the sweetly rank smell of fresh droppings, she finds only dust and cobwebs, the earthen tang of moldering wood. No trill of disfavor from disturbed roosting chickens. Only the wind chattering through a gap in the roughhewn cladding. Her second step kicks into motion an old glass bottle. Like some witch's diorama, the brittle mummy of a mouse trapped inside rides a brief, centrifugal wave until inertia brings it to rest.

A reciprocal roll of disorientation sickens Ida's stomach as her weathervane memory spins back to face the present. She has no chickens left, of course. They died off years ago. So what on earth is she doing out here? The forgetting is bad, but the remembering is so much worse. Just as a thick slab of defeat settles onto her shoulders, suggesting she sit down–perhaps forever–she spots the hunched form again through the henhouse slats, zigzagging a silent retreat into the woods.

Knowing she won't relax until she gets some answers, she follows as fast as the wind and her stiff legs will allow. She expects another arduous march, but when she passes through the first ranks of trees, the strange figure is suddenly there in the foreground, standing with its back to her like a human blank. The air between them seems to darken in response to Ida's ramping dread. She clenches her teeth as it turns to face her. Even from some distance away, she can see that its head lists hard to one side, nearly resting on its shoulder. As if, in considering Ida, it has found *her* to be the uncanny thing in this encounter.

Ida calls to it, "Who are you? What do you want?"

When no answer comes, she raises the shotgun and takes a

few steps closer. Halfway to it, another wave of vertigo nearly knocks her over. She is at last close enough to see it clearly, but still she can make no sense of it. Blood loss and exposure have blanched its skin to a nearly translucent pallor, but try as she might, she cannot deny that she shares the face on its oddly angled head.

Instinctive revulsion sends her groping for the trigger. Sighted between the barrels, her wounded double raises one hand and tries to say something, but it is impossible to know whether in warning or petition because it keels over before it can speak. The mind-splitting crack attending its fall echoes over the entire property, and for a moment Ida fears she has inadvertently fired. The whine of bent wood tugs her head around just in time to see a snow-laden section of the oak tree break away from the trunk and crash through her kitchen like a cleaver through cornbread.

Something about the slow-motion surrealism of it drags her back to the moment she found Earl beneath the overturned tractor. That strange sense of life unfolding like a cardboard box and showing all its faces at once. The weight of death sitting down to talk. The burden of bearing witness, of being the eyes of tragedy.

But the wind, it seems, doesn't want her to witness. The wind has more devious designs. It whips down the hill with demonic speed and whirls about her like a frantic bird defending its nest. Roiling her ears. Lashing her face. Clawing at her mind and trying to make her forget. Ida hunches up and turns against it, refusing it entry.

"No!" she growls. "No! No! No!" Desperate to hold on, she drops the shotgun and hugs herself so tightly she nearly dislocates both shoulders. If she can just hold on to herself, she will remember and get out before it's too late.

Without arms for ballasts, the next gust gets the best of her balance and knocks her flat. On her back, the wind cuts out like a severed audio feed. Within that cold pocket of silence, the cruel gray sky seems poised to fall on her like a splitting maul. Shrieking and scrambling, she manages to sit up and dodge it, only to find herself alone again in the cold and thickening silence.

SHE WONDERS WHY SHE IS OUTSIDE AT ALL, LET ALONE SITTING beside her father's shotgun in the snow. It takes forever to get herself upright and moving again. As she trudges back up the long slow hill she ran down so many times as a child, she admires the old oak standing watch over her house and thinks perhaps a hot cup a tea will help her gather her wits and remember why she ever left her favorite spot at the window.

Michael Gray Baughan writes weird fiction and manages a tree farm in central Virginia. When he isn't ruining his eyesight at the computer, he enjoys shaping wood from felled tree to finished piece. Born and bled on the outskirts of Philadelphia, he studied English Lit and Creative Writing at the University of Virginia, where he was awarded the Wagenheim Prize for best work of short fiction. His stories are featured or forthcoming in a number of magazines, podcasts and anthologies, including Pseudopod, *Surreal South*, *Richmond Macabre* (Vols. I&II), *Monsters of Any Kind*, and *Tales of Sley House 2022*. Michael's first collection,*The Ana Log & Other Anomalies*, was published by Independent Legions in late 2022.

THE LAST STAND OF WILHELM VON BERLIFITZING

Jonathan Olfert

With apologies to E.A. Poe.

The new body–a swaybacked gelding–is nothing like my last, but it gets me thirty precious miles before they corner me. The year is 1832, and such fairy-tale things should not be possible in these modern times. By refusing to die, this is the world on which I've stumbled, and I will cling to that world until my strength is spent.

I've ridden this poor old horse's body mercilessly. When I leap from his heart to a crow, high in an icicle-draped oak, the gelding totters away. His chest heaves, breath steaming, in a way that says he'll never run again, that I should never have pushed him so hard, the poor old fellow. Perhaps my enemies will kill him. Perhaps they'll realize I've jumped to a new body. They're wise to my trick.

I am Wilhelm, Count Berlifitzing, and unless I can foil my pursuers, it may be their turn for a satisfying revenge.

Ah, here they come: the last Metzengerstein retainers, the hoofprints of their horses forge a clear dark trail in the snow.

They can't be here to avenge their lord, that debauched little bastard. As his favorite horse, I burned his castle and him with it, along with my pursuers' friends, perhaps, even family. A castle is a town writ small. The Chateau Metzengerstein burned very hot indeed.

They spot the crippled gelding in the gloom and rein up beneath the oak. The crow is my fifth body, but my first bird since learning to be more stubborn than death. I find it difficult to hold still on my high branch. The crow is clever, aware its own thoughts have changed. It bucks against my will.

"The old witch jumped again," says a Metzengerstein man. There are five of them, all weathered veterans of hellholes like Raab and Wagram. They look around sharply, wisely. If they were men of mine, I'd give them better than they got from the Metzengersteins. Instead, I've brought them–unintentionally and maybe a bit callously–as much evil as their master ever did. My revenge begets theirs. I can't blame them.

I'll still kill them if I must. I've died in agony four times, and I'm not keen on repeating the experience.

One of them spots me, the crow I am. Instead of raising a cry, he brings up his rifle, a fine modern flintlock. The ball rips through the air without mercy. Its torrential wind shatters icicles and tugs feathers free as I scramble for altitude. Another shot. I wait for more, but the other four riflemen are taking their time, lining up their sights just so. In moments, I will be dead again.

The crow fights me, but I dive, skimming through the branches of the oak and over my pursuers' heads. I move too quickly, and too close, for them to track me with their rifles.

As a third bullet roars past me, I jump again. Not to one of the men or their horses this time. They know the signs too well: the shaking, the blaze in the eyes. Instead, I occupy the tree itself.

Why not become a tree? It's alive, is it not?

All too soon, the men understand why the naked branches tremble, why the ice shivers off the naked limbs. My enemies' attention is on the oak as the crow, sensibly, hurries away.

I have no eyes or ears, just a vague sense of the cold wind tugging at my branches. I'm unsure how it will feel if they take axes or torches to my flanks, my roots. That seems inevitable. But I have the tree's resilience now, which buys me time to consider my next move.

I can endure without a body for a time. I once haunted a certain tapestry. Another time, I brooded over my victory as a torrent of smoke. However, it's taxing and comes with great risk. My life, my future lives, all depend on stubbornness.

Numbly, I feel the first bite of axes. Reverberation shakes my boughs all the way up. It's a shame to sacrifice this grand old tree, yes. No more shame than the lives–both human and animal– I've spent to last so long, though. I feel as bad for the tree as I do the swaybacked gelding I've broken. I never would have ridden him so hard, but his fear got in my heart, and we ran together, barely lucid. I can still feel the *being* of him, the panic and the pain and the longing for comfort.

In the few days since I burned the Chateau Metzengerstein and my true enemy with it, I've chosen bodies by sight. I can only dimly feel my five pursuers and their tired horses around me now. I'm loath to interfere with the latter. Perhaps, though, it's time to take a chance on the former.

To steal a human body is a terrible, draining task. I've done it just once before: to a Metzengerstein retainer like these five. It was a gamble that earned me precious little time or distance, but rather a lingering heartache. The memory of his son's wide eyes…

I jump from the tree to the heart of another man. He fights me, shaking in the saddle. I force his head–now my head–away so the others won't see the telltale burning in his eyes. I absorb him. His name is Sandor. He has four children. He is a Protestant, but tells nobody, not even his wife. His knees ache with the cold.

And his brother died when I burned the castle.

Sandor and two others are in their saddles. Their focus rests on the two men chopping down the tree. The effort of keeping this body is sapping my energy, along with my will. I review my options: ride hard, fight, use Sandor as a platform for another jump before I lack the strength to do it. I don't know what will happen if I weaken too far to jump. Perhaps I'll fade to nothing. Perhaps I'll haunt this man's thoughts until his death, trapped in the deep places of his heart. These fates seem equally horrible.

Skipping from body to body requires a certain wilful moral blindness. Now that I'm tired, I'm less able to avoid unpleasant truths. There's dishonor in what I'm doing. Oh, any number of the landed gentry might not see it that way, but I fought, myself, against Bonaparte in much younger days, just like these men did. Perhaps I commanded them. We had sharp words for officers who spent their men in vain, who threw them headlong into canister shot for dreams of glory. *Gyáva*. Recreant. Craven.

There are two kinds of honor: the glory bestowed by others and living at peace with yourself. Honor is too broad a word to fit both, and yet here we are.

I've lingered too long in my weakened state. The man I'm inhabiting, Sandor, shakes me off and slides bonelessly from his saddle. He coils and gyrates in the trampled snow. I'm just a presence in the air, a wisp of cloud, a flurry. The others take his seizure to signify my arrival, not my expulsion. They raise their rifles and shoot poor Sandor dead. His victory over me killed him.

Attention turns to me now, to whatever I look like. I stare them down.

The tree groans. Frosty bark splits and crumbles from the

warping trunk. That great weight of ice-clad limbs bears down toward the party, and they scatter on foot or by spur. Their attention diverted, I could inhabit Sandor's terrified, riderless horse, drive him another twenty, thirty, forty miles and into the ground. Perhaps this time I'd get away. I am more stubborn than death itself. I've proven that, if nothing else. I could outlast them across five, ten more little lives, creating tragedy for more Sandors, more swaybacked geldings.

They're as tired as I am, these four men. One gets another glimpse of me, whatever shred or silhouette I am now, some cobweb form of interrupted snowflakes on the breeze. He shouts to gather his comrades back to the broken tree.

They don't know what to do with me. So in the end, they just watch, clutching hats and rifles and rosaries, as I fade. As I let myself let go.

Jonathan Olfert's short stories have appeared in *Beneath Ceaseless Skies*, *Dark Recesses*, *Radon Journal*, and other markets. He generates vast quantities of spreadsheets and wood chips, and holds a Master's degree in political science. Jon and his partner live and work near Halifax. You can find him on jonathan-olfert.carrd.co.

THE HIVE

Jacqueline West

No one had seen an ice bee in a lifetime.

No one—no one living—had found a hive, not even in the farthest reaches of the forest, or tasted any long-hoarded honey. Whether the bees had died off or merely disappeared into some perfect hiding place, no one could say. But in the stories told around smoldering fires, their honey was as clear as water, and it burned on the tongue like frost. Warriors who had eaten the honey of ice bees would charge into battle without boots or furs, their bare feet leaving steaming tracks in the snow. Anyone who tasted that honey would never feel cold again.

Anya knew what it was to feel cold. And she had no time for stories.

Just now, she only had time to gather a few more of the freeze-dried berries still clinging to their canes. Her pack was less than half full. Not a good day of foraging; not a good sign for the long winter to come. But the angle of light in the sky, the hazy shift from white-gold to white-blue, told her it was time to hurry home.

She would follow her own tracks back. This was a rule she'd learned as soon as she could toddle on tiny legs through the endless white of the Northwood. Now, with longer, stronger legs, it should have been easy enough. The snow was deep and fresh, her footsteps as clear as the trails of a sleigh. But when Anya turned around, she didn't see her tracks at all. She saw something else. Something she hadn't noticed as she'd trudged past it before.

It hung from one branch of a leafless oak, dancing prettily, almost flirtatiously, on the wind.

A length of dark pink ribbon.

A flash of color in the white and black winter woods was irresistible. Like a cardinal darting between branches, firelight behind a windowpane, a cluster of berries against brittle snow. Life, it said. Life.

Anya stepped closer.

She had to tug off one thick leather mitt to unknot the ribbon from its branch. In seconds, her bare hand was numb and her fingertips tingled, but the ribbon was hers.

For a moment, she could only stare at it, its rose-rich color fluttering from her icy fingers.

Then she forced herself to glance around. There were no cabins anywhere in view—no cabins for miles, as far as Anya knew, and she walked these woods daily. So who would leave a ribbon here? A ribbon like the heart of an apple blossom. A ribbon a father or mother or lover would save precious coins for, to buy at the market for a midwinter gift.

Who on earth would leave such a gift here?

At least taking a gift wasn't theft, Anya told herself. Things found in the frozen woods belonged to the finder. As she slipped the ribbon into her pocket, she could have sworn that she felt a faint warmth, as though she had slipped a tiny bottle of tea or a few glowing embers inside her coat, too.

Anya scanned the snow, making sure her tracks were still within view. Only a fool would wander too deep into the trees. But just a few steps farther off, in a dense knot of trunks, lay a fallen oak. Its branches stretched above the snow like frozen fingers, dry and brittle. Perfect kindling. Rushing nearer, Anya snapped a few of them. The cracks of breaking wood echoed through the cold. She was turning back toward the spot where her tracks had been when another flash of color caught her eye.

This flash was smaller than the ribbon, and stiller, closer to the snow. It was the color of an egg yolk in sunlight: a warm, impossible yellow-gold.

Without thinking, without choosing, without realizing that she'd dropped her armload of kindling, Anya stumbled toward it.

The golden flash was a flower.

The kind that villagers called sun-melts-the-hillside. The kind that sprouted a few weeks before spring began, pushing its vivid face through the drifts. But this was midwinter. Spring thaw was months away. And there wasn't another blossom or shoot anywhere in sight—just this single, full-blown, glowing beauty.

Anya couldn't resist. Taking the other mitt off this time—the hand she'd used to grab the ribbon was still numb—she broke the flower from its stem. Snow rasped against her fingers. Cold chewed at her bare skin. Quickly, she tucked the flower behind her ear, inside the shelter of her hood. The flash of gold in the corner of her eye could almost have been the sun itself.

But the true sun was sinking low. The air was growing swiftly colder. Tugging her mitt back on, Anya turned around.

Lengthening shadows threw their gray nets through the trees. Her tracks were lost somewhere in the tangle. Before she could unknot them again, a blast of wind rushed up, scratching her eyes with stinging white. It blew hard enough to push her off balance, hard enough to loosen her grip on her leather mitt. Anya squinted through the snowflakes. Her mitt had disappeared into the drifts.

She had never made such a foolish mistake. Never.

The Northwood didn't allow mistakes.

With her one covered hand, she dug through the snow. She still hadn't found the mitt when the wind rose again. White blades slashed her eyes, shoving her forward. Anya caught herself on both hands, mittened and bare, drifts swallowing her up to her shoulders. Icy crust broke under her knees. She fought to pull herself upright before the snow could slip around her collar, into her sleeves.

Not fast enough. Ice shards scraped her hands. Clumps of snow reached her elbows, melting just enough to cling. She made another dig for the lost mitt, but whirling snowflakes blinded her, and all traces of where she had been—footsteps, lost leather—had vanished in the white.

And now she had kept still for too long. She was shivering hard enough to rattle her own teeth. Too hard to do anything else.

Through the shaking and the dimness, she heard it. A soft, strange sound.

A delicate sound. Like tiny bells ringing, or like miniature cups tapping miniature saucers. A sound like icicles struck by a silver wand.

Anya listened, shivers slowly dying away. She could sense the brittle emptiness inside of her boots, the hollows in her sleeves. The slowing of the blood that washed under her skin.

But she hardly thought about these things.

She thought only about that small, ringing sound.

On stiff legs, she turned toward it.

The sound grew louder, clearer. It tinkled and hummed and chimed and wrapped its silvery hooks around her limbs and pulled. Anya took another lumbering step, the body that had always been her best tool now just freight to drag along.

She followed the sound onward, through drifts, between tree trunks, through frozen twigs that splintered like glass.

A tree loomed through the shadows ahead of her.

Its bark was the gray of winter, its limbs leafless and stark against the snow. And hanging from its branches was a hive.

Anya stopped, staring. Her feet, if she still had them, were buried deep in the snow. Her hands were dead things. Her eyes were mirrors, dry and hard, ready to shatter.

But this thing was alive.

The hive was so large, she couldn't have wrapped both arms around it. It was made of something that looked like linen, or thick, un-inked paper, or perhaps like pale skin. It rang and chanted and sang. It was a heart, a miniature cathedral. It buzzed with life.

Here, in the frozen woods, in a world made of snow. Alive. How alive.

Anya couldn't feel herself moving closer. The blood inside her slowed to a sticky crawl. Still, somehow, she took the next step. The next.

Until she'd come close enough to see them.

The ice bees.

Like crystals, like the facets in a snowflake, they were more light than substance. They were silver and paleness and pearl, with a blur of wings, and dancing bodies, and voices that sang one endless, ever-changing chord. They flew from the hanging hive too fast for her to do anything but stare. Their song grew louder.

They stopped inches from her face, one chiming, glinting, white swarm.

Anya opened her mouth. Gasping. Astonished that the world could contain this. That winter had brought her here to witness it.

That it was not just a trick of a hypothermic brain, a last, dazzling kindness passed between her body and the world.

The bees came to her.

One by one, hundred by hundred, they flew into her open mouth. They moved smoothly as a string of beads, lightly as petals. Inside, inside. Filling every frozen vessel. Every airless sac. Every space.

Still they came.

Anya wasn't breathing anymore.

She couldn't have even if she had tried.

The bees filled the chambers of her lungs. Their song rang against her ribs. They danced beneath the stopped lump of her heart.

She was their home.

When the old hive in the tree was just a husk, Anya closed her lips.

She turned around.

Her legs were weightless now. Her feet and hands. Her blood and bones. The bees hummed inside of her. They would carry her, their thousands of lives tucked inside of her paper-white shell. They would tell her where to go.

She would never be cold again.

Jacqueline West's work has appeared in journals including Strange Horizons, Liminality, Mirror Dance, and Star*Line, and in the recent anthologies *Chromophobia* and *Into the Forest*. Her books for younger readers include the NYT-bestselling dark fantasy series *The Books of Elsewhere*, the YA horror novel *Last Things,* and the middle grade ghost story *Long Lost*. An award-winning poet and active HWA member, Jacqueline lives with her family in Red Wing, Minnesota. jacquelinewest.com

HIBERNATION

Ashen Speir

And let them bury me in winter
where dark, fragile limbs can hold me,
kissing dewdrops of snow into my hair
and onto skin, icy not just from cold,
grazing frosted lashes and eyes ever closed;
my last gentle, lifeless, soulless embrace.

Let them bury me in everything I loved:
the snow, the dark, the tundra wasteland
that always felt just like home,
where no sun will ever find me,
and where frostbite will claim me
piece by unwanted, unlovable piece.

Let me lie in silence and in solitude,
abandoned in a land without color,
in a land without warmth,
where no one can disturb me,
and where I can be selfishly at peace
alone.

Ashen Speir writes haunting short stories and poetry with emphasis on queer and neurodivergent representation. They went to Bloomsburg University, where they studied too many languages and earned a degree in Creative Writing. Now, they live in central Pennsylvania trying to turn daydreams into stories.

PAID ON DEATH

Geri Copitch

Marsh Times
November 21, 2052
Skeletal remains were uncovered today by divers in waters near
the island once thought to be owned by the wealthy recluse,
Edwin Xavier Piry. An underwater survey was being done in
preparation for the transfer of title of the island from Marsh
County Trust for the new children's hospital. The forensic
pathologist is still trying to determine how long the body was in
the water and the source of the unusual, deep grooves found on
many of the bones.

October 31, 2022

O   I should never have agreed to take on the job.
When my agent, Maggie, called me out of the blue
and told me she had a wealthy client who wanted a ghostwriter
for their autobiography, I should have been suspicious. I'd never

written a biography, autobiography, hell—anything based on reality. I was a fantasy writer, and my agent knew that.

My next clue should have been the whole secretive non-disclosure thing, but I thought, "Well, that makes sense. Since I'm going to get up close and personal with this client, they don't want me writing a tell-all later with the scandalous details they wouldn't let me put in their book." Then I met the solicitors.

Maggie had texted me, saying I needed to get to her office right away to sign forms. Knowing I don't drive, she usually just sent that stuff via email. When I complained, she'd responded with only one word: "OFFICE." So I went. Staring out the window of the Lyft, I hoped that maybe the client wanted to offer a cash advance—like real greenbacks cash. I mean, you can't really email cash, right?

I owed money all over town. I hoped once I'd settled with my creditors, not all of them the friendly type, I'd have enough left over to buy a few boxes of mac-and-cheese and pay last month's rent. It wasn't always this way; looking forward to mac-and-cheese like it was Lobster Thermidor. Once I was almost a Somebody. But, ever since I'd become YouTube famous for an unfortunate incident on BART, I hadn't been able to sell a book anywhere. So, I was really eager to hear what my agent had to say.

We pulled up in front of Maggie's two story walk-up. The lone scraggly city tree that looked anemic and half dead at the best of times, now drooped its bare branches over the sidewalk as if it was trying to snatch bundled-up passersby. I edged my way around the hanging branches and scooted in the door. When I got to Maggie's office, the bolt clicked and a man in a three piece opened the door. Odd. Maggie never locked the door, even when she went out. When I asked where Maggie was, he said, "Gone."

"Gone? Gone where? When's she coming back? She just told me to be here *post haste*. We have business."

"Gone," he repeated. He motioned for me to come in. That's when I saw the other one sitting behind Maggie's desk.

"Ms. Stygian, please sit down," they said. "I'm Shade, and this is Harrow. We represent Mr. Edwin Xavier Piry, the subject of the ghostwriting project that your agent contacted you about." They gestured again. "Please, sit."

I looked from one to the other and sat down. This wasn't how Maggie usually operated, but I figured that this Piry must be some rich eccentric. Never argue with a rich eccentric who wants to hire you.

"You've been told there's a non-disclosure?"

I nodded.

"Good. Sign this, please." Shade pushed a leather bound folio across Maggie's desk. In doing this, they uncovered a large stain on the blotter that I hadn't remembered seeing before. It still looked wet, but before I could study it more closely, Shade leaned forward, covering it with their body.

"You need to read this Very closely, Ms. Stygian. Mr. Piry's privacy is Very important to him, and this contract is Very specific. Don't worry, you will be Very well compensated for the inconvenience."

That last part got my attention. I decided to study the contract and stop wondering about the damp, red stain on the blotter.

I had signed a couple of NDAs before, back when I still did research for my books, back when they were selling, back before what everyone else called "stress induced hallucinations" started. I wasn't under any stress now, but I could swear that blood had oozed out from under the blotter and was dripping down my thigh. I wasn't going to look. That just encouraged *Them*. Instead, I tried to focus on the papers in front of me.

Shade was right. The contract was Very short, Very specific.

This non-disclosure agreement is entered into willingly by Fiona Stygian and Edwin Xavier Piry, and his representatives from Shade & Harrow, LTD, on this day of Samhain, January 31st in the year of common reckoning 2023.

Term: life

Covered information: Everything heard from the time Fiona Stygian entered into the offices of Maggie Villane until termination.

Exclusions from confidentiality: None

Obligations of Receiving Party: Fiona Stygian will live and work out of E.X. Piry's home on Brasil Island until completion of the book. She will speak to no one not acting on his behalf.

Severability: Failure to comply will result in early termination.

Termination was such an interesting word.

A rapping at the window made me jump. Who could be rapping out there, two floors up? I ignored the sound, but then it happened again. Over Shade's shoulder, I saw the branches of the tree pressed against the window. Just a few minutes ago, they had been inches from the sidewalk. I should have ignored *Them.* As I watched, one branch tapped the window like a finger pointing at the desk.

I forced myself to refocus on the contract. If I wanted this job, I needed to appear like I had my shit together. New game plan: first, ignore further communication from the tree and dripping "blood." Part two, I should draw things out and ask for a few details. No sense in coming across too desperate. I cleared my throat.

Shade answered before I could open my mouth. "$350,000, POD."

Shit, that would buy a lot of Xanax. I could keep my demons at bay for a long, long time.

"Where do I sign?"

Harrow reached out a pale, crooked finger and pointed. When had he moved that close to me? It gave me that weird creepy feeling at the base of my neck that traveled up my scalp. Still, I signed.

"When do I start?"

Shade smiled, "Now."

"Okay. I'll just go home and pack—"

"No need," Shade pulled a small leather duffle out from behind the desk. "We've packed for you." That unsettling smile again.

"But I'll need my—"

Shade produced a laptop. "With retinal display. I assume it will do?"

I nodded, dumbfounded. I did a reality check. My hallucinations were usually of death and gore, so this part had to be real.

"We've also settled accounts with your landlord. He won't be asking you for rent again."

"You mean for the duration of the project?"

Shade offered me a smile, which was somehow creepier than their stare. "Shall we go?" Shade stood and gestured towards the door.

As we stepped out of the building, I ventured a sideways glance at the tree. Its branches pointed upright in a normal tree shape, nowhere near the window. I looked away before it sensed my attention. A cold gust that carried the crisp smell of snow sent icy fingers down my back. I regretted not grabbing my scarf. We headed down to the pier: Shade sat in the front, Harrow in the back with me. I had the odd feeling that he was here to make sure I didn't jump out. I took the Xanax out of my pocket and popped one in my mouth. Better safe than sorry.

We crossed a web of train tracks as we entered the marina. This had once been a thriving port, but now only a few small fishing boats set out each day. Grey skies indicated a winter storm was rolling in. I hoped we'd make it to the island before it did. We pulled up to a boat idling at the far end. The captain–do you call a guy who pilots a two bench motor boat a captain?– kept shifting his weight from one foot to the other and glancing around. The wind had blown the collar of his jacket up on one side where it lodged under his beard. When Shade approached him, he stepped back, nearly falling off the edge of the pier. Shade smiled.

"This is Mr. Smith. He'll be taking you over to the island. He lost his ability to speak some time ago, so no need to engage him in idle chit-chat." And with a nod of the head, Shade and Harrow climbed back into the car.

I tossed my duffle in, handed my computer bag to the captain, and carefully climbed into the boat. I didn't want my new toy winding up in the drink. Smith tossed off the mooring ropes, and we were away. We hadn't gotten very far out when there was a long blast of a train horn, a squeal of metal brakes and a loud crash, a crumpling sound, and finally, the screech of metal being scraped down the tracks.

I looked back at Smith. "Did you hear that?"

He kept his eyes ahead and said nothing. There hadn't been any other signs of life at the marina. I kept wondering if the train had hit... *No*, I chided myself. *You don't even know if it was real. You're just imagining death and gore again.*

A man waited at the dock for us, a lone tree looming over him. I resolved to ignore the menacing vegetation and tossed my bag onto the wooden deck. Captain Smith responded with a curt nod to my thanks, and I scrambled up to join my belongings.

When I stepped off the boat, waves of decomp in the air washed over me. Every sane voice in my head agreed: I should jump back in the dinghy and head for the mainland. But I was too intrigued. Instead, I switched to mouth breathing, picked up my duffle, and followed my guide up a winding path.

As we rounded a sharp bend, I heard the motor boat rev its engine. I guess I wasn't the only one getting creepy vibes from this place. I took stock of my surroundings. We were far enough out into the bay that I could just make out some of the taller buildings on the mainland. The rocky island had little growth on it aside from patches of dead sea grass and some scraggly brush no taller than my knees. I didn't count the tree. It had been too oddly out of place at the water's edge to be real. From this vantage, I didn't see any buildings, and I began to wonder if this was some kind of elaborate hoax cooked up by one of my creditors. I was startled from my reverie when the sound of wood splintering violently against rock cut through the cold air. An engine whined briefly before cutting out. I looked at my escort, who seemed unperturbed.

"Did you hear that?" I asked. "Do you think we should go back down and check it out? Maybe he needs help?"

No response, he just kept walking. Had I forgotten to take my Haldol this morning? Even if I had, I usually needed to miss more than one dose before the hallucinations become more than whispers in the background. I remembered the advice my therapist had given me: If no one around you seems disturbed, keep your shit together. So, I forced myself to ignore what had sounded like the certain destruction of the boat. I decided it wouldn't hurt to practice my deep breathing the rest of the walk.

We rounded another curve, and I saw the manor for the first time. It seemed to grow out of the craggy rock behind it. As we approached, I realized it was part of the rock; like a festering zit on a teenager's face. The smell wasn't as bad here, but the air felt thicker.

My silent companion led me into the residence. It wasn't as gloomy as I had expected, but it was damp. The walls had a shimmer to them. A door opened, and a tall grey-haired man in a brocade smoking jacket emerged.

"You must be Ms. Stygian." He extended his hand and gave me a firm, but damp, handshake. "Edwin Xavier Piry. I'm so glad that you've agreed to write my autobiography. Please, why don't you come join me in the study? We can get to know each other over some refreshments."

He seemed pleasant enough. I wasn't sure if I should bring up the boat, I mean, what are the odds that I'd really heard two accidents, that by the sounds of them must have led to the deaths of those involved, in the course of one hour? And the silent type who'd brought me up here hadn't seemed concerned. So I put it down to a little bit of stress, and maybe not enough antipsychotics.

We chatted for several hours, and I took notes on a pad I got from my host. Computers are great for typing up final drafts, but for all the rest I like the comforting sound of pen scratching across paper. Around eight o'clock, a slithering sound coming from the hallway distracted me from what my host was saying. My eyes were glued to the door when it swung open, revealing my taciturn guide from earlier. He nodded at Mr. Piry.

"Ah, good. Dinner is ready," Piry said. "I hope you like fish. We eat a lot of it."

What crossed my mind was that this was something that should have been brought up before I agreed to the job. What I said was, "Fish works for me." As I crossed the room, I noticed something on Mr. Piry's writing desk. It was a leather bound folio that looked a lot like the one Shade had presented the NDA in. I wanted to ask how he had gotten the folio, given that Shade and Harrow had stayed behind.

"Will Mr. Shade be joining us?" I asked, gesturing to the item.

"Ah, no. I'm afraid not. They were my grandfather's

solicitors. They were getting careless in their work, so I had to terminate them. Your contract seems to be in order, however." He smiled and ushered me out of the room.

Terminate. These people liked that word.

I mulled over the part about Shadow and Harrow being his grandfather's solicitors. I must have misheard him. Neither of them had looked over forty. But Piry chatted away throughout the meal, and we drank quite a bit of wine. By the time we said goodnight, my head felt a bit fuzzy and my questions about the solicitors were long forgotten.

———

I woke up with a start. My watch showed three A.M. The silence in the house was broken by the sound of something moving down the hall. It was… squishy. Not like the squishy sound sneakers full of water make. There were no footfalls. Just a squelching, slithery sort of sound moving away from my room. Voices bounced off the stone walls. I was pretty sure one was Mr. Piry. Assuming he had everything under control, I fell back to a fitful sleep.

———

Every morning, Piry and I ate smoked fish and eggs in the 'breakfast room' before moving into the study, where he would ask me to remind him of where we had left off the day before. Then he would spend the next few hours telling me more about his life. Often vague on dates, he waved me off when I tried to pin down approximate years of occurrences, saying they weren't really key to his story. I didn't press. After all, it was his autobiography. After lunch–usually some sort of broiled fish–he would lie down until early evening. We'd finish the day chatting through supper, which always included a great deal of very good wine.

I used the time he rested to review my notes on the laptop and flesh them out. I was surprised I hadn't heard from Maggie. With my other books, she'd rarely gone two days without pestering me about my progress. After a week of silence from her, I grew concerned. That strange stain on her blotter haunted me. I tried to track down the jeans I'd been wearing the day I met Shade and Harrow at her office, but I couldn't find them. I wasn't sure I really wanted to know what, if anything, had dripped on my leg, anyway.

A few times, I thought about going for a walk and stretching my legs during our breaks. But whenever I got close to the doors, I got the heebie-jeebies. I was taking my *Halies* religiously every morning, and popping *Xens* like they were PEZ candies, but they didn't seem to be working too well anymore. The doctor had said that might happen. When this project was done, I'd have to make an appointment to see her.

My lack of sleep couldn't be helping. Two, three times a night, I'd wake up to strange sounds in the house. Slithering, slapping, squelching sounds. At times, right outside my door. More often, coming from further down the hall, or as if they echoed from some other part of the house. Then I'd hear muffled voices, and the noises would stop. It was taking longer for me to fall back to sleep each time.

And I could swear that the walls were getting slimier.

I tried to push Mr. Piry along a little faster. But he said, "There's no rush. This will all end soon," before returning to his reminiscences.

After a fortnight of this routine, an odd sloppy sound against my door woke me. I sat up, my heart pounding in my chest. I pulled my sheets up to my chin, as if they could protect me from whatever made that sound.

Without warning, something burst through the door and landed on top of my legs. I screamed and grabbed the closest thing to me, the bedside lamp, and began beating the thing on my legs. It stopped moving, and I wriggled out.

Shaking, still holding the lamp, I heard a weak, muffled voice. "You fool, you don't understand. I was keeping you alive."

Now the real panic set in and my legs threatened to give way. I'd just killed my employer. My hand started to cramp and I realized I was still clutching the lamp. I slowed my breathing and focused on unclenching my hand, sending the murder weapon crashing to the floor.

Barefoot, wearing only my thigh-length sleep shirt, I ran downstairs looking for help or an escape. A shadow undulated across the foyer and toward the open doorway to the kitchen. Curiosity outweighed logic, and I followed, careful not to make a sound. Whatever it was exuded liquid as it moved along the floor, leaving a slimy trail. Some part of my scrambled brain told me not to step on it.

Ahead, a door banged closed.

Adrenaline spiking, I ran into the kitchen and wrenched open the door to the basement. Mr. Piry's silent companion turned and stared at me from the second step. His tongue flicked out like a snake's.

Without thinking, I shoved him. His flesh was pulpy, oozing around the skin on my outstretched hands. He teetered for a moment, grasping at my arms before falling backwards. I listened to him bounce down the stairs, and then the distinctive sound of his neck breaking as he hit the cement floor. I turned my head and vomited.

Something stirred from a far corner in the basement, a soft sucking sound, which moved closer and closer to the steps. A putrid smell smacked me in the face. I slammed the door and ran.

I tore out the front door, propelled by the fear of the sounds building behind me. My only thought was to get to the pier and hope that I'd find a boat.

As I reached the rocky shore, the moon broke through the clouds. A figure lay sprawled on the rocks. The face had been eaten away, as if by birds. There was no mistaking the clothes. It was Captain Smith, surrounded by the splintered pieces of his boat. I searched the shoreline, but if Mr. Piry had a boat, he didn't keep it here. The oozing sounds behind me were getting closer. I dove into the water. I knew I had no chance of swimming all the way back to the mainland, but I wasn't sure how much of what I'd seen and heard was real, and how much was my brain creating its own reality. Either way, I sure as hell wasn't staying on that island one minute longer.

I made it about fifty yards when something snatched at my foot, but I kicked it away. I tried not to think about what it might be. Focusing on things only encouraged *Them*. I swam another few strokes when cold, clammy fingers gripped my bare leg like a vice. More hands took hold of me, pulling me below the surface. I wished then that the moon had stayed hidden behind the clouds, that it didn't allow me to see the face with protruding eyes. And its teeth. Rows and rows of sharp dagger-like teeth. My final thought was to hope I'd drown before I felt them tear me to shreds.

Geri Copitch is an editor for Chutzpah Press, as well as *Gold Man Review*. Two of her short stories have been published in anthologies by Owl Hollow Press. Her novel, *Rule Number One: Know Thy Enemy*, is available on Amazon.

MY PURPLE CRASHING SEA

Elizabeth Suggs

I emerge from an ancient grove
to stand upon a steep snowy cliff,
overlooking crashing purple waves,
as a single black snowflake kisses my cheek.

The pink sun sets across the green sky;
my heavy feet hug the frosty grass.
The world is not my own,
like a distorted bedroom mirror.

Only I am the same.
I've got my hair, my clothes,
but I don't have my grandfather's necklace—
the golden #1 pendant that sparkles on the seafloor.

I could dive into the water to retrieve it,
but who knows how deep
or how cold the water is
or what rocks lay at the bottom.

If I stay,
I am safe,
but incomplete—
lost.

I had strayed from the path,
through twisted,
frozen trees,
a broken road caked in snow.

The path holds memories,
echoes forgotten whispers.
The creaking cracks of trees swarm,
threatening to drag me back.

When the leaves tickle my neck,
I leap over the edge,
breaking through the icy water
sinking to the rocky bottom.

I resurface,
with my grandfather's necklace in hand.

———

Elizabeth Suggs is the founder of the LUW Romance Writers
Chapter, co-owner of the indie publisher Collective Tales
Publishing, owner of Editing Mee, and is the author of a growing
number of published stories, two of which were in a podcast and
poetry journal. She is also a book reviewer (EditingMee.com),
popular bookstagramer, and cosplayer. When she's not writing or
reading, she's playing video and board games or making cookies.

THE WINTER LIGHTS

Craig Crawford

M ary and I stopped at the trail entrance. It represented a ten-minute shortcut home from school, but we sized up the caution tape blocking our path. During a winter lull, the massive snow piles melted down several inches.

Enough for someone to discover a body.

Along the trail, no one even knew how many snowfalls had occurred since the person died. It could have been weeks—our part of the country sees snowfall from November through March. Some years it snows into April. Rummaging through my memory, I counted the number of snowfalls: a lot had dumped on us. Even since Christmas.

We chose the trail most days, so the caution tape disturbed us. We'd doubtless walked by the body without ever knowing it. It could easily have been us who discovered the corpse if we'd happened by at the right time.

"All they say is it's a teenage girl," Mary said, her eyes peering down the path.

"It's been over a week," I answered. "They must know who it is. If it was a kid, they had to live in the neighborhood."

"No one's disappeared from school," she answered. "People have been out sick, but I talked with Chenise and Katy. They can't think of anyone who's been out more than five days. This would have been weeks back."

Conversation on the body ran up and down the halls daily, rumors bubbling. Teachers started cutting talk short during class because everyone wanted to discuss it and go over the few details. We chatted about it nightly at our houses. The authorities released no further information, either. The news updated nightly, which meant mostly two minutes of empty air time as the police and coroners continued their 'ongoing investigation.'

"I heard two guys talking in the lunchroom," Mary said. "They heard a rumor someone dumped the body from another state."

"Who said that?"

"Gavin Parish and Mully."

Not the most respectable sources to my mind. I seriously doubted Gavin or Mully knew the truth. "I suppose," I said, considering a more likely scenario. "If it wasn't someone from our school, it could be someone from one of the other two high schools."

"Yeah, but this trail is just down the hill from Windham. Who would be over here screwing around if they didn't live nearby?"

"I don't know," I said. "I kind of want to go past the tape."

"There's nothing there," Mary told me. "They removed any evidence when they found the body. We'll get in trouble for no reason."

"I know," I said. "I just want to see it."

"Yeah, no," Mary said, taking my hand. She tugged and drew me away from the trail. "We'll find out when they release it to the papers, eventually. If it's a school kid, then they probably had a backpack or an ID with their name on it."

"Unless it's like Gavin and Mully said: someone dumped the body and stripped them of anything giving away their identity."

"Who doesn't go to the dentist, though?" Mary asked, showing off her white, even teeth. "They'll still tell the papers when the body's been identified. Let's go, Martin."

Mary and I started dating almost six months ago, and she always called me by my proper name, even though everyone else called me Marty. It was just one of the things I loved about her. Our sense of humor ran the same, and we both liked spooky movies and playing board games. Her short, red hair only added to her cuteness, and I spent every moment with her I could.

We followed the road cutting back and forth around the trail, instead. We passed my street and climbed the last four blocks up the hill to Mary's house. Mary barely closed the door before her mom's head sprouted up from behind her laptop screen. Her bright orange hair matched Mary's, only longer. They shared the same sharp nose and cheekbones.

"They know the name of the girl they found along the trail," she said.

"Who is it?"

Mary's mom shook her head. "She's only seventeen, so they won't release her name. The news said the family was being located."

"Same age as us," I said. "Did they say which high school she went to?"

"Nope—no details. They dated the death to the blizzard three weeks back."

I remembered it: nasty cold and Mother Nature dumped close to twelve inches on us. The wind got so bad I couldn't see the street from our window. "They don't know how she got there?" I asked.

"They didn't say, but the FBI is involved." Mary's mom eyed us both. "That means it's more than just some girl getting lost in a snowstorm."

Mary and I traded looks. "Did they say if she was murdered?" I asked.

"The official cause of death right now is cited as 'exposure,' but I can't imagine some girl just being out in that weather. It was a bad storm."

"So weird," Mary said, cutting off the conversation between me and her mom. "Hey, can Martin stay for dinner?"

"Sure. Be in about an hour. I take it you're going to spend the hour doing homework?" she asked expectantly.

"Yes, Mother. We both have a paper to write for English Lit."

"Fine, but keep the door open."

I held out my hands. "Cuffs again?"

It was a regular joke between us, and Mary's mom only rolled her eyes.

We headed to Mary's room, and I tossed my bag to the floor, sighing and sitting against the side of her bed. Mary kicked off her shoes and sat on the bed. "I seriously have to get a good grade on this. I've screwed up a couple of the homework assignments, and I want to keep an 'A' or Mom and Dad will cut our time."

I sighed. "I got the same lecture. They act like you're my pet or something. 'If your grades suffer, your friend won't be able to come over.'"

She grinned. "Suppose there's some parents' manual they all read before having kids?"

"If there is, I'm pretty sure my parents didn't read it. They half-ass everything."

The doorbell rang. We heard the front door open, and Mary's mom talking to someone. I strained my ears and picked out more than two voices. I didn't decipher even a single word, but the door closed, and the conversation continued.

Mary bounced off the bed. "I'm seeing who it is."

She disappeared out the door, and I heard her sock feet plodding down their stairs. Mary's voice added to the mix, and the conversation picked up. I dug out my notebook, but I kept trying to catch bits of the conversation.

Mary's footsteps thumped back upstairs, faster this time. "You have to go home."

"Why?"

"I don't know," she said. "The police are here."

"What? Is your dad—"

"No, he's just pulling up," Mary said. "Mom won't tell me what's going on. She just sent me back up to kick you out. That's all I know. I'll call you later when I can."

"Okay," I said, packing up my stuff. "I hope everything's alright."

"Me, too."

I hugged and kissed Mary before heading downstairs. I spotted three people in the main room, along with Mary's mom: two uniformed police officers, one woman and one man, and a second woman in a dark suit. Mary's mom glanced up on my way by. "Sorry, Martin. Something's come up."

"It's okay, Ms. Templeton. I'll talk to Mary later. Hope everything's okay."

She mumbled something, but immediately turned back to the woman in the suit.

Once outside, I passed Mr. Templeton, who hurried inside after only a nod. I flitted through scenarios and ideas about what might have happened. Reaching my house, my own dad peeked out from the kitchen as I entered, mixing salad with his beefy hands. "Hey, Marty. I thought you were staying for dinner at Mary's."

I shrugged. "I was, but the police showed up."

His big, dark eyebrows dented. "Police? Was there an accident?"

"Don't know. They rushed me out. Mary's dad got home as I left, so I know everyone there is okay. I'm thinking maybe it's a family member."

"Odd," he said. "Well, Mom's on her way home. Ted's finishing wrestling practice, but he's eating over at Brace's. I hope you like manicotti."

"You know I do."

He grinned. "My psychic powers must have kicked in because I cooked a bunch."

AFTER DINNER, I TEXTED MARY THREE TIMES. NO RESPONSE. I considered calling, but she kept her phone close like a police officer packs a pistol. Whatever happened wasn't good, because Mary usually texted me constantly. A call would likely not be welcome.

I slogged through my assignments, my eyes glancing at my phone every few minutes. Afterward, I got on Discord. She didn't show up there either. I made small talk with some of my other friends as they came online, but I kept looking for her.

The digital clock edged toward ten when my phone finally lit up. I snatched it from the desk. "Mary?"

"Hey," she said, an edge in her voice.

"What's up? Are you okay?"

"We're fine. Mom said she has an aunt who died, and we have to be gone for a few days. Did you finish your science assignment?"

I bristled. 'Science assignment' was our code word for parents listening in. "Yeah. Is it okay for me to share answers?" I asked—my code to ask if they were hearing my end of the conversation.

"It's okay. I finished it already," she said.

"Is there trouble?" I asked quietly.

"Yes, I finished my paper," she answered. "They already called me in sick for the next week. I guess we're leaving tomorrow."

"Do you know what kind of trouble?" I asked.

"I don't know. I didn't get the notes for Government. Can you email them to me?"

"Okay, I'm guessing there's nothing else you can tell me. Call you tomorrow?"

"Sure," Mary said. "I'll call you before school." Muffled conversation erupted in the background and then Mary fired out, "What? What do you mean no phones? We're going to a funeral. Of course, I'll have my phone. Martin, hang on…"

I heard Mary's dad talking in the background, his voice sharper than either Mary's or her mom's. I definitely picked out the word, 'police.' Concern reared as I caught his next word: 'dangerous.'

"Mary, what's going on?"

Another heated exchange erupted in the background. "Martin, I'll call you back… oh yes I am!" she barked. "I'll talk to you soon. Sorry," and she hung up.

My brain kicked in and I reviewed everything I'd heard. Had one of Mary's aunts gotten mixed up in something dangerous and gotten killed? I decided a relative would have called if someone died of normal causes. The police didn't get involved in deaths unless something criminal happened. Between the dead girl in the snowbank and whatever was happening in Mary's family, it weirded me out. What was going on lately?

The next morning, I immediately checked my phone, but I

had no missed calls and no texts from Mary. I hopped on Discord, but she didn't put in an appearance there either.

When Mary didn't show up at school, I asked around, but no one else had heard from her. I sent three texts. No answer. After school, I skipped the trail again and walked straight toward her house. Oddly, I saw her mom's car in the driveway. Usually, they parked their cars in the garage, and if they left town, I doubted they'd leave one in the driveway. Quickly, I doubled back toward home.

All evening, I monitored my phone and Discord. Nothing but radio silence from Mary. I checked the news, having little better to do. They ran another story on the body of the girl along the trail, but didn't offer any new details. Bored, I headed upstairs and started fishing around on the net for more information.

I found several news articles on the body, which were a rehash of everything I already knew. I did discover one new detail: an older man spotted the body while cross-country skiing along the trail. He glimpsed part of a purple coat in the thawing snow.

One crackpot site ran an article on the weird stories surrounding our town. It said people saw strange lights in the wooded areas from time to time. People referred to them as the 'Winter Lights.' According to some unnamed "expert," several strange disappearances occurred too, going back decades.

I rolled my eyes. As kids, Ted and I walked the trail and played in the creek all the time, and we never saw anything. I'd never even heard of anyone disappearing in my entire life before this. It had absolutely nothing to do with the body as far as I could tell, but sites like this loved digging up stuff to keep people interested.

I texted Mary again but received nothing.

The rest of the week, I received no calls or texts. I broke down and tried calling again on Saturday. Her phone diverted me straight to voicemail. I walked by the house but saw no cars this time. Curtains shuttered all the windows.

Worry settled in big and bad. Dad and Mom tried looking from their end. Dad knew where Mary's dad worked and he called over, but only learned he took an emergency leave of absence.

I distracted myself by shopping online for a six-month anniversary present for her. I found a necklace with a Celtic cross. Mary loved history, and she especially liked reading about 'Old World" mythology. I knew it was perfect and hit the 'buy' button. Three days later, it arrived.

Still no word from Mary.

Days ticked by, and I noticed strange cars in the neighborhood. Two black sedans with tinted windows trolled the streets. The license plates contained only numbers, with nothing identifying which state the car had been licensed in. Federal maybe? It added weight to my idea that Mary's family was somehow mixed up in something bad, something with mobsters or drug dealers.

Fifteen days after Mary first went quiet, I signed onto Discord, joining up with two of my other friends. They'd been grilling me about Mary, but I still had nothing. A friend request popped up from a new player: MerryTemptress04. Normally I'd have dismissed it, but I read enough into the name. I accepted the invite, hoping.

Two minutes ticked by, and Mary answered. "Can't stay long. They're watching me."

"What's up?" I immediately typed back. "Where are you?"

"We're still home. Didn't leave. No dead relative. Authorities involved, but don't know why. They won't let me leave the house."

I shook my head, unsure of what to say. "I miss you," I typed. "Get back on tomorrow?"

"YES!" she typed. "7ish," and she disappeared.

I stared at the screen for a long time. All this time, she was right up the street.

All the next day, I watched the clock, just counting down to seven and ignoring everything and everyone else. Walking home after school, I eyed the trail. Still cordoned off, I thought it odd after so much time. I decided to finally take the shortcut home. I slowed, allowing a car to pass by on the street. Looking behind me, I waited for the car to veer around the bend. I ducked under the caution tape and sprinted down the path.

Further down, I stopped and scanned in both directions, but I stood alone on the path. I spotted another square shape of caution tape just off the trail. I approached, but the previous evening's four inches of snow blotted out everything. There was a scoop in the frozen snowbank, where I assumed they'd dug out the body. Now that I was finally at the site, I suddenly felt the creeps settle over me. The quiet all around sent my eyes darting. I lurched into a jog toward home, which quickly became a dead run. I ducked under the yellow tape at the other end of the path. I allowed myself one glance back along the trail but saw nothing.

Reaching home, the TV announced another snowstorm on its way. I headed upstairs to finish my homework, constantly eyeing the time. I joined Mom and Dad for dinner, but it only served as another distraction to eat more time off the clock. I logged on at six-thirty and stared at the screen.

At just after seven, MerryTemptress04 joined my server. "How are you?" I typed.

"Something weird is going on," she wrote back.

"???"

"Parents scared," she typed. "And they won't leave me by myself. Always one of them with me."

"Scared for you?" I asked.

154

"Don't know. People at the house aren't police. They send me upstairs when they talk."

"Mobsters?"

"Unknown. Meet me tonight at 11?" Mary asked.

My mind raced, working through the logistics. Dad always went to bed early, but Mom usually fell asleep on the couch. My room sat over the garage and it was a far drop to the ground. But then again, we had a lot of snow piled up, and I could aim for the snowbank. Still, I liked my chances of getting past Mom without waking her. I didn't need a broken leg on top of everything else.

"I'll try. Where?" I typed.

"My backyard."

"Ok."

I received a thumbs-up icon, and MerryTemptress04 disappeared.

The light shone from under Ted's door. I headed over and knocked. It took four raps before his door opened. Ted cast suspicious eyes at me from under his brown mess of hair. "What?"

"I need help."

Ted fully opened his door. I never, ever asked him for help with anything. He motioned me inside, and I proceeded to confide in him on what was up.

"Weird," he answered, looking me over. "They catch you, and you'll be screwed."

"It's why I need you to cover for me if she comes to check on us."

"If she does, I'll tell her you already went to bed. So get your door closed and your bed set."

"Thanks, Ted."

"All good. I'll need a favor someday."

The snow cavorted with the wind outside, and I stashed a coat and boots for my trek. I bided my time until Mom finally fell asleep around ten-forty-five. I put on my coat and slipped out as quietly as I could. I darted into our backyard and out the gate.

The wind pushed on me, pelting my cheeks with snow, but I was about to see Mary for the first time in weeks.

I walked toward Mary's street. Remembering the black cars, I stopped on the sidewalk. I couldn't have them catch me approaching her house. Running the layout of the neighborhood inside my head, I planned a route requiring me to hop a few fences. A few of her neighbors owned dogs, but judging the weather, I figured they'd all be inside.

I walked swiftly, eyes on the lookout for cars. I stayed at the edges of the streetlights, prepared to dive over piles of snow if I spied a car. I made two blocks and cut through a backyard. Working my way uphill, I pulled myself over two wooden fences and a shorter chain link.

Slipping over the last, I crouched down inside Mary's yard. I wanted to text her, but I feared they might have her phone. I didn't understand why they kept her from me.

Unless.

If she was in trouble with someone dangerous, meeting her could cause trouble for me too.

A shadow moved in the backyard. My eyes widened. Dread and defeat washed over me. I'd missed someone staked out in the backyard—probably FBI. My stomach churned as I expected to be caught.

A lone figure approached, and I recognized Mary's gait. She wore her dark purple parka—a good move for hiding. She attacked me with a hug when she reached me. She kissed me, too. I had a million questions, but they could wait.

She finally released me, and we crouched in the snow.

"What's going on?" I whispered.

"No one will tell me the truth."

"Who won't?"

"They're from some federal agency, I think. Mom said there's a dangerous person after me, but she won't say who or why. It's stupid. I haven't done anything to anyone."

"Didn't they tell you *anything*?"

"No. We're supposedly waiting it out. They won't even tell me what we're waiting for."

"Speaking of waiting. I've been wanting to give you this. I fished a box out of my pocket and handed it to her. "Happy Anniversary," I told her.

Mary's eyes lit up. The smile on her face told me everything I needed to know as she opened it. Unzipping her coat, she put the pendant over her head and hat, and hung it over her sweater. She wrapped her arms around me, squeezing tight. "I love it. Thank you, Martin."

I held her. It felt so good to have her back.

"Let's go for a walk," she said.

"Can you? They're probably watching. How did you sneak out?"

"They've got people out front, but no one inside. I slipped out after Mom and Dad went to bed."

"Why the Feds, you think?"

"I do *not* know, but I wish this was over."

"It's got to be the mafia, or drugs," I said. "Do you think one of your parents' siblings got involved in something?"

"I don't know. I don't care anymore. I'm sick of being cooped up in the house. Let's go for a walk. Please."

"They've got cars on the streets. They might spot us."

"I'm inside," she said, grinning. "They're not expecting me outside, and especially not with a guy."

I wavered. "I don't know. If someone *is* after you, this is a good way to give them a chance to get you."

"Why would anyone be after *me*?" she asked. "I haven't done anything. Neither have Mom and Dad. I think they're worrying over nothing. C'mon. Just a short walk. I need the fresh air."

Those large brown eyes killed my resolve. "Just around the block," I said.

She squeezed my hand, and we slipped over the fence. Heading away from her house, we walked hand in hand, ducking against the frequent rough wind gusts. We didn't talk. I kept an eye out for cars, but saw no one.

Passing a stand of trees, a flash of light caught my attention. Stopping, we both saw it. Mary sucked in a breath, pointing. "I've heard of the Winter Lights," she whispered, "but I've never seen one. Have you?"

I read about them on the internet the other day, but I thought it was crap." The light shifted and moved, killing the rest of my words.

A bluish light meandered in between the trees, further back from the road. It looked like the light of a giant firefly. A brilliant pale blue, it bobbed and lazily floated waist high off the ground. Mary grinned at the sight, but I shivered.

"We should go," I said.

"No way," Mary said. "I've always wanted to see one. Let's get a closer look."

"Mary, no," and I grabbed her hand. "I don't think they're friendly."

"Oh, come on. They talk about them in the legends around here. They're fun, but they're just superstitions. A bunch of old stories to scare kids and keep them inside."

"Mary, please."

The blue light brightened and whisked behind a tree. I looked around, but we stood alone on the street. Squinting, I didn't see anyone back in the trees playing a trick on us. The light didn't come from a flashlight. It bounced, too animated and too quick to be someone running in the snow-covered woods.

Mary pulled me forward.

The wind whipped down on us, and I shifted sideways to cut the cold against my face. "Mary."

"It's okay," she said. "I don't have a bad feeling at all," and she wriggled her hand loose from mine.

"No," I told her, grabbing at her hand.

She turned on me, her defiant look in place. "Look, I won't go into the woods. Just to the edge. I won't leave your sight. It's… so pretty." She trudged through the snow—no more than ten steps. Looking back at me, she smiled against the gloom. "See, I'm fine. You can see me. Just let me look at it for a second."

My instincts told me to grab her, but a dread crept over me. The wind whipped again, but the blue light cut through the haze of the blowing snow.

Her back to me now, Mary clasped her hands together. "It's so cool. Martin. It backed off when I stepped forward. If it is actually something, whatever it is, it's shy."

I couldn't move. I willed myself forward to join her, but my feet disobeyed. I stared at the back of her coat, looking like a shadow against the night. The blue light cavorted, shifting back and forth, weaving in and out from between the trees. It mesmerized me.

A rush of wind hit us. Sharper and stronger than the last gusts. I squinted, turning sideways, shoving my backside against the gale. It pushed on me for several seconds before relenting.

I sucked in a breath. "Whoa," I said. "That was a bad one. Mary..."

She was gone.

"Mary!"

Wildly, I jerked my head back and forth, but Mary was nowhere. The light in the trees disappeared, too. I called her name again and ran forward to where she'd stood. I followed her tracks, but they ended the last place she stood.

"*Mary!*"

I called her name over and over, but she didn't answer. I saw no sign of her in the trees. Panic poured into me. I didn't know what to do. I took four steps toward the trees, but fear stopped me. Something about the stand of trees warned me; scared me into stopping short.

I remembered my phone and pulled it out. I knew Mary's parents' numbers, and I called her mom. I scanned the trees, shouting Mary's name again until her mom answered. I don't know exactly what I said, but I vomited out words, apologizing but getting out the story of what happened and where I was. I don't know how much Mary's mom actually deciphered, but it only took a few minutes before I saw headlights.

One of the dark sedans pulled up, followed by Mary's mom's car.

Her parents jumped out, and they pounced on me, pelting me with questions I couldn't answer. *What's going on? Where is she?* A woman and a man in dark coats exited the black sedan. "Where is she?" the woman called.

I pointed to the trees, but I didn't know if she was in there or not. It's what my fears told me, but I hadn't seen her run toward them.

Strong twin beams shot out from powerful flashlights, running over the stand of trees. The two immediately stomped forward, pausing for a couple of seconds on Mary's tracks before heading in.

Mary's dad grabbed me. "Where did she go?"

"I don't know," I told them. "She snuck out because she wanted to see me, and we went for a walk. We saw a spooky light," I answered, gesturing to the trees. "Mary wanted to get closer, but I only let her go this far," and I pointed toward her last two prints. "A gust of wind hit us, and then when I looked up, she was gone."

Mary's mom started sobbing. She dropped to her knees in the snow. Mary's dad ran to her side. "We told her not to go out!" he shouted at me. "Why didn't you keep her there?"

"I didn't know," I tried. "Mary said you wouldn't tell her anything."

Mary's dad wrapped his arms around his wife, who cried into her hands. All at once, she rifled into her coat and pulled something out. Thrusting her arm out, she shouted at me. "Do you know where she got this?"

Looking down, pins and needles flushed my cheeks. The creeps crawled down my back, and I felt sick to my stomach. Mary's mom held out the pendant I'd just given Mary only minutes ago.

"Where did you get that?" I asked.

"They found it on her," Mary's mom said. She buried her face in her husband's chest and cried harder.

"When did you give it to her?" Mary's dad growled.

"I… what do you mean they found it on her?" I asked.

"The body on the trail," he whispered. "It was Mary–even though it couldn't have been. That girl had been dead for weeks, but we saw the body. It was her. It was her coat, and her wallet in her pants pocket."

"How?" The only word able to leave my lips.

"They don't know. No one knows." He gestured toward the two in the trees. "They found her dead in the snow weeks ago. And now our Mary is really gone."

Growing up, **Craig Crawford** read constantly. After being wowed by so many great novels, he wondered if he could do it too. In the last three years, he's published fifteen short stories, including a novella with another due out in December 2022, another in 2023 and a serial coming out in 2023. He writes in fantasy, sci-fi, YA, horror, humor—whatever his imagination gives him. You can learn more about his writing and what makes him tick at craiglcrawfordbooks.com.

PART 3

FROZEN IN TIME

C.R.J. Smith

C.R.J. Smith is a writer and photographer from Navan, Ireland. He has had several short stories published and is currently working on a novel when he's not running around after his son and his cat.

LIFE SAVER

Bev Vincent

For days, forecasters had been warning about the Arctic vortex descending on Southeast Texas, predicting that it would cause a multi-day hard freeze, but Bryan hadn't taken them seriously. He'd been living in the state for several years, and the worst he'd seen were a few flurries. There was no way he was going to change his plans simply because it was going to be a little chilly.

However, Mother Nature had plans of her own, and she didn't consult Bryan. What started out as sleet soon changed to freezing rain. The extra weight on the branches of the massive old oak tree beside the driveway—a tree he should have removed a year ago—pushed it past its tipping point. From his secret room behind the pantry where he was preparing for his monthly excursion, Bryan heard the enormous tree come crashing down. His SUV, parked in the driveway, proved an irresistible target for the falling oak. The tree landed across the hood of his vehicle—crushing it, shattering the windshield, and blowing out the two front tires.

Bryan stormed to the front bay window, switched on the

outdoor floodlights, and stared at the wreckage. His house was two miles from his nearest neighbor, set well back from the county road that was his only route into the city. There was no way he was going to be able to rendezvous with a subject tonight.

It took every ounce of willpower to stop himself from breaking something. It was all about self-control. His ability to rein his emotions in during heightened situations meant he'd been able to continue doing what he'd been doing for so long without getting caught. Conditions had arisen in the past that prevented him from carrying out his mission and he'd survived those, but there was always an emotional toll. For the next thirty days, he would be out of sorts. Fortunately, no one had to live with him to endure the repercussions of these frustrations. He would have been hell to live with. Sometimes he didn't enjoy living with himself.

He shook his head at the sight of the destroyed vehicle. Now he was going to have to deal with the fallen tree and the wreckage it caused. The tree he could handle easily enough. He was an expert at reducing things to a manageable size and making them vanish. Give him a couple of days with his chainsaw, and he'd have a generous addition to his stockpile of firewood. It might not get cold in this part of Texas very often, but he did enjoy sitting in front of the fire on a cool evening, revisiting his souvenirs. Getting the shattered SUV repaired, though, was another matter. That would involve people, and Bryan avoided people as much as possible.

He regretted his earlier skepticism about the severity of the storm. He should have paid more attention, especially when they gave the storm a name.

He was still commiserating with himself over the interruption to his plans and the inconveniences he now faced when the lights went out. He waited for the generator to kick in. After a momentary, distant whine, the lights flickered on for a moment, and then darkness prevailed once again. Bryan didn't mind the darkness—he usually worked at night—but he didn't relish the idea that he might lose everything in his fridge if the power stayed off too long. Maybe even his deep freeze, and that would be really bad. He stored precious things in there.

It had been a while since Bryan had needed the generator, and he'd been lax about servicing it. Before going outside to see why it wasn't running, he spent a few minutes in the living room starting a fire in the fireplace. Once he was sure it wasn't going to go out, he grabbed a flashlight and a heavy coat from the closet, then pulled open the front door.

A young woman was standing on the stoop, shivering, her hand raised as if about to knock. Wearing jeans and a flannel shirt, she was woefully underdressed for the weather. Her clothing provided virtually no protection against the—yes, he had to admit it—the Arctic blast that also greeted him through the open front door.

Although Bryan was momentarily speechless, his unexpected visitor was not the least bit lost for words. "Oh my God. I'm so glad someone's here. I thought for sure I was a goner. I saw your lights, but then they went out and I worried that maybe I'd imagined them, or they were fairy lights and I was being lured astray. It's so cold. Can you believe how cold it is? I mean, what the hell, right? This is Texas, last I checked."

She was still standing on the stoop, arms wrapped around herself to ward off the cold, and yet she was talking a mile a second through chattering teeth. Bryan stepped back. "You'd better come inside." He affixed his most congenial smile to his face, uncertain if she could see him in the dark. Maybe his evening plans hadn't gone up in smoke after all. Maybe Lady Luck had delivered exactly what he needed right to his front doorstep.

The woman hesitated a second before following him into the dark house.

"Power's out," Bryan said. "I was just going out to check the generator." He pointed toward the living room. "There's a fire in the fireplace. Get yourself warm. I'll find something for you to eat when I get back. If you're hungry, that is."

"Famished. Thanks. You're a real lifesaver," she said.

Bryan shot out the open door before she could launch into another long-winded speech. He picked his way around the fallen tree toward a small shed beside the house that held the gas-powered generator. It was indeed brutally cold, which made him wonder why this woman was wandering around in the dark. There was nothing beyond his place—the road dead-ended at a barricade a dozen yards past his driveway. He'd have plenty of time to figure that out once he got back inside, he decided. At the moment, he was on a mission, although not the one he originally intended.

Before he even reached the shed, he sensed something was wrong.

Tracks in the frost-covered gravel led up to the shed door, despite the fact that he hadn't been in this part of the yard for several days. As he drew closer, he saw that the padlock was missing, and the shed door was ajar. With only his flashlight to use as a weapon, it would require getting into close quarters with a potential burglar. Still, he didn't want to go back inside for a gun. That would raise questions he didn't want to have to answer.

He flashed the light around the perimeter of the shed to see if anyone was lurking in the shadows. Then he pulled open the door—the hinges squealing like a stuck pig—and pointed the beam inside. To his amazement, the generator looked like someone had taken a sledgehammer to it. But hadn't he heard it whine to life briefly just a few minutes ago? Had that been his imagination? It didn't seem likely. That scrawny young woman couldn't have done this, could she? Maybe she had a companion.

Something was very wrong, indeed.

There was nothing he could do about the generator. It would be impossible to repair the damage, and he had no intention of calling the cops. The last thing he needed was to have them sniffing around his place. Staying off their radar was crucial. And there was no chance of getting a replacement. People had probably been buying up every available backup generator in the county for days. Time to take care of his unexpected guest and find out if someone else was with her.

On the way back to the house, he remained on high alert in case the vandal was skulking in the darkness, waiting for him to relax his guard. So far, there were no other signs of anyone else, though. He ran his flashlight across the front of his wrecked SUV once more before entering the house, locking and bolting the door behind him..

"I saw the kettle next to the fireplace," the girl said when he returned to the living room. She was wrapped in a comforter that was normally spread across the back of his sofa. "I filled it with water and hung it from the hook to make tea. I had a couple of spare bags in my purse. I hope you don't mind. I'm just so cold."

"No, that's all right. Tea sounds like a fine idea." His eyes scanned the room for signs of anyone she might have let in while he was outside investigating. Nothing. He needed to relax. "Would you like me to make you a sandwich?" he asked, his voice practiced at projecting calm. "I have tuna. Or peanut butter. With the power off, my options are a little limited."

"Tuna salad would be great. Just mayo, nothing else. Don't you hate it when people put nasty things in food you really like and ruin them? Like onions or pimento or celery."

"Just mayo it is." As he headed toward the kitchen, he asked, "Was there someone else with you?"

"No. Why do you ask?"

"No reason," he said. It sounded like she was telling the truth, but he couldn't be sure. If she had a partner, the other person would be stuck outside in the cold and probably wouldn't survive the night. Another kind of coldness was about to descend upon his guest, who had chosen the wrong door to knock on. The kind of cold from which there was no return.

He could easily have overpowered her while she warmed herself in front of the fire, or shot her while she wasn't looking, but that wasn't his way. He wanted her to go peacefully while he talked her into the darkness.

He set aside half the tuna salad mixture for himself, then took a small bottle of clear liquid from his pocket. He'd been planning to use it in the city right about now. Instead, he added several drops to her tuna salad. He put the assembled sandwiches on a tray, then added a couple of mugs, a small pitcher of milk, the sugar bowl, and a bottle of honey. If it was going to be her last meal on earth, he wanted her to have her tea just the way she wanted it.

"Oh, you're a lifesaver," she said for the second time since she arrived. "Let me pour."

She put a generous dollop of milk in the bottom of her mug and gave him a quizzical look, the pitcher hovering over his mug.

"Black for me," he said.

She poured tea into both mugs and wrapped herself up again in the blanket. Then she grabbed the sandwich he offered her and took a big bite.

Satisfied everything was going according to plan, Bryan took a sip of tea. The warm liquid felt good, dispelling the chill that had set in after his venture outside. He moved his chair closer to the fireplace and took another sip. "What were you doing way out here in the dark anyway?" he asked.

She finished polishing off half the sandwich. "We'll get to that in a few minutes," she said.

That struck him as highly unusual. He had let his guard down, and now he had the feeling that something was very wrong again. He tried to put his teacup on the coffee table when a profound lethargy overcame him. The cup tumbled from his hand and fell to the floor with a crash.

Then he knew no more.

———

HE AWOKE IN HIS SECRET ROOM, STRAPPED TO THE SAME operating table to which he had strapped so many others. Several candles illuminated the room with flickering light. Where had they come from?

It took a while to fully regain his senses before the realization struck.

"The tea," he croaked. "You put something in the tea."

"I did indeed," the young woman said. "Just like you put something in the tuna."

"But how…?"

"I asked you not to add anything but mayo. Bad boy. Bad, bad boy. Fortunately, your potions have no effect on me."

"Who *are* you?"

"I guess you could call me a nemesis."

"A… what?"

"Some call us avenging angels. You've been on our radar for a long time, Bryan. There are so many bad people in the world, it's just taken me a while to get to you." A profoundly sorrowful look fell over her. "If I'd gotten here sooner, who knows how many lives could have been saved?"

"The generator. That was you?"

She nodded. "And the tree, of course."

"I don't understand. No one could have been watching me. The storm took down the tree."

She gave him a wan smile, as if she pitied him. "Look what I made for you."

When she stepped aside, in the shimmering illumination of the candles, Bryan saw something on the counter. A long row of objects, all very similar but each uniquely different, too.

His trophies.

She'd been in his deep freeze. How could she possibly have known about them?

He flexed his muscles and tried to twist himself free of the straps that bound him to the table, but he knew that was futile. He had designed the setup himself so that there was no chance his subjects could wriggle free.

"So many bad people out there," she repeated. "Mostly men, if I'm to be honest. We try to do what we can to restore balance, to make sure as many of the greater demons in the world pay for their sins, eventually. Seriously, though, Bryan—it's almost impossible to keep up. The scales are so heavily tilted in favor of evil. But we do what we can, even though it feels like it's never enough."

"What are you going to do to me?"

"You'll see. Soon enough."

"Who are you?" he roared. "Who the hell are you?"

"I'm a life saver, Bryan." She smiled, revealing a mouthful of impossibly sharp teeth. "Only yours isn't one of the lives I'm going to save. Now close your eyes. It will be easier for you that way."

Bev Vincent is the author of *The Road to the Dark Tower* and *Stephen King: A Complete Exploration of His Work, Life and Influences*, as well as over 120 short stories, including appearances in *Autumn Noir*, *Summer Bludgeon*, *Ellery Queen's*, *Alfred Hitchcock's* and *Black Cat Mystery Magazines*, and *Cemetery Dance*. His work has been published in over 20 languages and nominated for the Stoker (twice), Edgar, Ignotus and ITW Thriller Awards. In 2018, he co-edited the anthology *Flight or Fright* with Stephen King. Recent works include the novellas "The Ogilvy Affair" and "The Dead of Winter," the latter found in *Dissonant Harmonies* with Brian Keene. bevvincent.com

NOW, DESOLATION

Avra Margariti

Where you now stand
A tree had stretched
Skeletal fingers
To puncture bone-white heavens
Like a wineskin masqued
Erebus black in winter breath.

And farther down, following
Your tresses windswept,
Uprooted from your
Bleeding scalp,
A copse had aggregated:
Oppressive canopy, a coven
Stealing oxygen
Like ghosts from sleeping infants.

What did we do, you ask?
We felled every frost-stripped tree.
Their hollows replete

With secrets, split down
The middle; the conspirator
Rings plotting our downfall;
Fey wraiths and birds speaking
In anthropolalia, annihilated—
Nothing but mulch
And splinters.

You can still see the boughs
And bark, you say?
Merely a snow mirage, child
For nothing survived
Our righteous slaughter. Not even
The timber, turned into
Rafts, set ablaze in the ocean,
Flames blue with salt
The way the old prophets
Taught us, even as we shivered
In houses devoid of hearths.

You can hear the roots murmur
In self-healing dreams?
It's only the wind, child,
Fluting our triumph,
Its threnody.

Avra Margariti is a queer author, Greek sea monster, and Rhysling-nominated poet with a fondness for the dark and the darling. Avra's work haunts publications such as *Vastarien, Asimov's, Liminality, Arsenika, The Future Fire, Space and Time, Eye to the Telescope,* and *Glittership. The Saint of Witches,* Avra's debut collection of horror poetry, is available from Weasel Press. You can find Avra on Twitter @avramargariti.

THE ROOTS OF SILENCE

Ryan Kirk

I t never occurred to us, in our times before, how memory is tied to our bodies, to our senses. The scent of garlic and onions sautéing in butter. The laughter of the girls across the street as we stretched out after a long run. The sound of hospital monitors going silent as nurses unplug the machines after the final fight is lost.

Take the bodies away and the memories become unmoored, like unanchored ships carried away by gentle tides. Such are ours, now. Sometimes they strike with a startling clarity, so vivid as if they had thrown us back in time to relive the mundane moments of our fleeting existences. More often, they are like mirages in the desert, vanishing at the barest hint of our attention.

Mostly we don't mind.

Because emotions, like memory, require flesh. The beating of the heart, the quick intake of breath as the shadows jump at you.

Some of us once wished for peace. For the end of worry and heartache.

No longer.

Because all the concerns, all the frustrations, and all the fears mean you're alive. And sometimes, it's good to fear the shadows that reach for you in the night.

I REMEMBER THE FIRST TIME I SET EYES ON THE OAK. IT WAS OLD when I was a child, gnarled branches twisting in the sky above me, shading me from the burning summer sun. It grew deep in the woods behind our cabin, offering me protection when no one else would.

I relive that day in my dreams. My heart pounded as I ran, my chest on fire with every step. Though I never lifted my shirt, I was sure that if I did, I would see the outline of my father's boot.

He shouted after me but didn't pursue. Why should he bother? That deep in the woods, there was nowhere to run. I'd have to return, eventually.

But he had been yelling, upset at how his food was cold. His deep voice, echoing in the small dining room, hurt my ears, and in my pain, I cried for him to stop.

The ground was rugged, and I tripped and fell, cutting my left hand on the sharp edge of an exposed stone. As I stood, I held my injured hand to my chest.

Then I saw the oak, quiet and lonely, surrounded by taller, straighter brothers and sisters. It was ancient and knobby, its bark twisted in intricate patterns.

I walked toward it, drawn to it like iron filings to a magnet. I reached out with my injured hand, then pulled it away as my blood seeped into the cracks of the bark. It was absorbed into the tree like rain in the middle of a drought.

I returned my hand to the tree's bark. When I removed it

again, I found no visible blood on my palm. The tree's leaves rustled, as though in thanks for the small offering.

Driven by a desire I didn't fully understand, I opened my arms and embraced the oak. Its bark was rough against my skin, but still far gentler than my family. In return, it offered me silence.

Blissful tranquility.

THERE IS A SEASON FOR ALL THINGS.

A season to work and one to play.

A season to love and one to mourn.

A season to live.

And a season to die.

He is the only person we know, and there is no seasonality to his visits. He joins us often, embracing and whispering to us.

But he only brings the voices in the spring, summer, and fall, when the ground around our roots is soft enough for the cold steel of his shovel. There are rings of overturned earth around us, and we now contain multitudes.

We drift in lifetimes of memories, but he is in none of them. In our times before, we did not know him.

Sometimes, when he comes, dragging yet another voice down the well-worn path, we scream, but all he hears is the rustling of leaves.

THERE ARE DAYS I WISH I COULD LIVE IN ETERNAL WINTER.

Let everyone else have the spring songs of cardinals and blue jays, the joyful squeals of children on summer break, and the crunch of leaves underfoot in autumn. Winter is silence. The snow muffles all sound, and people hide in their homes. Give me the days where the air is so cold it feels like it might crack, like thin ice. Give me soft, thick snowflakes that cover the ground like a blanket.

If not for the needs of the old oak, I would be content to live in an everlasting snow globe.

But it is hungry. Always hungry. In the winter, I cannot bring it the sustenance it craves. The ground freezes, and I cannot break it with my shovel. So in autumn I bring extra, hoping the oak can store the surplus for the long midwestern winter.

It doesn't speak, of course, but its silence says more than most humans do in their entire wasted lives. I hear its leaves rustle, even on windless days, and I know it is thankful.

THE NEWEST VOICES ARE ALWAYS THE LOUDEST, THE MOST confused. And we are beyond full. Dim as our memories are, there are just so many. Lifetimes stacked upon lifetimes, each of his rings of overturned dirt pouring more into a cup that overfilled ten summers ago.

It's worst in the autumn, as our leaves fall to the ground and he visits so often. So many unfamiliar voices, all so loud.

We can feel ourselves becoming something more.

Something that desires.

All we want is silence.

But we are trapped, and he cannot hear us.

IF I HAD FRIENDS, I ASSUME THEY WOULD ASK ME WHY I RUN A crematorium. So many of us are terrified of death, we can't imagine working around it every day.

The answer is simple: it's quiet.

I don't understand how people don't realize how loud their lives are. Their favorite celebrities are always shouting, their newscasters are always in a panic. The wails of sirens fill their streets, and the deep-throated roars of jets pollute their skies.

I think, somewhere deep in their bones, they do understand. They know their lives are noisy messes.

But what do they do? They drown it out with more noise. Headphones blare voices and instruments into ears that crave only a moment's rest. It's all noise, all the time. Until death intrudes.

It's a patient teacher, visiting friends and family, reminding us that silence is our natural state.

My work is quiet by design. A funeral director deals with the grieving families, leaving me to work in peace. The crematorium is a silent workplace, and a constant source of food for the oak.

No one questions whether the ashes they receive are the remains of their loved ones. No one weighs the urn, wondering if some part of their dearly departed is missing. I've developed a dozen techniques to fool the grieving.

It's easy to find bodies, if one knows where to look.

———

HE DIGS ANOTHER HOLE AND PLACES ANOTHER VOICE WITHIN. We scream, but he only looks up at our rustling leaves and smiles.

We do not know him, but as he adds more and more voices, an emotion takes root, as strong as any we felt in our times before.

Hate.

All we want is silence, and he is the bearer of voices.

We stretch our branches toward him, but he doesn't notice.

Soon he is gone, but he will return.
Thankfully, winter is near.
It is the closest we get to peace.

I SHUFFLE FORWARD, HAND AT MY SIDE. THE RIB GRINDS WITH every step.

I've lived in apartments my whole life, always close to the crematorium. They're the places I've slept and ate, but they aren't home.

Since that day as a child, my home has been here, at the foot of the old oak. I knew it felt the same. I've seen the way it reaches for me, bending its limbs as I near.

The food I've been supplying isn't enough. It wants me. It's always wanted me.

I don't know how they found me. Perhaps I got sloppy, or perhaps someone was just too curious. I hear the sirens in the distance, and it won't be long before they arrive.

This was the only place I could come, the only protection that remains. I don't know how I'll escape, but I know the oak will keep me safe.

My boots sink into the soft snow. Dark clouds gather to the west, and I know more is on the way. It'll blanket the world in silence, and I'll be free. I run my fingers over the gun in my pocket. I've never used it, but I know I'll never let them take me to prison. Too many people in small spaces.

It would be nothing but noise, all day, every day.

I gasp as my rib shifts again. I drove too fast and hit a stump by the old cabin. The rib is probably broken. It doesn't matter, so long as I can get to the tree.

There it is. As beautiful as ever. I shuffle up to it, wrapping it in an embrace. It welcomes me, as it always does, with a groaning of cold branches.

I turn, lean my back against my friend, and slide painfully down to the ground. Freezing water soaks my pants as my body heat melts the snow.

It's so quiet here. Not even a breeze whistles through the bare branches of the oak. My breath comes in ragged gasps, exhalations visible on this gelid morning. How I'd loved to pretend I was smoking as a child.

I laugh, even though it hurts. My lips draw into an O, and I puff, just like I was six again. The sirens approach, and I hate them for disturbing me here.

I barely feel the movement. The tree is silent, even as bark and trunk crack open. I turn and see a hole in the tree where none was before.

It will protect me, just as it always has.

I scoot back, curling my legs in tight. It's dark. As the tree closes around me, wrapping me in its stiff embrace, I smile.

Soon, it will be silent forever, just as nature intended.

HIS IS THE LAST VOICE, TRAPPED AMONG DOZENS, ALL SHOUTING at him. A never-ending outpouring of emotion.

And he screams, just like us all.

But he is the loudest.

Ryan Kirk is an author and entrepreneur based out of Minnesota. When he isn't writing, he can usually be found hiking outdoors or playing disc golf. Even in the winter. ryankirkauthor.com

IF A TREE FALLS IN THE FOREST

H. Dair Brown

"If a tree were to fall on an island where there were no human beings would there be any sound?"
-*The Chautauquan* magazine, June 1883

On a late summer day in Virginia, more than a century since it had been a mere seedling, a Wolf Tree spread its crown wide above the younger, smaller trees below. It was one of many species typically found along that portion of the Appalachian Trail. A man and a woman struggled below. Having no ears to intercept sound, the tree didn't hear the woman's fierce attempts to fight for her life, or the man's grunts as he shoveled the dirt over her. The tree didn't know that this was the first in a series of similar scenes that would repeat in the coming years, like a brutal echo. Different women, different times of year, but always the same man.

Less than a dozen years later, a windy autumn followed on the heels of a soggy summer and the Wolf Tree fell. Having no other large trees nearby to help protect it from the storm, its roots were no match for the wind. It lay across the graves of three of the man's victims. Arborists would classify the Wolf Tree's cause of death as *windthrow*.

IN THE WINTER OF 2007, A MOTHER BEAR AND HER TWO yearlings made their den under the protection of the downed tree's crown. It was conveniently located far enough from the trail itself to avoid the risks that came with human interaction. They'd only just settled in when the sound of the man stashing his tarp-wrapped shovel under the fallen trunk of the Wolf Tree disturbed the mother.

Going on instinct to protect her cubs, the bear charged, chasing the man back towards the hiking trails. She'd barely taken him down to the ground when she, too, was felled. Cause of death: the well-aimed bullet of a retired policeman out doing some winter birding. Lt. Pat Boniwell had hoped to snap a picture of a Yellow-rumped Warbler nibbling on the pale greenish-blue winter berries in a stand of wax myrtle shrubs on his morning hike. Instead, a local newspaper reporter captured images of Boniwell and the rescued man posing near the large, forever-stilled body of the mother bear. It made the front page, and Boniwell's friends affectionately referred to him as "One Shot" after that. David Rucker Leeds, the man he saved, would later be referred to as Inmate #4221237.

WHEN P.J.'S DAUGHTER WAS MURDERED, SHE SUBSISTED ON THE scraps of information from the police investigation. Once Leeds was caught, she consumed every detail of the court case. After the jury handed down a life sentence without the possibility of parole to Leeds, she gorged herself on the court transcripts and her own notes. She wasn't attempting to fill the Amalie-shaped emptiness, knowing the futility of that. She was working to pinpoint the exact moment when she could go back and undo everything without causing too much other disruption.

There were too many people involved, and the timeline was too vague for her own daughter's murder. She kept looking for another, earlier event that she could affect. She kept gleaning information, harvesting as much as she could from the seemingly endless array of true crime tv shows and podcasts, which continued to unearth details about the slayings by "The Beast of the AT." It still wasn't enough. She would have to talk to him directly.

She pretended to make peace with her daughter's killer. She wore her "forgiveness" like a corset: it molded her into a shape pleasing to others, but her insides were contorted and crushed. Sometimes she felt she couldn't draw a full breath. She did her best to duck the attention and praise generated by her visits to him on Death Row. She focused her energy instead on pulling stories out of him with the patience of a huntress and the methodical nature of a scientist.

When she heard the story about the bear, a little glimmer of excitement bubbled up inside her. Could this be the moment she'd been looking for? She gave him a nudge, which was all he ever needed to talk about himself.

"I'd just finished burying the third—no, the fourth one. Kara. She was a real fighter," he said, staring at her with his transparent, faux repentance. "God forgive me. I was a monster back then." He reached over to squeeze her hand. The guards had long ago stopped admonishing them for such things. She fought back the revulsion his touch gave her, focusing instead on her performance.

"Well, that was then. This is now," she said.

"That's right." He continued, not letting go. For a moment,

she glanced down at their hands: one had tended to her daughter's wellbeing, and the other had squeezed the life out of her. She shoved the thought down, smiled at him. "You were telling me about the bear."

"Well, it was quite a thing. I'd finished what I was doing at one of my favorite… burial spots…"

Dumping, she thought. He'd been about to say *dumping spots* and caught himself. For the millionth time, she squelched the desire to bury her thumbs in his eyes.

"I was on my way back, almost in sight of one of the markers on the AT, when all of a sudden, this big old black bear comes up out of nowhere and charges me. I start running, but they're faster than you'd think. She took me down from behind, and I thought I was a goner. Just then, some off-duty cop out for a hike spots it. He pulls out his handgun and *blam!* Dropped that bear in its tracks just in time. Right between the eyes. Saved my life."

He looked at her then, waiting for her to express gratitude for the officer's lucky timing. She needed more information, so she indulged him, as always. "It's so fortunate he was there."

"Yeah. Hardly a scar on me. First time I was in the paper, actually. Me and the cop shaking hands over the corpse of that bear. Not the last time, though."

He was on a roll now, didn't even notice the look of disgust she was trying to mask.

"At the time, I was a little afraid they'd ask me questions about what I was doing. I worried they'd find the graves. But everybody just focused on that bear. Still, I never went back to that spot. That's why I took the others after that to… other places. Like with Amalie."

When P.J. was pregnant with Amalie, she and her husband weighed the pros and cons of countless names for their daughter. They'd settled on a name that felt both special enough to convey their love for her and mainstream enough that she wouldn't hate it. Amalie meant "work" in German and "hope" in Arabic. It was also the first name of Amalie Emmy Noether, widely considered one of the most important women in the history of physics. When they said her name the first time, it felt like the most fervent prayer they could muster to the universe.

In Leeds' mouth, Amalie's name sounded like a perversion, a sound unfit for human ears.

She redirected him to details about that earlier site where he'd encountered the bear. Why he'd chosen it. What he remembered about the place. What he'd done before he'd gotten to the fallen tree. She followed behind him on his stroll down memory lane, plucking useful details from the otherwise useless chit-chat.

"You know, come to think of it, I almost didn't find the right spot. The big old tree I used as a landmark had fallen over in a windstorm. Covered up the graves of the first three, actually. Saved me a little trouble later. Between you and me, it probably kept the needle out of my arm. They never did find them. It's alright. It's nice out there. Peaceful. You should go there sometime."

He looked at her, completely oblivious to her true feelings for him. In those moments, he looked almost guileless and young. Once or twice, it had caused P.J. to struggle and lose focus. She'd even once convinced herself that Leeds was an intricate piece of the math that made up life. Him, a motherless, unloved boy. Her, a mother without a child. They made their own sort of equation, she supposed.

But then, P.J. would think about the way that Amalie's laugh used to erupt out of her or the way she would scowl in determination or thought. And that this shell of a man had stripped the world of Amalie's goodness and all the goodness that would come after her. Every time, it restored her resolve. She would bring Amalie back.

She stubbed out the flicker of compassion she felt for him and kept the raging fire of hatred camouflaged, as always. She smiled and nodded, as if he'd given her something to think about. "That's a good idea, David. I was thinking I just might do exactly that."

IN FACT, SHE WENT TO THE PLACE COUNTLESS TIMES. SHE TOOK A leave of absence from her post at the Kuamua Institute and rented a small house near the place where Kara Waters took her last breath fourteen years before Amalie would cross paths with Leeds.

If Amalie's dad were still here, he would waste his time trying to talk P.J. out of her quest. And he would fail–just as surely as he had when trying to talk Amalie out of hiking the Appalachian Trail solo in the winter. Amalie's disappearance nearly killed her father. The Leeds' trial finished the job. Being alone, like anything else, had two sides. It was lonely, but your choices were always entirely your own.

P.J. befriended "One Shot" Boniwell and heard his side of the story, mining it for every detail. Every day for a month, she hiked. She went to the spots where Boniwell and Leeds had parked their cars, to the AT marker where they both left the official trail, to where Leeds had left his victims, to where the bear had been brought down. She used her notes, the photos from the article in the local paper at the time. She walked until she knew every curve and turn, until she knew the best place from which to watch.

And then she put her plan in motion.

When P.J. was a child, there was a famous commercial that asserted, "Membership has its privileges." Being a world renowned expert in String Theory brought its own perks. She had her pick from a handful of devoted and brilliant associates she could tap to help her pull off her mission. In the end, she chose Nicky, who she knew would remain entirely focused on the science–and not the philosophy or ethics–of what P.J. wanted to do. Nicky didn't hesitate to accept P.J.'s offer to put theory into action. She'd been an unrelenting detail-oriented sounding board, catching a few things P.J. had missed, asking good questions, and always willing to go over the logistics and the math.

In the moments just before the jump, P.J. said, "You know I couldn't have done this without you. How will I ever thank you if this works?"

"Well, if it doesn't work, we have a lot bigger problems. Who knows? If we did the math right, there's a pretty good chance I won't be here or I won't remember it. Either way, It's been a pleasure to be your Igor."

P.J. laughed. "I think Igor had to dig up bodies and stuff. I just had you doing math and helping me–"

"Plan a murder?"

Hearing it put like that, P.J. almost lost her nerve. Nicky read the room and waded back in quickly.

"Proud to be your accomplice, Doctor. Seriously, it's been an honor. Now go erase this bastard and get your family back. Okay?"

"Okay."

"And even if I don't remember, be sure and tell me what happened."

A FEW HOURS BEFORE DAWN ON DECEMBER 8, 2007, P.J. CREPT into the garage where "One Shot" Boniwell–still known by everyone as just Pat or Lieutenant at this moment–kept his car. She pulled a screwdriver off the pegboard. She chose the front tire on the driver's side, hoping he'd notice it right away. Easing the air out as she'd practiced countless times before, she still had to stop twice when she thought she heard Pat or his wife moving around, fearing the sounds of her sabotaging the tires had awakened them.

Through her research, she'd learned that Pat's wife had gone to work that day sometime before Pat left for his hike. She was tempted to disable Angie's car, too, but didn't want to risk the ripple effects a change like that would make. She just needed to delay Pat. That was all. And before he could drive up to his favorite entrance to go hiking on the Appalachian Trail, he would have to change the tire.

She left the garage as quietly as she'd entered and walked the route she and Nicky had mapped out. It had the least risk of disrupting anything else. And failing a disaster, she should be there well ahead of Leeds's interaction with the bear.

As P.J. hiked her way to the location, she marveled at how ordinary it all felt. And yet, five states away, another P.J. was there, sleeping next to her husband of only a dozen years. Their beloved daughter, Amalie, all of nine years old, slept down the hall, surrounded by her favorite stuffed animals. P.J. was overwhelmed by the desire to ditch the plan and make her way to this other place where Amalie lived. The desire to simply lay eyes on her family nearly made her abandon all the careful work it took to get here.

She thought of Kara Waters' mother, whose nightmare was just beginning right now, without her even knowing it. Kara was likely already dead by now. Leeds had indicated that after one of his earliest victims had awoken and nearly escaped during this part of his "process," he'd changed how he handled the "disposal of their remains." There would be no more scuffles in the woods. P.J. had met Ms. Waters a few times. She'd been nice enough, if a tad vacant. The medication, which had been prescribed to combat Kara's mother's obvious depression, sometimes caused that effect. She'd seemed hollowed out, aged into a fragile husk by the trauma of it all.

P.J. couldn't bring herself to watch him bury Kara, purposely taking her time as she got closer to the spot. She'd long since dealt with the stinging guilt associated with not going back earlier in Leeds' life and changing his course. She simply couldn't run the risks associated with a change like that, with too many variables to count. Even this narrow slice, this relatively perfect "Target Moment," involving the fewest number of people possible, brought an incalculable number of risks. She didn't care. If it meant getting Amalie back–as well as her husband–it was worth it. Someone was going to be the first to time travel. It might as well be her. This was her best shot at doing something meaningful with it without disrupting too much at once.

She found the spot she'd chosen where she'd watch what would happen next, a rocky perch allowing her to take in the whole scene from above. She spotted him then, catching his breath after he finished filling in Kara's grave. He looked up at the crisp winter sky, and she could see his face. Younger than the man she'd spent so many hours talking to and mining for information. He looked smug, wearing a self-satisfied grin. He scattered some of the surrounding leaf litter over the bare ground, then unzipped his pants and pissed on the freshly covered grave. In the quiet of the night, P.J. could hear it hitting the dry leaves. Her fury brought her vision to a pinpoint, and she struggled to calm herself. She slowed her breathing and watched him wrap the shovel before stuffing it under the upper branches of the felled tree. He turned and walked back towards the path, less than fifty yards below where she hid.

A spider ran across the back of her hand. She jerked and tried to stifle her surprised yelp, but in an instant, she knew that he'd heard it. His head snapped up and their eyes met. In all the times they'd met, she'd never seen him with the expression he wore now. The predator within him shone through. The idea that Amalie and others would be forced to face him if she didn't do something converted her fear into a fury born of protective maternal instincts. She searched around for a rock or a large stick to hit him with. She didn't know if she could overpower him, but she knew that one of the two of them would not emerge from this.

That was when she finally saw the movement, heard the crashing from underneath the downed tree. The bear. A fellow mother, P.J. knew—something she'd later learned from the newspaper articles about Leeds' rescue. She'd left behind her two yearlings in the den to protect them from a potential threat to their safety. Leeds hadn't bothered with that detail in his story, of course.

Leeds didn't hear the bear at first. He was already running toward her spot on the ledge. By the time he realized it, the bear was already gaining. He tried running faster—something she knew from her own research is the worst thing you can do. It only excites the bear, igniting its predatory instincts. And a man will never, ever outrun a mother bear. As the morning light broke, with no sign of Pat Boniwell emerging for his morning birding hike, the bear easily took Leeds down from behind.

P.J. dropped to her knees, exhaling the breath she didn't know she'd been holding. She listened to Leeds' unanswered cries for help as the bear tore into him and chewed at the back of his neck. She watched, a hand covering her mouth, as the black bear flipped him over like a rag doll. Leeds swung wildly and screamed as the bear ripped through him. The sow seemed to take a moment to catch her breath before tilting her head at an angle and opening her mouth until Leeds' head more or less disappeared into it. The last echo of his pleas was overtaken by the sound of the bear's jaws cracking his skull, effectively ending Leeds' timeline.

And restoring others'.

P.J. remained on her perch, shaking and watching the mother bear drag Leeds' body deeper into the woods. She heard the sound of the bear feasting on him before lumbering back toward her den under the tree, where her two yearlings rested.

Together, they would all awake in the spring.

H. Dair Brown's short fiction has appeared in *The First Line, The Grief Diaries, Hope Screams Eternal, Summer Bludgeon,* and *Autumn Noir*. Her novel-in-stories, *Molly Bright*, was a top finalist in the Colorado Gold Fiction Contest. In between ballgames with her family and belly rubs for her dogs, she works on her unsettling novels and stories. hdairbrown.com

THE YULE LOG FIRE

Sam Claussen

Holiday neared its festive demise. Ravaged wrapping paper littered the wine-stained rug in the Bellow family's living room, warmly lit by a log smoldering in the blackened chimney. Coffee-laced tobacco smoke drifted around the curly brown hair of the two Bellow sons: Jonathan, aged twelve, and Benjamin, aged six—the latter with drool caked to his rosy cheek. Their dad snored in the adjacent dining room, reclined uncomfortably in a wicker-backed chair, the half-eaten ham congealing in a cherry-charred puddle before him.

Their mom stood at the frost-nipped bay window, watching as neighbors emptied out of their homes, dragging their felled Holiday trees with hay hooks. She held a pink quartz ashtray in one petite hand, a half-smoked cigarette in the other. She smoked it to the filter, left it smoldering in the ashtray, and closed the dusty green drapes.

"Go and get your dad up," she said to Jonathan.

The elder brother stood, ruffled Benjamin's sleep-matted hair, and slid across the reflective hardwood floor in footed Holiday pajamas, wool-warm and itchy, steadying himself upon the dining room table (and almost unsettling the whole glassware buffet in the process). He tapped lightly on his dad's shiny, bald head.

Dad snorted. His brown eyes flickered open. Their frosted glaze diminished with every blink. "Hey, Jonno," he said through blubbery lips.

"Time to burn the Yule Logs," Jonathan said, glancing at the family's Holiday tree towering in the corner like scalped Samson. Mom was stripping it of its garlands of lights and fragile ornaments. "Think you'll need help this year?"

"Give me a second." Dad stood and placed both his dirt-colored hands on his lower back before straightening abruptly; a skeletal crack echoed in Jonathan's ear drums, sending a chill down his own spine.

"Can I help this year?" Jonathan repeated.

"I don't see why not."

"I'm not so sure about that," Mom said as she rushed by with mopey Benjamin, hands red and sticky from the candy canes he had snuck off the Holiday tree throughout the day. "I don't like Jonny playing around with those hooks."

"I won't play around!" Jonathan said. "Charlie is a year younger than me. He helped his stepdad last year, *and* he got his own hook for Holiday this year."

"*Alright*, Jonno," Dad said, holding his hand up to Mom, quieting the rest of her objections. "You can use my old hay hook. Go grab them from the shed."

Mom brushed a graying lock of sandy hair behind her ear. "Just be careful with those rusty things," she said.

His father had received a new hook two Holidays ago, so only Jonathan's was rusty. The brick coloring of the hand-me-down tool pegged Jonathan as lower middle class, but he was too excited to be ashamed. He'd been practicing with hay hooks for many years in the shadow of parental ignorance, playing both pirate and Pan with the neighborhood kids and covering the suburb's backyard trees with sappy scabs.

The Bellow Family, dressed snugly against the cold, followed in their patriarch's surefooted gait. Jonathan lodged his hook firmly in the family's tree and lifted his end. His father's new hook was buried in the other end. The family joined the others on the crowded suburban street, which was lit dully by yellow streetlamps and gutter-latched Holiday lights.

Children scurried through the maze of dragged trees–snatching branches every now and then from those they passed–before gathering beneath a streetlamp, where they traded matches and branches like drug peddlers. Benjamin broke from his mother and joined them. He struck a red-tipped match against the lamppost until it flared into its short, fiery existence. Its hellfire soul duplicated in Benjamin's eager brown eyes.

Quickly, Benjamin lit a lush, green branch that produced fluffy clouds of white smoke. Other boys gathered around and nearly snuffed out the original source, but he shouldered them away fiercely. He'd inherited his father's prickly confidence, a trait that had passed over the elder, Jonathan. Led by Benjamin, the children darted through the crowd of half-inebriated adults, whipping their torches to-and-fro, casting cinder-snowflakes in their wake.

"Jonny!" Marcus shouted above the crowd before rudely shoving his beefy body through it. He popped up next to Jonathan, red-faced and out of breath.

"Hiya, Mark," Jonathan's father said, turning around.

"Hello, sir."

"How's your grandpa?" Jonathan's mother asked from behind. She slowed her pace and lit a cigarette.

"Alright," Marcus said, shrugging and going quiet for a moment before returning his attention to Jonathan. "You got a hay hook this year?"

"Nah. It's my dad's old one. I'm just helping."

"Can I?" Marcus asked.

"Not without your parents' permission," Mom interjected.

"Can I help carry the tree, at least?" Marcus asked Jonathan.

"Sure."

Marcus crouched beneath the tree and emerged opposite Jonathan, grabbing the sticky trunk with his pudgy bare hands. The procession continued down the Bellow's street before turning left onto Ashland Avenue. The crowd followed Ashland a short distance to the designated burning zone: a frost-famished midwestern field. Each year, the town council chose from an abundance of similar fields, rotating the burning zone location.

"They got so many logs in New York this year," Marcus said in a breathless whisper, as if what he was about to say had not been heavily reported in the many jovial weeks leading up to Holiday. "I heard they're going to light it from the top of the Empire State Building this time."

"I know," Jonathan said. "I'm the one who told you."

"Oh," Marcus said, deflated. "Know anyone else with a Yule Log this year?"

"Nah. Your grandma is the only one from our street. Sorry about that, by the way." Jonathan said, as much a peace offering for being snippy with Marcus as it was a condolence.

Marcus sighed. "Yeah, well. I'm just glad we don't have to keep her at the house anymore. Anyways, I better go find my family."

As quickly as he had appeared, the pear-shaped boy disappeared into the dense crowd. Jonathan and his father unhooked their tree and stood it straight. Surrounded by the more affluent totem poles of neighboring families, it looked embarrassingly diminutive. Jonathan focused instead on the growing pile of parched conifers just ahead of them.

Short-tempered firefighters unceremoniously yanked the

trees held out to them by eager citizens and tossed them on top of a neatly stacked pile of Yule Logs. The neighborhood was a relatively new development, inhabited mostly by young families with children, so there weren't as many logs as other older communities; but occasionally grandparents resettled there, and some died in accidents. These were mostly who the suburb gathered each year to cremain.

Approaching with his dad, Jonathan peered as hard as he could through the interlocked maze of furred conifers and barren branches–all soaked in flammable chemicals–to see Marcus's grandma. She had passed in February. To store a Yule Log properly, and for that many months, was complicated and expensive. He wanted to see what she looked like. The firefighters reached down and grabbed the Bellow Family tree from Jonathan and his father. Jonathan made one last attempt to see one of the bodies buried within the unlit bonfire, though he knew he wasn't supposed to call them that. They were simply Yule Logs now, saved throughout the year, to be burnt on International Holiday Day.

"Jonno." His dad nudged his shoulder. "Make room for the rest."

They retreated to the outskirts of the gathering. To Jonathan, the lumber pillar before him was a Babel-like tower of potential. It almost looked like if scaled, he could reach the full moon blazing not so far above its peak. Before he could even consider an attempt, however, the firefighters climbed down the yuletide pyre and drew gas torches from their utility belts.

"Thank you for your warmth, in life and death," Jonathan and the crowd said in unison as the firefighters touched their blue gas flames to the pile. Instantly, what had seemed like a secure staircase to an untapped universe only seconds before now buckled and compromised, as the whole structure erupted into hot, licking flames.

The crowd, cheering, backed away from the kindled bonfire, with the heat quickly becoming too much to bear. Jonathan watched as a group of teenagers remained, their skin soon reddening. Despite this, they danced around the flames like ambrosia-fueled demigods, daring one another to get closer. He longed to join them, oblivious to a future where they are no longer relevant, where they are nothing more than kindling for the Yule Log Fire.

Jonathan spotted Benjamin and the other small children scooping ash and tossing it into the air. They made snow angels. They mixed the ash with saliva and pasted it on each other's cheeks like war paint. They were giddy flames destined to be extinguished.

Jonathan wondered which ash specs originated from Marcus's grandma. He watched as the cremated were swept up in a frigid breeze and driven into the saturated midnight, void of life and dark as oil, as the moon's light disappeared behind black clouds of smoke that hung above the crowd like a stench.

Sam Claussen is a fortunate father, humble husband, and weary writer from Des Moines, Iowa. Tweet your favorite examples of #WordArt to @writeclaussen.

HOW I BECAME THE REAL ELIZABETH FINCH

Karol Lagodzki

T he day I arrived in Summit Point, the only liquor store in town had closed for a funeral. I could beeline right to it because my new landlady had sent me a Summit Point Chamber of Commerce town map that seemed drawn by someone who couldn't have been a day over five. That, a key, and a sheet with a list of commandments for me, her only tenant, all in a padded manila envelope. So now I was in Summit, while she vacationed in Florida.

Instead of overshooting my place and going to the grocery store for a bottle of something, I moved in first. I had seen the house in photographs. A two-bedroom log cabin, it sat on the western outskirts of Summit on seven acres of dense, hilly woods. Quiet. The directions called for driving a mile north from the regretful note on the door of Edgar's Fine Liquor and Vape, down a county road pockmarked by potholes and scars of failed past repairs, and then turning off onto a gravel path. The path had a name—Knife Ridge Lane—but would lack a sign, so I watched my odometer and paid attention.

I almost missed it anyway. Had it been after dark, I would

have. It came in a blink. I stood on the pedal. The rapid-fire staccato of anti-lock brakes mixed with my curses. The car stopped.

I sat level with the turn onto the gravel road, breathing in the acrid fumes of burned tires. Stupid. With this crappy asphalt, I could easily have swerved into the ditch to the right or, worse, down the ravine to the left. When my breath slowed down, I coaxed the station wagon onto the gravel.

In the glare of the early-afternoon December sun, the path was a tunnel carved through the sky by a crumbling roof of black, leafless canopies. The contrast was stunning, and on another day, I might have been tempted to stop and draw it. Then a smile lifted my cheeks despite the tire stink still filling the car. I *would* draw this landscape. Tomorrow or next week. And if I wanted, I'd draw it again. This was home now. For the next three months.

I hadn't intended to winter in an Appalachian cabin. Only this past summer, I had been running one of Chicago's most celebrated art galleries, lived in a Wicker Park limestone walkup a five-minute stroll from work, and had been happily married to a man my so-called friends drooled over, but couldn't have. Or so I had thought. I had everything, except a baby, but at 32, I'd surely still had time.

Now, I was driving a beat-up Subaru down a wooded alley, with all of my belongings in two suitcases in the back. But the tug of a smile still tingled my face. I had a plan. Everything would be as it should.

The path wound along the ridge until it morphed into a driveway that then swelled up into a circle in front of the cabin. From here, the building seemed not much larger than one of those tiny houses everyone's talking about. But I knew that in the back the cabin opened up onto the ravine below. From the front, I saw only one level, but a second, lower story, with a bedroom and a study, had been chiseled into the limestone. A wooden deck jutted out of each floor. There, I intended to enjoy my morning coffee and an afternoon glass of good wine—just one—and I wouldn't care if it snowed.

I dragged the suitcases up the stairs to the front porch but had to give in to the urge to turn around and calm my thoughts by taking in the trees, the rays of sunlight, and even the ugly, beige car. After a few deep breaths, I turned to the door and unlocked my new home.

Everything was as advertised. I found the promised pillows, blankets, and linens. Tons of blankets. The Wi-Fi password on a card resting on the bedside table. On the kitchen island perched a bottle of The Prisoner chardonnay, a 2019 vintage, with a bow tied around its neck holding down a handwritten note:

Dear Elizabeth,

I hope you enjoy the house. When you settle in, call Alva Norvell. She'll show you around.

God bless.

Ethel.

A local number followed. I forgave my landlady her three-month South Beach vacation right there and then. Gifts of good white wine go a long way to improving my opinion of the giver. I stuck the bottle in the freezer to cool it down pronto, then dialed the number from the note.

"Norvell family," a woman said, "Mrs., Mr., and his four cats." The voice didn't have the drawl I'd expected.

I stifled a giggle. "My name is Liz Gr…, Finch. Liz Finch. I'll be renting Ethel Dalrymple's cabin."

"Right, Ethel said to expect you. Glad you called. Remembering the right name will come easier, I promise. I've been married three times, so I should know."

"Ethel—"

"You have nothing to worry about, my dear. I'll take care of you. Ethel is my best friend in the world—the third wife of my first husband, you know—and the sweetest woman the good Lord ever created. But she can hold a grudge worse than my old dog's ass can hold on to a cocklebur. I wouldn't want to disappoint her."

"Thank you."

"You come right over. You'll meet everyone. I won't hear no for an answer. We're having a little reception for poor Abner. Write down this address. You're young, so you can use the Google. Better than me trying to give directions. I would have gotten you lost for good. Don't dally, dear."

And at that, she hung up. I needed a shower, so I made it a quick one, but not before moving the chardonnay from the freezer to the fridge. Fifteen minutes later, I was driving on the gravel path again, then on the familiar county road.

AFTER I PASSED A "PRIVATE PROPERTY" SIGN AND DROVE AT least a third of a mile down a paved road, I had to stop in front of an iron gate that would have been at home in Malibu. The gate swung in without making a sound. There was nothing that looked like an obvious camera. I was impressed, and I don't impress easily.

Minutes later, I arrived at a sprawling white colonial mansion, inexplicably fitted with a gothic turret on its left side. The turret was half as tall as the rest of the building and brought to mind damsels with unnaturally long hair. I parked the station wagon by the ten or so cars lined up on the grass to the side of the driveway. The driveway continued, widening to the size of a piazza that surrounded a stone fountain shaped like a candle with a wax catcher at the bottom. As I walked by, I saw the fountain was dry. Wisps of dead vegetation stuck out of the ring around the base. I approved of not wasting water on a fountain.

There was no one outside. A sudden breeze reminded me it was December, and I wrapped my coat around. I wondered if we'd have a white Christmas that year, even though I hadn't celebrated in a decade. Hadn't believed in anything for much longer than that.

Given few options, I walked along the side of the pavement, up a few stairs, and across a stone terrace, until I reached an immense front door. It was too grand, too important for knocking, but there didn't seem to be a buzzer. The thick wood rattled my knuckles and appeared to muffle whatever noise I might have managed to make. A minute later, I was about to bang on the door with my fist when it cracked open. I hid the poised fist behind me.

Murmurs of conversation and classical music full of strings and piano reached me first. Schumann's Fairy Tales. A bit flighty for an after-funeral reception. All of this, the house, the music, even the sense of unease I was starting to feel had not been on my bingo card for a tiny mountain town one had to make a point of zooming way in to find on Google Maps.

When the door fully opened, an old woman beamed at me from the doorstep. Her crevassed cheeks and gray hair made her appear in her late eighties, but a tremor in the smile added a decade. Her back had bent, making her appear shorter, but she was easily as tall as I. I hadn't seen a person this aged outside of a wheelchair, and the last time was at The Altenheim, my great-grandmother's nursing home, back when Starbucks was still an *avant-garde*, cool coffee house.

"There you are," she said. It was the voice from the phone call. Mrs. Norvell. I hoped my face didn't betray me. She sounded half her age. Strong, confident, and in control of her warm alto. "Come in, come in. You're one of us now."

I crossed the threshold. The empty hallway let the conversations from beyond bounce around, amplifying the noise, but not making the words any clearer. Alva Norvell shuffled away to the right, and I followed. After a couple of turns, the voices became easier to make out. We entered a large room—a ballroom by any measure—where several women of various ages, dressed in simple black, loitered around in clumps of twos and threes. A similar number of men in matching black suits stood to the side, snifters in hand, seemingly in quiet contemplation.

"Friends," Mrs. Norvell said. "Friends," she repeated with greater force. The conversations sputtered, and the women's heads turned toward us. The men didn't seem to notice.

"Friends," Alva Norvell said again. "This is Elizabeth Finch."

Some of their eyes lit up as if they had met a minor celebrity. Others barely bothered to hide smirks behind their palms. I heard a stifled snicker. And then they came at me as a wave. Black dresses swayed toward me like a tide of silk tornadoes. The women offered only the politest greetings and introductions. I would have doubted the scorn I'd seen a second earlier had it not continued to heat up my blood. These faces chatted me up with delight, open and sincere.

I'm good with names. You have to be if you run a premiere art gallery. But when we were done, I had no idea what any of theirs were. No memory of any interesting anecdotes. I shook my head, then stopped when I felt a hint of vertigo. Something was wrong. I hadn't been drinking. Had I eaten something I shouldn't have? I couldn't recall the last thing I ate.

A voice penetrated the fog. "You've gone pale as a sheet. Too much too soon. My fault entirely. I hope you can forgive me. At my age, you become impatient. To think of it, I've never enjoyed waiting much." That name I could recall. Alva Norvell.

Mrs. Norvell took my hand and coaxed me out of this space, down another corridor, and into a small, cozy room with a sofa and two low armchairs. I was leaning back in one of the chairs before I knew it. Soon, a drink materialized in my hand, and Alva Norvell shooed away the man who'd brought it. Something, a sense of déjà vu, tickled my mind. Then we were sitting opposite each other, with the door closed, glasses in hand.

"Take a few deep breaths," the old woman said. "You've been through much these past few months."

I followed the directions, then added a sip of the cocktail. I thought I could make out peach, pomegranate, hints of lemon, and something savory and mineral that was quite pleasant.

"Thank you," I said. "I don't know what happened. But I'm starting to feel better now." It was not a lie. My thoughts were becoming solid again, connected. "Whatever this is," I raised the glass, "it seems to be working."

"An old family recipe. Some fruit juices, spices, honey, this and that, and a ton of vodka."

"I don't drink," I said. "I mean, I'm trying to get a handle on it. Cut back. It got to be a bottle a night, and then I'd open another. No more." This felt right. I could tell Alva anything at all.

"I don't judge, sweet." She drained half of her drink in one go. "I'm having something simpler," she said. "Bourbon. Though I should probably take my time, sip, comment on the complexity, seeing as this bottle would have cost a fortune now. But I'm not a patient person."

"I couldn't save the gallery," I said, and felt tears drip down my cheeks. "Couldn't save my marriage. My husband traveled more and more–for work, he said–and then, one time, he never came back." I scoffed at myself, wiping my tears quickly. "He sent a damned text."

"And then you did what you could to get your life on track, didn't you?"

I nodded.

"You might have had a drink, but you haven't been drunk since then."

I nodded a lie. "He's here somewhere. In Summit Point. I paid a small fortune for an investigator. Why he's here, I don't know. Maybe he wanted the opposite of what our lives had become? Maybe he met another woman? I don't know."

"And now you want to find this asshole and show him what he's missing."

I nodded. Then I jerked my head up and shook it.

"What? No. Not at all. I love him. I want to give us, what we used to be, one last chance."

"You've got chutzpah. But we'll need to teach you to make smarter choices. Look at that wall." Alva pointed straight ahead at a framed portrait of a middle-aged man. "See that picture? That's my Abner, my dear. He was the sweetest of my husbands, yet."

"Oh. Oh, no. I'm so sorry."

"Why? I didn't die."

I struggled for anything at all to say.

"See?" Alva said after a few gulps of her drink. "You must move on to something else. Probably something better. There is nothing but pain in trying to hold on to a man."

"You don't know my husband."

"Hmph." She looked at me sideways. "My glass is dry, and I'm still thirsty. Do you want another? Yes, you do." Alva pushed her chest out like a diva, and called out, "Richard, sweetheart, bring us two more!"

A man stepped into the room, carrying a tray. I was on my feet before I knew what I was doing. Slapping him. Trying to kiss him. Pulling at his hair. The tray and the glasses tumbled to the floor. Slap. Kiss. Slap. And then I couldn't move. The man had slipped behind me and held me tight. Richard. My Richard.

"Richard?" I whispered.

He didn't let go. Didn't say a word.

"He'll do as he's told," Alva said. "By me. We'll teach you how to manage them."

"Richard?" My chest had grown tight, and not because he held me too hard. My fingers tingled. I was panting, and yet could not get a deep enough breath.

"If we let you go, will you sit and stay calm? That would be the best for everyone."

"What's happening? Richard!"

I screamed. I wailed loud enough that her guests must have heard.

No one came. No one was saving me from this woman, and from the man I thought I had known, the man who'd sung me lullabies and held my hair when I sicked up sour prosecco. I worked to gather air for another scream when Alva came up with a napkin in her hand and pushed it in my face.

I thrashed. I bit. I struggled for air, for dignity. Then everything faded.

I WOKE UP ON SOMETHING SOFT, WITH GENTLE LIGHT ON MY eyelids. I forced them open. Candlelight, but still a bit much. My head pounded. I could move my arms. My legs were free, too. I was naked and covered with a comforter that was light and thick enough to be a cloud. My head—if not the surroundings—felt unfortunately familiar, but I was fairly certain I hadn't earned this headache and the acid in my belly. How had I gotten here? I could recall being upset, but not why. Not until I closed my eyes again. Everything came back. Mrs. Norvell, Richard, the sensation as if I had moved through those moments in a blizzard. I still couldn't say how I came to be in this bed. I opened my eyes again and scanned the room. The candlelight was warm, playful, and my headache was already subsiding. The space was circular. Two windows, now blackened with night, were set into the wall close enough to each other to bring to mind empty, dark eye sockets. On the surfaces all around me, dozens of candles flickered as if straining against an invisible breeze. No door anywhere. *No door.* I scrambled out of the bed and spun around.

No door, but an opening in the floor revealed a couple of steps leading down. There was a way out. I dropped back onto the mattress and rubbed my head. The veins in my temples throbbed, but my heartbeat slowed down.

There was a way out. But if there was a way to leave, there was also a way in. Anyone could ascend this staircase at any moment. I had never been modest, but I tossed the bed linens and was pulling a sheet to wrap around when I saw a chair with a dress draped over it. The color of red ochre, like burned clay squeezed out of a New Holland oil paint tube—or dried blood—it was finer than anything I'd ever owned. Under the dress, there was a pair of standard underwear and a soft, off-white blouse. In a moment, I threw the clothes on. The dress and the blouse felt custom-tailored for me.

No matter how hard I looked, I could find no shoes and had no choice but to go without. I put my foot on the first step, then down to the next, and then crept on, descending in a spiral, one narrow step at a time, until I reached a landing illuminated by electric light coming through the opening to the hallway. I peeked in and recognized it. The same main hall I had seen earlier.

"Awake?" The voice, booming in the silence, made me flinch.

Before I blinked again, Mrs. Norvell was halfway to me. She must have come from one of the side doors.

"Ready to talk?" she asked. "Calmly? Like reasonable women?"

I swallowed. Nodded.

Soon, we sat in the same armchairs. I still hadn't come up with anything to say.

"I'm glad to see you have spirit," Alva Norvell said, "but I hated to use chloroform. Takes work, time, and feels much too Victorian. I have left those years behind me, and good riddance." She took a sip. "Ask me a question. The first question that comes to mind."

First? My mind was a subway turnstile during rush hour. One thought, though, finally slipped in. "Richard? That was Richard?"

She *tsk*ed. "Do your best to get him out of your mind. He no longer belongs to you. Although, if you stay with us long enough, who knows? He may again one day. But by then, you probably won't care."

She had to see the confusion on my face. "Men who come here, my dear, have a purpose. A better purpose, I believe, than they think they have outside. You're about thirty, in your prime. How long do you think you'll live? Another forty to sixty years? You'll die just as you become the person you were always intended to be. It's an awful waste. Our way is better."

"I don't understand," I said, but I had begun to guess, and a war had started in my mind between curiosity and fear.

Mrs. Norvell seemed to sense it. Her lips curved in a tiny, sympathetic smile.

"Let's get you some tea," she said.

When Richard brought in two teacups, I forced myself to stay in the chair. Our eyes met. He smiled, but I stayed put, offering the same neutral smile in response.

After he left, Mrs. Norvell arched her eyebrows and cocked her head. "Good. Very good. Well done." She took a sip. "Nice. Now, where were we…"

"Right," she continued. "Humor me as I tell a little story, dear. My family came here from Pennsylvania by way of Cincinnati. My parents, my aunt and her husband, their parents, my siblings, cousins. More than twenty of us. Years passed, the children aged, and yet no babies were born. A curse, they thought. Some sin they had committed, yet no one knew what that could have been. The forest in these hills blessed them with food and water, but seemed to have taken their future. Four years in, during a snowy winter, they decided they'd leave the following summer. They were going to go, but no one knew where. They had nothing to go back to out East. Nothing specific to seek further West, other than the hope of children. They were likely to find starvation first.

"That's when my aunt talked my mother into going into the woods. To pray, they had told the rest. My mother's first-born son and my aunt's oldest boy went with them. For protection, they said. The four were gone a day, then two, then a week. That night, when the family had lost all hope, two women entered their cabin. At first the men didn't recognize them, but, in the light of the fire, they had to accept the women's word: these girls, neither older than sixteen, were the same women who'd gone into the woods. When asked about the boys, my mother and my aunt wept, wailed, and the men stopped asking. Both women were with child by April, and the family didn't leave that summer. I was one of those two babies, and our family has been here since."

"When?" I asked, though I feared the answer.

"The year of our Lord 1798. Give or take a year. I am the oldest here, and I feel it in my bones."

I wanted to ask how, but I could already sense it, and a confirmation would have made it real. I kept my jaw clenched.

"Richard, dear!" Mrs. Norvell called out.

He came in. The man I had thought I knew.

"Take a close look," she said.

The same face. Dark hair. Brown eyes, blinking at me at a lazy cadence. The mouth relaxed, as if the tension had gone out of it. Peaceful. Not the same. The Richard I knew *was* tension, strife, desire. The man standing in front of me was fulfilled and wanted nothing. The lines in his cheeks were deeper than I had remembered from only a few months earlier. The corners of his eyes flared into tiny wrinkles that seemed to bestow wisdom. This Richard had aged a decade or more.

"How?" I couldn't resist asking.

"None of us really know. My mother never said more than she had to. I was born into it, and it comes no less naturally than breathing. Richard, once he found his way to Summit, couldn't have stayed away from here if he tried. The sweet boy gave me some of his time. His ten years is twenty or thirty for someone like me. They live longer, more happily if we share them. Another woman will get him once I'm done. Then maybe you, who knows, but only if you stay."

Richard smiled and nodded. "I really don't mind," he said, the first words I heard from him since he'd left. "You wouldn't believe how good this feels."

"A man. A creature that'll risk his life, and yours, for an orgasm. And compared to a climax, the pleasure we give them is like a sun flare next to a lightning bug. I really think he finds the deal fair."

"What do you want from me?"

Instead of responding, Mrs. Norvell rose and waved for me to follow.

Outside the room, two women and an ancient bent man waited, and as we headed for the front door, they trailed. Richard, silent, rushed ahead and threw open the door. Snowflakes drifted in. My bare feet ground to a stop on the terrace outside, my eyes disbelieving the view. The old, dry fountain had sprouted branches of light. A tree now stood where the stone column had been before. Made of shimmering ice, it seemed just as alive as the firs around my cabin. It grew in front of me until it would have put the Rockefeller Center Christmas Tree to shame. The tree illuminated the night through the falling snow far into the property's grounds.

A finger poked me in the back. "Remarkable, isn't it?" Alva Norvell said. "Remarkable what a few generations of powerful women can accomplish." Then she poked me again. "This isn't the time for gawking, dear. We are expected."

Richard led. The three unnamed people now surrounded us, and Mrs. Norvell shuffled next to me, continuing to talk.

"Once we get there, follow my lead, and Richard will help, too. As will the rest of our friends. You haven't tried to run. That's good."

I had thought of running, but my mind felt soft, as if a more concrete thought would plunge beneath the surface and disappear. Escape seemed an abstract concept, one I could not define, let alone put into practice.

"Not that I really thought you would," Alva Norvell continued. "Around so many of us, an uninitiated often feels confused. But you *do* have spirit. Once you're fully with us, you'll be sharper than you'd ever been."

"Will it hurt?" I asked.

"Oh, my, no. It won't hurt you. To the contrary. Now, hush. It's time to collect our thoughts."

We walked in silence long enough that the needling of the snow on my bare feet punctured through my numbness. A flickering light appeared in the dark. The light grew. A few minutes later, it resolved into a bonfire. It roared. Lonely. Untended.

Mrs. Norvell, Richard, and I came as close as the heat allowed. The old man stopped behind us. The two women edged to each side of the fire, and it seemed to intensify until I expected my eyelashes would singe.

Alva Norvell's voice rose a couple of decibels over the roar. I struggled to hear and understand. "Despite Richard's sacrifice, I am running out of time," she said. "Ethel will take my place. And a new one must be made. Here's where we make you, Elizabeth."

She turned her head to the old man behind us. "This is always hard. Poor Edgar. He's been a good, faithful man. But a rib, or a few years, is not enough for this. For the making."

Edgar's jaw clenched, his shoulders set.

"You mean to kill him," I said.

"Sacrifice is the word." Something shimmered in the corners of her eyes. "I'm afraid you'll need to take off this pretty dress. It will get in the way, and you'll want it later for the celebration."

Too much. Without further thought, I grabbed Richard's sleeve and bolted between Alva and Edgar. The snow needled my feet again. Richard didn't resist and sprinted behind me. As we put distance between us and the women at the bonfire, my mind grew clearer. A few minutes later, we threw ourselves, panting, into the Subaru.

I pulled the keys from under the floor mat, started the car and peeled off down the path, seatbelts be damned. The gate. I gritted my teeth and scrunched my eyes as it grew in the windshield. A hammer blow, and the gate flew out sideways. The station wagon barely slowed down.

We were on the county road before I thought to turn on the heat. Soon, my feet thawed, and I did my best not to writhe in pain.

Richard's gentle palm touched my shoulder. "I am so sorry," he said. "I never meant for any of this to happen."

"These witches won't get you back. We'll get to Chicago. Get some help. You and I, we can handle anything together."

"You may need to tie or lock me up. Something in me wants to go back right now. Like a dog. Or a pigeon." He cleared his throat. "I do love you, Elizabeth. I'm so sorry."

I clasped his hand and brought it up to kiss it.

"Between your friends—Susannah and that other one—and me, that was nothing. Just physical. I swear on my life. And we'll get the gallery back."

I lifted my hand off his. I suspected Susannah. *The other one?*

"The gallery? Back?" How could that be? The court had declared it forfeited.

"Before they cast their damned spell on me, I was beginning to feel out of time. Me, in the rat race. You, always busy and stressed. Or in the bottle. I resented you for those lost years. I am so sorry." He paused and cleared his throat. "Elizabeth, I put up the gallery as a loan collateral to pay for Susannah's... whatever. It was madness. I don't love her. I love you. You have to believe me."

I kept my eyes on the road. Susannah had mentioned she'd started fertility treatments.

When it seemed safe, I slowed down and pulled over.

Richard glanced sideways. It was a relief he remained silent. I pushed open the door, staggered around the car, and threw open the trunk right before I threw up into the snow. My stomach heaved until nothing else came. Before I returned, I grabbed the tire iron from the back.

"I believe you," I said, as I got back in. Then I swung the metal right into the middle of his forehead. He crumpled, but breath continued to lift his chest.

I believed him. Still do. That night, I turned around and headed back to Summit Point. Down the path and through the busted gate. To the house with the ice tree in bloom.

To Alva and Edgar waiting right inside.

The bonfire still burned hot enough for the job.

Karol Lagodzki left Poland at twenty. His non-writing careers have ranged from fixing stucco while dangling from roofs in Paris to sorting through human cadaver heads in Jacksonville. His stories have appeared or are forthcoming in *Storm Cellar*, *Panel Magazine*, *NUNUM*, *Streetlight Magazine*, and elsewhere. One of Karol's stories won the 2020 Ruritania Prize for Short Fiction, and he has been nominated for the Pushcart and the Best of the Net anthologies. He holds an MFA in fiction. Karol lives halfway down an Indiana ravine with his family and a large dog. Find him at klagodzki.com.

A DESPERATE PLEA TO THE RULER OF ALL THE PENGUINS

Christina Bagni

please sir
please, emperor
please, ruler of all the penguins

we have done all you asked
we have gathered pebbles in groups of three and five
we have sacrificed legions of fish in the name of the gods,
praying and begging
we have stopped fishing in certain waters, stopped eating certain
fish
we have herded our children away from the areas where the
ground crumbles beneath our feet

what more can we do?
what will help?
what will make the sun weaker? the snow last longer?
what will make you finally help us?
what are you waiting for, your majesty? your grace?
what will you do to help us? you must be able to help us?

do you need more fish? more pebbles?
do you need more praise, more time, more space?
do you know what to do?
do you know what is wrong?
do you know how to fix it?
do you want to fix it?
do you know how badly we are suffering?
do you listen, when we cry out to you?

we were told it was demons
we were told we were to blame
we were told to do something about it, to clean the waters, to
clean our bodies
we were told to be good, to be conscious, to be gentle.
we have done that.
we don't see a change—in fact, we see it getting worse.
we see our children dying, choking on strange materials,
swimming poorly with weaker wings
we see fewer fish in our ocean, less snow from the sky, less ice
on the ground.
we need an answer.
we need you, emperor.
we need your help.
we need to know what is wrong.
we need to know how to stop it.
we can stop it. right?
we must be able to stop it.
we just need you to tell us how.

Christina Bagni's creative work has been published in Brigids Gate Press, Writers Resist, and Flora Fiction, among others. She's a professional editor and ghostwriter with a love of mythology and buying too many books to ever actually read. Her first novel is forthcoming with Deep Hearts YA (2023). https://linktr.ee/christinabagni

PART 4

TWO-HEADED TREE

Lexie Carver

Lexie Carver is an American horror writer and photographer. Lexie's love of all things horror started early. Always drawn to dissecting the psyches of villains, able to name the culprit in any film or story within 5 minutes, she prefers vampires to zombies, coffee to tea, 90s slashers to extreme horror and dogs to cats. Her two books, *A Fine Day for Murder* and *Into the Dark* are available on Amazon. When not writing or reviewing movies on Twitter, you can find Lexie taking photos, walking her dog or wandering in what remains of the city's bookstores and coffee shops. lexiecarver.com | https://linktr.ee/lexiecarver

THE CHORUS OF THE TREES

Shaun Horton

C harlie hopped out of the truck, his shoes crunching in the layers of snow. Fresh flakes drifted down around him, draping all the trees in a thin layer of white that reflected the weakening sunlight.

"Ya know, dis place is real pretty. I'm glad I came by here." He hefted the chainsaw and lantern out of the bed of his old Toyota, hung a length of rope off his shoulder, and looked around. The truck was twenty years old, with spots of different shades of blue covering up scratches and dents. It was the same truck that had carried him and everything he owned from Wisconsin.

He stood on the side of the road, in a little pull-out on the edge of the Olympic National Forest. Back across the country, it had been a family tradition to head up into the woods and cut their own Christmas tree. No tree farms, or pop-up lots for him. This was his first Christmas up in the Pacific Northwest, the land of year-round green trees, and he wasn't going to let an unfamiliar location keep him from the customs.

The chainsaw was full of gas and fresh oil, and Charlie

relished the weight of it as he walked through the snow and into the forest. Most of the trees by the road were older, and much too big for his small living room. He also didn't want anyone to just drive by and catch him cutting one down, in case there were rules he wasn't aware of in Washington State. Charlie figured a short hike would lead him to one small clearing or another where he could find the perfect sized tree to take home.

As darkness descended, he flicked on the lantern, casting white LED light around him. It wasn't a big deal. He was used to the dark, and he could follow his footsteps in the snow back to the truck afterward. If it was snowing harder, he might have been more concerned, but the light powder falling wouldn't pose a problem.

The forest was silent, except for the sound of his boots in the snow. There wasn't any breeze blowing branches around. Occasionally there was a soft *whump* as a pile of snow broke through the cover of the trees and fell to the ground in one large clump. The hike was easy, slowly sloping uphill, without lots of dips, holes, or branches to trip over. He half wondered if he was on a trail or a path that someone took care of.

Twenty minutes into his hike, he found a small clearing. It wasn't much–maybe six or seven feet across–but it was exactly what he was looking for. Around the edges, several smaller pine trees huddled together, all between five and ten feet tall. Each had a thin layer of snow glittering in the lantern light. In Charlie's mind, he could already see how gorgeous they would be if he could just take them home exactly like that, add bulbs, lights, garland, and a small angel on top. Any of them would be perfect.

Charlie walked the perimeter of the clearing, inspecting each candidate. As he walked past one, it seemed to shiver, snow falling off its branches to the forest floor around it. Across the clearing, another one of those *whumps* answered it. Charlie paused and looked around, wondering if there was a breeze building up high in the air. A sudden wind could be a problem, bringing in more clouds with fresh dumps of snow. As unfamiliar as he was with the area, he didn't want to be caught in a sudden blizzard.

As he paused and looked around, he noticed a feeling in his stomach, a small knot that had settled in. Combined with the silence of the forest, it unnerved him a little, but he considered it just another sign that he shouldn't spend too much time out in the woods. There were bears and cougars out here, after all.

After another lap, Charlie settled on a pine near to where he had entered the clearing. It was just over six feet tall, with a good spread of branches. There was a small bald spot on one side, but he could just turn that to face the wall.

He hung the lantern from the branch of a larger tree next to his chosen prize and set about priming the chainsaw. He yanked on the cord, but the saw sputtered and fought against the cold, refusing to start. Several more *whumps* echoed around the clearing. Charlie looked around and saw nothing. He suspected the strange noises of the chainsaw had startled a few squirrels or an owl, who then knocked the snow loose.

Another pull and the saw started up, the sound echoing around the clearing. The deafening noise sliced through the silence of the snow-covered forest as Charlie leaned under the branches, pressing the whirring teeth to the trunk.

Pieces of bark and wood flew as the saw chewed its way through the small tree. Wet splatter flew out of the cut. Thick, dark liquid flowed down the blade, dripping down and staining the snow. Charlie noticed, but continued on, ignoring the sap which flowed freely from the cut.

A howl resounded through the clearing. It echoed, bouncing around and coming from all directions at once. Charlie stopped the saw and crawled out from under his prize tree. All the other trees were now clear of snow. The white powder was piled up around them as if they had just shaken it off their branches. None of the small trees in the clearing had a speck of white stuck to them, and even the branches of the larger trees that overhung them were clear. The howl had dissipated, leaving only an unnerving silence as snowflakes continued drifting down from the now black sky.

"Dat's interestin." Charlie stood and reached up to grab his lantern. It wouldn't come down from the branch. He pulled harder. The branch it was on bent, but it wouldn't release his light. He pulled it down to look at it, to try to work it free. The wire handle of the lantern was embedded in the branch, as if it had been left there for years and the wood had grown around it. A second small branch had also wrapped itself around the wire, gripping the lantern and refusing to let go.

He stepped back, letting the branch resume its natural position, and stared at it for a minute. That had to be one of the most bizarre things Charlie had ever seen. He'd seen a few pictures of trees overgrowing things. An internet story of a soldier in World War II who'd left his bike propped up against a tree, and then never come back for it. Fifty years later, the tree had continued to grow, absorbing the bicycle and lifting it fifteen feet into the air. That took years, though. This had happened in minutes.

Charlie reached for his utility knife on his belt. No matter how it happened, he needed the lantern to find his way back. The blade slid into place with a satisfying click, but the knot in his stomach suddenly tightened.

He was being watched. That's what the feeling was. Eyes staring him down, taking in his every motion. It wasn't just a squirrel or bird, though. No small animal could make him feel so on edge. A bear he would have heard. They weren't exactly known for their subtlety. *So, a cougar then.* Charlie swore at himself for not bringing his forty-five with him. He'd just have to work quickly, hope the sound of the chainsaw scared it off, and then get back to his truck as fast as he could.

Grabbing the lantern, he pulled the branch down within reach of the knife. Before he could cut it, the light came loose, sliding down off the branch. Charlie was so surprised he didn't even catch it, letting it fall to the ground.

Grateful that it didn't break, Charlie brought the lantern with him back under the tree this time. He picked up the chainsaw and started it up again, kneeling down under the lowest branches of his prize tree. The cut he had made before still dribbled thick, brown fluid, which created a puddle around the base.

Another howl echoed through the clearing, but this time Charlie ignored it, remaining focused on his task. The whirring teeth made short work of the wood that was left and the tree fell into snow.

The howling increased, but the echo was gone. The sound now seemed to be coming at him directly from all sides. He grabbed the rope and looped it around the tree, trying to move as fast as he could. Tree secured to a rope around his waist, chainsaw in one hand, the lantern in the other, he turned to head back down the path.

His footsteps were gone.

Not just the way he came, but all around the clearing. The snow, which had been light to begin with, had completely stopped, so it couldn't have filled in his tracks. Charlie scanned the ground with his lantern, but couldn't find a path or anything that looked like the way he had come. He stepped further under the trees in one direction, and the knot in his stomach tightened, almost pulling him back into the clearing.

Panic gnawed at his mind. He wasn't prepared to spend a night out here in the cold, wet, and snow. He had no food or water, nothing to start a fire with, and his clothes weren't good enough to stave off hypothermia for more than a few hours. Plus, that unrelenting sound still came at him from all directions. He needed to get back to his truck *now*.

Holding the lantern up high, he thought he could make out a shoe print deeper beyond the edge of the clearing. Deciding it had to be from his trek in, he started towards it. But the tree wouldn't budge. Charlie looked back and saw it tangled in the low-lying branches of another small tree. He pulled, but the branches refused to give, holding on tightly.

Charlie set down the lantern, hefted the chainsaw, and started it back up to cut the branches away. As he moved towards them, though, the branches slowly moved, releasing his prize and withdrawing.

This froze him in place. *The tree was moving on its own.* It was moving in response to him revving the chainsaw. The branches slowly drew back until they disappeared among the other branches. And yet, it looked for all the world like an ordinary tree.

Charlie turned and ran, aiming for the path he thought would lead him back to his truck. His prize dragging behind him slowed him down, catching on branches, bushes, and rocks. Then it caught on something hard enough to yank him off his feet, putting him flat on his back in the snow.

The tree could stay if it wanted to so badly. Charlie threw off the rope attaching him to it and pushed up to his feet. He picked up the lantern and peered back to see what it had caught on.

The tree was gone, and the rope was wrapped around a body. It was like someone had carved a life-sized body from a tree trunk, and then glued branches and twigs sticking out all over it. Layered pine needles even formed "hair." One "arm" reached out and grabbed a root sticking out of the ground. That was what it had caught on. The only things missing were the thing's feet. Just above where ankles would have been, two stumps oozed thick, dark fluid.

Pieces were moving about in Charlie's mind, trying to come together in a way that made sense. The image couldn't actually be real, no matter how well they fit together. He held the lantern higher and looked back beyond the body. There was a trail of the dark sap—*blood*—leading back towards the clearing.

He spotted more movements in the shadows. Other people? No, their general outline was humanoid, but they were more like the creature at his feet.

"Hey! Yous guys! I don't want trouble! Just tell me what'cha want!"

As he watched, what looked like a tree branch reached down, wrapped around the body on the ground and picked it up, drawing it back into the shadows.

He turned to run again, stumbling off the path and against a tree. Pain shot through his arm as he fell back onto the ground. He looked up and saw the tree had a small stub from what used to be a branch. It was short, and pointed, and glistening red. Already, he could feel the blood running down his arm, soaking into his shirt.

Something was moving under the bark, but the bark itself was moving too. It was fluid, like watching paint swirl. Then it changed. Holes opened in the bark, revealing pitch blackness inside. They twisted and contorted until Charlie saw the shape of a face form in the dark hollows of the tree. For a moment, it pinned him there with a glare of pure rage and hatred.

He couldn't get to his feet fast enough. Terror powered his legs as he plowed headfirst through the undergrowth. Branches lashed out at him as he ran, grabbing at his arms and legs. The lantern swung wildly in his grip, casting long shadows between the trees surrounding him. It gave the impression that more of the creatures were silently striding along around him, but Charlie didn't dare turn his head to look. He squeezed his hand tighter around the handle of the lantern. The blood running down his other arm made the chainsaw's handle slick, hard to grip.

Another inhuman howl rose behind him, and a branch lashed out, catching his cheek and drawing fresh blood. Then he felt something wrap around his left ankle, squeeze, and pull. Pain shot up his leg as the ankle snapped, and Charlie went down. The chainsaw skittered ahead of him along the ground, but his grip on the lantern held strong. He rolled over and watched as roots wrapped around his leg. They seemed to flow around, thickening, spreading up to his knee. Then it yanked him up into the air.

Charlie swung towards a large fir tree, towards another grotesque, twisted face leering out at him from the trunk. The dark, round mouth opened wide and the roar that bellowed forth pounded in his ears.

More branches and roots reached out, grabbing his arms and his other leg. Several of the creatures were now gathered around him, staring up at him, making strange noises of their own. All of them looked like wood-carved people, branches, needles and leaves covering and hanging off of them. The branches holding him continued to thicken and twist, squeezing him tighter.

Swung through the air again, and then suspended, Charlie looked down at the ground underneath him. He feared a large rock or a sharp stump. Instead, in the swinging light of his lantern, he could see he was held over a sapling, barely a foot tall, stalk and branches no bigger around than his pinky. It had, at most, a dozen green and brown needles clinging to its spindly branches. In some corner of his mind where things were still normal, he was reminded of a sad little Charlie Brown Christmas tree.

Charlie's screams of pain mixed with the snapping of bones, as the branches and roots squeezing him twisted, pulling his legs in one direction and pushing his torso in the other. Shards of splintered bone broke the skin. Blood stained the snow underneath him red. His bonds started to push and pull harder, twisting first one way, then the other. Blood flowed faster, showering the sapling and the ground around it.

Some of the other creatures maneuvered underneath him, letting the blood rain down on them as well. A few reached up with long, thin, stick fingers and slashed at him, tearing lines in his clothes and flesh. Charlie's blood poured out of him, and darkness crept in around the edges of his sight. The lantern finally fell from his grasp, glowing in the bloody snow. The last thing Charlie saw was the sapling underneath him, twisting and squirming in the shower of warm, nutrient-rich liquid.

Charlie was spared the sounds of the creatures' howlings, which went into the night, as they mourned their loss and celebrated the sustenance that would strengthen their babies through the winter. The sound echoed through the trees, stretching out across the forest, finally washing over the old blue truck that sat on the side of the road.

Shaun Horton writes his horror stories, including the Alien novel *Class 5* and the Cryptid novelettes *Cenote* and *Burrows*, from the Pacific Northwest where he lives with his corgi, Quill. He continues to work on more Cryptid stories, and hopes one day to meet Sasquatch himself.

BEWARE THE SNOW BUNNIES

Danielle Davis

"Watch out for the snow bunnies," the shifty bartender had told her before directing her here. But as she looked up at the line of pines bracketing the trail, she couldn't imagine anything so intimidating attracting bumbling beginners who were more about ski fashion than actual ability. Not for the first time, she wondered why she'd even listened to him. But that thought was more habit than substance. She knew exactly why she was here.

It had started with small steps: a watercolor class at a local studio, which had really been just the artist's basement. But it forced her to leave the house once a week. Next, she'd taken a few piano lessons from the music minister at her church. She'd never gotten past learning "The Saints Go Marching." She realized all-too-quickly that she didn't really care for the piano. It had only been a new thing to learn, to take her mind off the ache that never seemed to go away in the eight months since the funeral.

And now here she was, in Alta, Utah all the way from Montreal, preparing to do something reckless and whimsical—

the whole trip had been planned in an afternoon—and out of the ordinary life she'd been living. She'd tried the regular slopes. And while they were fun, they were too safe, too ordinary. She never lost herself in the adventure of the trip, even on the black diamond runs. So far, it was exactly the kind of trip Grant would have loved–everything in bounds. It just made her miss him more. On her next-to-last day there, she asked the bartender if there were any hidden areas.

At first, she didn't know why she picked him to ask. Later, she'd think it was something about the furtive way he glanced out the windows at the long unmarred track of mountain rising next to the resort pub. What caught her eye wasn't that he looked out the window—lots of people were doing that—but it was the tightness around his eyes when he did it. Like he was wary of the mountain. Like he was waiting for something unpleasant to come skiing down. A thought bubbled: *That's a man who knows how to keep secrets.*

That last evening, she sidled up to the bar, trying to look both suave and trustworthy, and asked about places most of the tourists didn't go, didn't even know about. He was wiping down the counter and didn't even look up at her, just snorted in disdain.

"Why? So you can tell your yacht club buddies how *gnar* it was when you scored some *sick air*?" He shook his head like a bobble-head doll and made air quotes with his fingers while he said it.

"Not quite. I'm just a snow hound looking for some fresh territory. Thought you seemed like the kind of guy who'd know all the nooks and crannies around here. Maybe even know a secret powder cache that nobody might've roughed up so far...?" She raised her eyebrows and gave him what she hoped was an inviting half-smile.

He appraised her with a squint for a moment before wiping at the bar again. "There're lots of those around here," he gruffed. "What kind of cache are you looking to find?"

She leaned forward, too eager. "The kind that only a handful of people have ever even seen."

"Well," he drawled with a glance out the window toward the western slopes. "I've heard tell—no more than a rumor, mind you—of a few runs up past the Grizzly Bowl." He snickered suddenly, a sneaky, grunting noise. "One in particular...some of the locals call it Gnar-nia. Get it? It's not too hard to find, but it's... tough. Not a lot of people make it down. Most of the people who say they have are just spouting fairytales."

"Well, where I'm from is mostly just back-country, but I've run Jack's Bowl. You know, the double black at Sierra-at-Tahoe? And I've been around the slopes at Aspen Snowmass a few times. You familiar with those? I'll be fine."

She used the same off-handed tone that he'd used on her. He eyed her with a newly appraising glance and snorted at the barb. She raised an eyebrow and favored him with a look that said, *Two can play that game, can't they?*

"Alright, well, you still gotta watch out for the snow bunnies up there." He snickered again.

"You get joeys and snow bunnies that far up?" she asked. She could hardly picture a couple of coiffed ladies in tight ski pants and jackets with large, fur-trimmed hoods attempting to ease their way down a run like they were discussing.

The bartender laughed full out at her, with a mean glitter to his eye, like he was on the inside of a joke that she was the butt of, and shrugged a little, as if to say *c'est la vie* or *what can you do?* or *screw off.*

"Strange things happen up there. You're apt to see things you never imagined you'd see," he replied in a cryptic, ghost-tale-around-the-campfire voice. She realized he still thought she was just another adrenaline junkie out to find her next big fix. But that was ok. And not entirely untrue.

"So where can I find Gnar-nia?"

"Out past the Grizzly Cup area, to the west of it." She remembered her trail map indicating that as one of the areas designated for off-trail skiing, over the ungroomed, rough slopes of Little Cottonwood Canyon. "You know where that is?"

"The snow cat skiing?"

He nodded. "Gnar-nia's a fairly open path to head down. At least, open enough for someone who's skied a double black before. He smirked at her, as if he really didn't believe she had, but was humoring her nonetheless. "Just a twisting strip of all the pow pow you can handle. If you're *game* enough." And then he laughed again, like he'd made another joke.

———

SHE SIGNED UP FOR ONE OF THE RESORT'S SNOW-CAT adventures the next morning. She stayed with the group up to the summit of the Grizzly Gulch bowl, then, at the first opportunity, slipped away and headed farther west, out past the markers.

She was a bit winded by the time she found the strip of red trail marker tape tied to the base of one scrawny pine branch, fluttering in the wind like it was waving hello. The trail was extremely thin, but she'd found the marker and couldn't help the tingling thrill that skittered across the backs of her shoulders at the thought of the run that lay ahead.

The trail curved up the side of the mountain like a crooked question mark. Each side was, surprisingly, clearly marked with stones protected by the overhanging tree branches. Of course, one good snow dump and they'd disappear until the spring runoff, but apparently the snowfall hadn't been heavy enough to hide them completely. She picked her way up the mountain, relishing the way the air thinned and turned crisper with the higher elevation.

As she climbed, she became aware that the trees seemed to be noisier at this altitude. They creaked and cracked as if being pushed by a heavy wind at their tops, but she didn't feel even a hint of breeze. It was almost as if the trees were whispering to each other.

Occasionally, strange, rattling cries echoed from somewhere farther off in the forest, like a snow hare snared by some raptor, only they were too frequent. *It's the echoes distorting the sound,* she told herself, but there was a part of her—a small part that was steadily encroaching on the tingling excitement—that thought otherwise. That part thought the screams sounded feral and fierce, more like war cries than cries of pain. And then, once the thought took root, it wouldn't leave.

She knew she was doing something incredibly stupid. Grant had always been up for the rougher slopes, but only within the bounds set by the ski resort. "It's too dangerous to ski off-piste," he'd told her. "Too many bad things that can happen. What's wrong with having fun within the safety rails?"

There was a certain logic to it. *Besides,* the memory of Grant's voice whispered, *if you turned around now, you'd still be able to get in a few runs down the Grizzly Bowl.* It was an area that was pretty challenging, even if it was in-bounds. And she knew that nobody would think to check this far out if she got hurt or went missing. She'd be on her own.

But I'm already on my own. The chasm of despair that she'd been trying to close for the last eight months yawned a little wider, undoing some of her efforts. Everyone had been telling her to take her time, that the grief would fade, eventually. But waiting hadn't worked. What worked was doing the little things she'd never had the guts to before, of showing herself that she could be strong enough to survive his death.

She'd come to a different country to do it, and despite the fact that she was starting to cool down as the first bit of chill leaked through her layers, she knew she wasn't turning back. If she quit now, she wouldn't be going back to the Grizzly Bowl—she'd be going back to her quiet, empty home in Montreal filled with her quicksand-like bed and her grief, getting pitying looks from the neighbors whenever she took out the trash or fetched the mail.

"I can do this," she said in a firm voice to the empty mountain air. "Who needs safety rails?"

She kept walking.

It took her just over a half hour to reach the summit, but when she finally arrived, it was unimpressive: just an opening to the trail and the smooth white stretch of snow that would take her back down the mountain. It was relatively open, with few trees to dodge, though it looked like there was a fairly steep turn about a thousand yards down the trail. She could see the sun sparkling off the ice of the cornice that overhung the turn. It didn't look like the super-challenge the bartender had implied.

While she unloaded her gear and strapped in, she tried to squash her disappointment. "This is the first slope of your new life," she told herself. "This is just the beginning."

She started down the slope, pushing off hard with her poles so she didn't sink into the snow before she got up to speed. She tried a few looping serpentines to test the snow quality and had to admit that it was some awesome powder; the snow was so thick and fluffy it was like she was floating, weightless, down the slope. The wind cut at her cheeks under the rim of the goggles, but she grinned into it, savoring the feeling of needles on her skin.

But she'd only made it a few yards down when she heard a sharp crack, like a gun report, off to her right. Her stomach gave a nauseated flip. One word raced across her mind—*avalanche*—

and her eyes searched for a break in the tree line. But the trees stood close together like impassive, deadly sentries, and she didn't see anywhere she could duck into to take cover. *Gonna have to make a run for it.* She deepened her crouch, feeling the pull in hamstrings already tired from the hike up the trail, and felt her speed increase.

The first one appeared in her peripheral vision, loping almost casually through the powdery fluff like the world's biggest Saint Bernard. It was the size of a compact car and covered in thick white fur that looked dirty and gray against the white purity of the snow. When she turned her head to stare, slack-jawed, it snarled at her, revealing a mouthful of jagged yellow teeth set below blazing crimson eyes. But it was the two buck teeth in the front, each the size of a tombstone, that made her legs wobble a little off-track.

What the hell kind of rabbit is that? A noise exploded from her throat, not a scream but a high-pitched yip like a hurt dog. The tall ears, previously waggling like sunflowers in the wind, pinned flat to its head, and it growled.

With a practiced flip, she tucked her poles in her armpits, so they stuck out behind her, and crouched to become as aerodynamic as possible. As the massive rabbit angled toward her, she shot down the fall line, zooming like a bullet down the slope.

Another gun report, off to her right, followed by one more ahead on the left. Though she didn't dare look at the one behind her, she saw the one ahead of her as it came out of the snow. It rose like a submarine surfacing: ears-first, straight up out of the snow with a sharp crack of ice, then leveling out parallel to the ground as the giant furry body followed. It emerged running, as if it had been running the entire time below the surface of the snow. *And, oh God, it was fast!*

Its haunches pumped as it lunged towards her, and she had to angle sharply away from it. The lunge was over-eager, uncalculated, and it overshot her by several feet and crashed through the wall of trees like a bus. The tree trunks exploded into a shower of splinters. She angled back toward the center of the slope where the snow would be less deep, slaloming through the debris.

She risked a glance over her shoulder, and a weak moan escaped her as she spied the other two bunnies bounding afterward, legs folding and stretching forward in unison. Even though she leaned forward into a slightly tighter crouch, she had a sick feeling it wasn't going to be fast enough. Because as fast as she was rocketing down the slope, that quick glance had been enough to tell her that *they were faster*.

The pole in her right hand twitched and then was jerked backwards out of her grasp. The strap around her wrist pulled her along with it, flipping her in a somersault, and slamming her on her back in a burst of powder. The landing flung the goggles off her head and the air from her lungs as she skidded to a halt. She was dimly aware of her arm being jerked violently from side-to-side as she struggled to take a breath. Craning her head back, she managed to look along the length of her arm to where her hand hung limply in the crook of the pole's wrist strap. Beyond the strap, the hulking mass of a snow bunny crouched, crunching and bending the aluminum pole in its jaws like a dog with a stick.

It shook the pole again, and she cried out in surprise as it jerked her a few feet to each side. Something in her wrist popped, and she screamed. The noise was primal with pain and rage and startled the rabbit, who jerked upright and looked around in nervous, twitchy movements.

She used her good hand to rip the strap off her wrist, which felt hot and thudded with an angry ache. She heard herself gasping in short, quick breaths and realized she was going to pass out if she didn't get her breathing under control in the high altitude.

Holding her injured wrist to her chest, she looked at the rabbit as fire ripped through her calf. She screamed, instinctually swiping her other pole like a sword through the air near her feet.

She'd forgotten there was more than one.

The other rabbit jumped away with a nimbleness that shouldn't have been possible by something so large, its hungry eyes holding steady on her. A bright red stain splashed across the powdery snow of its mouth. It growled at her. She risked a glance at her calf, noting the bloody groove through the skin.

Move or you're going to die! Grant's voice screamed in her mind. She glanced back to the pole-eating rabbit. It was staring at her with the same hungry look, but hadn't come closer.

Yet.

She gave a half-hearted wave of her pole at the blood-stained rabbit near her feet. She struggled to untangle her skis so she could get to her feet, saying a silent, vague thank you for the fact that they hadn't popped off when she fell. If she'd had to get back downslope on foot, she knew she wouldn't make it.

She managed to keep both creatures at bay by making stabbing motions at them as she collected her equipment under her. As she straightened, she shifted her grip so that she held the pole like a baseball bat and tried to collect herself enough to plan her next move.

The blood-stained rabbit lunged. She swung, and the pole connected with the rabbit's face. A shower of powder exploded into the air as the head burst apart and the body crumbled in a pile at her feet.

The rabbit behind her snarled, and she swung at it, too, but missed. A quick glance over her shoulder confirmed she was only a short distance from the sharp turn of the slope. Could she make it before the rabbit took her down again?

There was only one way to find out.

She turned and pushed off as hard as she could. Though she didn't hear the rabbit move, she imagined she felt the air shift as it lunged to catch her. With a wild swing of her arm, she swung the pole over her shoulder and felt a small shower of icy clumps hit the back of her head as the pole connected. *Not enough to have gotten it for good*, she thought, remembering the huge pile of snow the first rabbit had made. Ignoring the burn in her calf, she lowered into a tight crouch and hoped she'd at least injured it enough to slow it down.

Her speed picked up quickly, but it still wasn't as fast as she'd have liked, given that she only had one pole to push with. She could feel her blood pressure pounding in her neck as the adrenaline rushed through her body. Knowing she would probably be face-to-face with a pair of wicked teeth, she risked a glance over her shoulder to see how far behind it was.

Nothing.

There's no way it gave up so easily. She straightened slightly and looked again. No large, murderous rabbit racing through the snow behind her. Only a clear set of parallel lines from her skis leading from the patch of roughened snow where she'd fallen.

She turned her attention to the path ahead of her, looking nervously along each side of the tree line for the waiting figure of the rabbit crouched to intercept her. *If it is, there's no way you'll be able to fight it off again,* Grant's voice whispered to her. *You'll have to get creative.*

A loud crack sounded ahead, but it sounded as if she was hearing it from a distance away. She braced herself and tightened her grip on the pole, but no snow bunny appeared.

She reached the turn and leaned into it. Her injured leg almost buckled, but she planted the pole in the ground and used it to pivot around the corner. The rest of the slope opened before her in a straight chute, empty except for the now-familiar hulking shape waiting in the center of the path. Not moving, but waiting with its ears raised in the air like lumpy antennae. *Not ears,* she realized. *Ear.* She must have clipped the other with her pole.

The thought filled her with a savage glee, but the feeling faded as she scanned the tree line: the trunks were packed as tightly as they'd been at the top of the slope. Given the narrowness of the slope, it was like the whole path was designed to funnel her right to it—there certainly wasn't any room to dodge around on either side.

A tear tickled the edge of one eye and then trickled its way down her cheek until it was blown away by the wind. So this really was it. She remembered the pep talk she'd given herself at the top of the slope–this hadn't been a beginning at all. She pressed her hurt wrist to her chest and tightened her hold on the ski pole, squeezing the handle as if it would bring her back to reality, to the real world where there were no such things as monster snow rabbits that killed unsuspecting skiers. Where the world didn't punish foolish women who only wanted to feel more alive by doing something they never would have suspected themselves capable of. To catch themselves by surprise.

Surprise, babes, Grant whispered. *That's it.* And she realized she had one card left: a last-ditch, desperate idea that she knew probably wouldn't work. But she didn't really have many options left.

She angled her course so that she was skiing straight down the fall line, in the middle of the slope, toward the rabbit. Then she lowered herself into a tighter crouch, making herself into the smallest ball possible on top of her skis. With a twist, she flipped her ski pole around so that it was pointing straight out in front of her, like a jouster.

Her stomach flipped like she might throw up as she flew toward the rabbit, so she concentrated on the tip of her ski pole, at the small circle of the basket that kept the pole from sinking all the way into the snow, and beyond at its pointy tip. And she flew like a small cannonball toward the rabbit.

The second before she hit it, she closed her eyes. But that didn't stop her from hearing the rabbit's snarl. The sound was louder than anything she'd heard, so close it was practically inside her head. Her ears felt like they would burst from the noise or from her heartbeat or just from her own terror.

The sting of a thousand icy needles pelted her skin as her pole pierced the rabbit's chest and she ripped through the body. Tiny flecks of ice and snow stung her face and hands as the avalanche of the rabbit's mass fell on top of her.

Then suddenly she was through!

She straightened and tried to open her eyes, but they were held shut by a thick crust of snow that clumped her eyelashes together in a hard shell. She scrubbed at her face with her good hand, and thin sheets of ice flaked away. When the cold air whistled across her skin, it continued to sting like a dry ice burn.

She opened her eyes to see the beautiful sparkle of sunlight on the unmarred path of powder before her. Turning her skis hard to the right, she came to a stop in a spray of snow and looked down at her ski suit. She took in the covering of snow from where she'd fallen and the tear down one leg that was bleeding in earnest now. If not for the injuries, it could have all been a dream. She passed her hand through her hair, feeling the hard crust of ice that had formed like a helmet on her head.

"I'm still alive," she murmured out loud. Her voice was hoarse, as if she'd been screaming, but she didn't remember doing so. It made her voice sound like someone else's, a bit huskier and more tired than her own. It fit with the way her skin felt: all rough and raw, like everything had been exfoliated down to something cleaner, down to something that had been under the surface the whole time.

"*I'm still alive!*" she screamed, ignoring the way her broken voice cracked. Her voice echoed back around her, and though the words of the echo were unintelligible, the fierceness in the tone seemed to amplify. It sounded like she felt—feral and a little primitive. She turned with a smile on her face, even though her face hurt more for doing it. Pointing her skis downslope, she made her way down.

THE CLOUDS UNFURLED BELOW THE PLANE LIKE WISPY BITS OF snow powder stirred up by the wind. She selected a window seat just so she could watch it. There were plenty of mountains to fly over between Utah and Montreal, and she liked how they lay like sleeping blue giants below her. She wondered how many snow bunnies were still waiting in places like Gnar-nia.

And, as always, she thought about Grant.

Thoughts of him—*jokes he would've liked, snatches of old conversations, the way he squinted when he was thinking hard, that funny voice he used to cheer her up when she was*—always hovered just on the edge of her mind, even when she was thinking about something unrelated.

She'd hiked up the hill, hunting for the next thing she could concentrate on long enough to not think of him. But she realized she'd been doing it wrong. Escaping the memories didn't make the hurt go away, but perhaps trying to live with them would.

Danielle Davis (she/her) is a liar, a cheater at cards, and a misrememberer of song lyrics: only two of these are true. Her horror and dark fantasy have appeared in *The Santa Barbara Literary Journal, Andromeda Spaceways Magazine*, and multiple anthologies, including Hungry Shadows Press's *It Was All a Dream: An Anthology of Bad Horror Tropes Done Right,* Black Ink Fiction's *Cosmic Menagerie*, and Wandering Wave Press's upcoming *Tumbled Tales: Stories that Upend Genre Conventions.* You can find her on most social media under the handle "LiteraryEllyMay" and at www.literaryellymay.com.

WINTER TREES

Amanda Steel

Shaking snow off their branches
And swaying in the wind
Almost in beat to the music below
Silent Night and Jingle Bells
Shouts of merry Christmas
And if you listen carefully
Rustling of leaves not shed in autumn
The winter trees held on to them
As if afraid to be stripped bare
Now they look through windows
At trees glistening in tinsel and lights
Decorated in baubles and wooden soldiers
I used to be pretty too, think the winter trees
It feels like so long ago now
My branches were a palette of greens
And flowers in all shades of red and pink
Regret keeps them from looking closer
Until one night, they notice those trees are dead
Cut down and carried home

By those who wanted to capture their beauty
The dead trees shed pine needles on the carpets
And the winter trees shed tears
Silently grateful to be alive

Amanda Steel is the author of *Ghost of Me* and *After the Zombies*. Her word has been broadcast on BBC Radio Manchester, and adapted on *The NoSleep Podcast*. She is also a freelance writer. Her credits include *The Sun Newspaper*, Ask.com, *Reader's Digest*, *Author's Publish* and *Introvert Dear*.

IN THE FORESTS OF THE NIGHT

David Daniel

"*Hylophobia.*" Ed pronounces it carefully. "A fear of forests. Robert ever talk to you about that?" Ella Rios is still as beautiful as she was back in high school.

"You mean like trees?"

"Big old trees. He ever mention it?"

Ella's tentative smile asks: *Is this a joke?*

Ed prepares to press his case, but just then he spies Robert in the distance, wandering in a forest. He blinks. *Can it be?*

He looks at Ella for confirmation, but she is gone. The air smells damp. He has not seen Robert in years, and now, here he is, in the forest. Ed shouts excitedly—explanations can come later, apologies—and runs toward his friend…

"Captain." Someone was gripping his shoulder, shaking him. "Sir, it's time."

Ed Cogan blinked awake. The sergeant stood over his cot, towering in the green, uncertain light. Wind buffeted the tent with gusts of winter rain.

"The storm's worsening, Cap."

Cogan groaned, rising, catching fragments of his dream, though what it'd been about was already fading. The smell in the air was real though: the dank, mingled scents of woods in the rain and water-repellent canvas. "How long was I out?"

"Twenty minutes, like you asked." The sergeant's name was Paddock. Water dripped from his helmet liner and poncho. He saluted and left the tent.

Cogan had napped with his boots on. He drew on his poncho, remembering as he did that Ella Rios had been in his dream. He tried to recollect more, but nothing came. He put on his helmet liner, opened the tent flap, and stepped out.

The wintery chaos of the storm continued unabated. The ground was slush and mud. Nearby, heavy trucks grumbled in idle, giving the air a metallic diesel perfume. Below this knoll, invisible from here, the river was a rushing roar. Cogan squinted at his watch. The projected flood crest was midnight, just two hours away. He set off to check the critical points.

―――――

THE GOVERNOR'S STATE OF EMERGENCY DECLARATION activated the National Guard. Now, thirty guardsmen under Ed Cogan's command were deployed along a sharp elbow in the river just above the bridge that linked the small towns. Swollen by the relentless storms of the past week, the river was topping its wooded banks, and high winds wreaked havoc with the trees. Already exposed roots protruded from the shore like claws.

The guardsmen needed to reinforce the southerly bank, where the rush from upriver made its fiercest assault. The bridge was a two-lane webwork of iron and concrete, constructed as a WPA project in the 1930s and minimally maintained in the decades since. If the surge continued to undermine them, the bridge-footings would likely wash out and the span would surely fall.

At best, Cogan knew, the sandbag barriers he and his crew erected would delay the flooding of the adjacent town–also under orders to evacuate. The road and bridge were the only means of egress. A second Guard unit was aiding in the evacuation. Cars and SUVs, their headlights made blurry by the rain-snow mix, were moving across the bridge in a slow parade.

Determined, he checked on the troops at their tasks. Working in the glare of generator-powered floodlights, some were filling woven fiber sacks with sand that had been brought in by truck earlier. Others had a brigade going, moving the heavy sacks down to where the river cut its sharp eastward angle, slashing now at the shore with floes of ice. For hours, the soldiers worked with Cogan moving among them, offering encouragement. And yet, the woody lowlands were already ankle deep in the flood. Small, uprooted trees flowed by in the boil of icy water.

If they could just endure the crest, Cogan thought, the bridge might be saved. His watch showed 10:15. He moved along the sodden trail toward the next point.

He grew up near the river just six miles upstream, but had not been in woods like these since high school. The town, once the sum of his world, hadn't been a part of his life in over twenty years. He lived downstate now, in the city, where the only water was in park fountains and swimming pools. He was a construction engineer by trade, and a proud captain in the state National Guard. His unit had been called up the night before last and, except for the brief nap, he'd been in motion since.

Darkness made the woods a place of hidden treacheries. Overhead, branches thrashed. As he trudged along the rudiments of a trail, stepping over downed limbs, pushing through brambles, a fragment from the dream reemerged.

Robert Trimble.

Robert had been in his dream.

THE SUMMER THAT ROBERT TRIMBLE'S FAMILY MOVED TO ED'S town from Boston, the two neighbor boys, both twelve, found an immediate intersection of interests: football, lifting weights in the backyard, Tolkien. On rainy days, they would lie under the sloping pressboard walls in Ed's unfinished attic bedroom and talk about Frodo and Gandalf, dreaming of grand journeys. By the time the junior high football team began its workouts in mid-August, the two were best friends.

Robert—always that, never Bob—was a study in contrasts. He was fearful of snakes and swimming in the river, yet on the football field, he was dauntless. He approached people with an easy, off-hand friendliness that won them over immediately, despite being plain-looking. From behind horn-rimmed glasses, he set his sights on Ella Rios, a popular, pretty girl. By sophomore year, Ella was his girlfriend.

A revelation was shared late one winter afternoon as the two walked home after school. On a stretch where the road curved alongside the old town cemetery, they passed the unpaved entry lane. It was lined with stately parallel rows of enormous sugar maples. In the fading light, the stark branches scraped against the sky.

"C'mon," Ed said. "Let's cut through. It's cold."

"No, man, let's not." Robert shook his head.

"Why? Scared of the graveyard?" Ed kidded.

"No, it's... I don't like those trees."

Ed frowned. "What's the matter?"

Robert looked around miserably. "I'm scared of them, okay? I'm scared of the trees."

"Seriously?"

"Remember that time we camped out in your backyard—near those old apple trees last summer?"

"Yeah." To be fair, the orchard had been spooky. Untended for years, the trees had become stunted, distorted shapes like something out of Disney's *Snow White*: spooky oval sockets of eyes, leering mouths, and long, ghostly arms with taloned twig-fingers. Still, Ed nearly laughed, thinking his friend was teasing, but Robert's pinched expression shut him up.

Ed remembered how Robert had cried out, shouting, "The branches... claws!" His best friend had sat up abruptly, hyperventilating in the semi-dark when Ed had shaken him awake.

"You talking about that nightmare you had that time?" Ed asked.

"It wasn't just a nightmare. It was the trees."

"No sweat," Ed said, unsure of what else to do. They crossed the road, taking the long way home.

"SIR, THE KNOLL'S GETTING SOGGY." PADDOCK APPEARED, HIS breath smoking in the cold night air.

In the storm-lashed woods, the familiar had become the strange. For the last two hours, Cogan had been working alongside the others. Around them, trees groaned restless sounds above the deeper pulse of the gale and the mad-rushing river. Occasionally, a tree, its roots undermined, crashed down, sending soldiers scrambling. With nerves scraped raw by the incessant wind and rain, they labored under a growing weight of dread.

"Several big pines are down," said Paddock. "I put guys on chainsaws, but I don't think we'll be able to get the vehicles out if we wait much longer."

Forty-eight hours ago, they had arrived in a convoy of heavy trucks and Humvees, with sand and lights, tools, and several high-capacity pumps. There'd been the flush of exhilaration a good storm brings, a can-do sense of mission. It was weather, for God's sake, not some heavily armed enemy force. The vehicles now sat parked on the high ground. The pumps hadn't even been unloaded. Gloom had gradually overcome unit cohesion. The storm was bearing with a growing ferocity, gummy with sleet, slashing them with gusts of branches.

Cogan considered all this. "Request for a transport chopper to be on standby. If we have to, we'll evac by air."

"Will they fly in this?"

"Get on the radio and find out. Until then, we stay on task."

ROBERT TRIMBLE'S FEAR OF SNAKES WASN'T HARD TO understand—he'd been a city kid—but a fear of trees? Ed probed him about it. Robert was vague. "There's just something about big, old trees. They're scary."

"How? It's not like they can chase you."

"Not that. It's more like... what they *know*."

Ed laughed. "Know?"

"Ancient stuff. They've lived a long time—much longer than humans have been here—just taking it all in. There's a kind of *consciousness* in their cells."

Ed mulled this over. Okay, on some level maybe. Response to stimuli. But consciousness? "That's a stretch."

"I'm telling you, trees *know* us," Robert insisted. "They've felt the woodsman's ax, the chainsaw. And I think they fear us."

Ed was starting to smile, but Robert remained deadly serious. "I believe trees *dream*. A different kind of dreaming than ours, maybe, but they try to connect with our dreams. It happens to me sometimes," he said, quieter now. "Like that night in the tent."

"You're saying those old apple trees were trying to get into your head?"

Robert was undeterred. "I think there's a gap between their dreamworld and ours, and that gap protects us most of the time."

"You've lost me."

"Okay, how about this: every year people die because of trees. Limbs fall, take out power lines, crush houses."

"You're saying trees do that on purpose? Why?"

"I told you. Because they fear us. And sometimes, they cross that gulf and lure us in." He'd grown animated. "Trees are beautiful. Those sugar maples you love in the fall. Or beautiful flowering dogwoods in spring. All that allure. They draw us in. And then…"

"What are you talking about?"

"Listen," Robert said. "Not every tree, just some. I'm pretty sure that in every forest there's one tree who's the *father* of all the trees there."

"Like the Ents in Tolkien? Treebeard?"

"Yeah. And maybe that tree's purpose is destruction. Or maybe protection of the other trees. Either way, it's at war with people."

"Robert," Ed said. "Treebeard is just fantasy."

Frown lines deepened above his glasses. "I know I'm sounding loony, but just come with me tomorrow. I'll show you."

It took some coaxing, but the next day, after school, Ed joined Robert, and they set out to find one of Robert's "father" trees. The town was surrounded by woods. They focused on a point of land by the river covered with old-growth forest. Just before sundown, which came early with the short winter days, Robert pointed. "There!"

Twenty yards beyond stood a vast-trunked pine. It was by far the most impressive tree they'd seen. A half-dozen people with outstretched arms might just have been able to link hands around its base. It was bare of limbs up to about forty feet. Its top, another sixty feet higher, had been blasted at some point by lightning. An enormous scar ran down its trunk. Limbs several feet in diameter had fallen away and lay dead beneath the pine, resembling bones, but there was still life and growth in the tree which towered over the encircling forest.

"That's got to be it," Robert said in a hushed voice, at the edges of which Ed heard a quaver. "That's the father tree."

"That's the badass, huh?"

"Shh—it may be able to hear us."

Ed didn't know whether to laugh or to try to talk sense to his friend. Instead, he started toward the tree.

"Come on, man," Robert said, "let's get out of here. It's getting dark."

Ignoring him, Ed made his way to the base of the tree. Thick vines of poison ivy, like twists of cable, were overgrowing the fallen limbs. Ed kicked the tree. It was like kicking granite. He kicked the tree again, then again. Robert kept his distance, imploring him to stop. Panting, struck with the futility of the afternoon's wandering, and his friend's naivete, Ed got angry.

"It's just a stupid tree!" And in a spontaneous act of frustration, he unzipped the fly of his jeans, stepped closer, and began to piss at the base.

Robert found nothing funny or freeing in this. On the contrary, he was terrified, pleading for Ed to come away. He didn't relax until they were far from there, headed home. "You took a huge risk."

"Yeah? What did you expect to happen?"

"I told you, there's a gulf... a chasm of—"

"Oh, yeah, I remember. Of dreams, right? Trees lure us in, because they want to kill us? Well, no limb fell on me. No creepy twig hands reached down and grabbed me, no roots twisted around my legs. It's just a tree, okay? The real risk I took? Getting poison ivy on my dick!"

AND YET, AT TIMES, THE NOW-GROWN ED COGAN CAUGHT NEWS accounts that brought to mind Robert's fears. Stories of trees that had fallen in storms, killing people, or coming down on houses, crushing occupants as they slept; or tearing out power lines, plunging communities into darkness and cold. And there were the fatalities of loggers, of do-it-yourselfers with their Home Depot chainsaws, the accidents on lonely wooded roads. Just the other week, in his city, there'd been such a crash. A young woman slammed into a huge oak and was dead at the scene. Texting while driving was the official determination, but a small, secret part of him wondered.

Just as he still wondered about what ultimately happened to Robert.

Sgt. Paddock materialized, cold rain sluicing off him, breathless. "Sir, word just came. The flood barrier upriver's been breached. The surge is on the way."

"How long?"

"Fifteen minutes. Maybe less. The chopper you requested is en route."

Reality hit Cogan. The sandbag reef they'd erected would be useless against the cascading water and ice. The bridge would almost certainly go. Thankfully, the evacuation of the nearby towns was complete. There was nothing else they could do. "All right, get everyone up on the knoll for when the chopper comes."

"What about the generators, the lights?"

"No time. Bring only what you can carry."

Nearby, a rending crash split the night, followed by frantic shouts, screams of pain. Cogan and Paddock hurried toward the sounds. A tree had come down, striking several guardsmen. A medic appeared and made her assessment. A dislocated shoulder, a fractured leg.

"Do what you can now," Cogan ordered, "then get them to high ground. Sergeant, get everyone up there and accounted for ASAP."

Most of the unit got aboard the chopper, but with two soldiers on stretchers, it was tight and there wasn't room for everyone. Cogan stayed behind to await a second flight. Two others volunteered to wait, as well. The aircraft lifted off with a thrashing downwash and soon faded into the scud. Cogan instructed the two volunteers to shelter in one of the Humvees. The engine was running; it would be warm and dry at least.

"And you, sir?"

"I've gotta get something in the truck." He pointed at a deuce-and-a-half. "Keep your radio on. Be right back."

Taking a two-way mobile unit himself, which he sheltered under his poncho, he headed for the truck. Pausing just a moment, he started down the trail toward the river.

ED CONCEIVED A PLAN TO HELP HIS FRIEND OVERCOME HIS obsessive dread of trees. Without making direct mention of Robert's phobia—*hylophobia*, Ed knew the term by then—he proposed an overnight camping trip. "It'll be like old times," he insisted before Robert could mount an argument. "Where?" Robert asked.

"The shopping mall. Where does *anyone* go camping, dummy? The woods."

Robert declined.

"What if it was Ella asking you to go? Would you then? Are you going to let this crap run your life?"

Robert's eyes narrowed behind his glasses. "All right. Screw it. Let's go."

"For real?"

"Yeah."

"Cool. We've got vacation coming up in a week, we can—"

"Tonight," Robert said.

"What?"

"Let's do it tonight."

"We have to plan, figure out what to bring."

"Plans are for the fainthearted, Frodo. When the call to adventure comes, you go, right?"

And so they went.

It was the end of winter, still chilly, especially after dark, but spring felt like it wasn't far off. They wore sweaters and their crimson football letter jackets and brought sleeping bags and a tent and groceries they picked up after school. They told their parents they were sleeping at each other's houses.

They hiked in on a trailhead near the river. Ed hadn't had time to chart the route, but without mentioning it he made a dead-reckoning attempt to put them in the vicinity of the old lightning-struck pine tree. At dusk, they set up camp. They prepared a supper of hotdogs and beans. Afterwards, they sat by the fire, talking and downing some beer Ed had liberated from his dad's stash.

"This is good, no?" said Ed.

"It is."

"Just a nice quiet forest." Ed watched the firelight glinting off his friend's glasses. "No fears, right?"

"No fears." Then, after a silence, Robert said, "You're the best friend I've ever had, man. The best I may ever have."

"Drink to it," Ed agreed.

Ed woke in the night—Robert was a shapeless hump in his sleeping bag—and slipped out of the tent to take a piss. A thin moon lent its milky light to the otherwise dark woods. He didn't go far, just to where he could lean against a boulder while he relieved himself.

He lumbered back and opened the tent to climb back in, eager for the warmth of his sleeping bag.

Robert wasn't there.

His sleeping bag was, along with his backpack. But his boots and the crimson letter jacket were gone. Had he also slipped out to piss? Or decided to play some sort of prank? Possibly, and yet, given his fears...

Something else caught Ed's attention: Robert's eyeglasses were hooked to the tent pole, where he had hung them before turning in. Without them, he was semi-blind.

Ed ducked back out of the tent. "Robert?"

He stumbled over the empty beer bottles, which lay by the remains of the campfire.

"Robert?" Again and again, he called his friend's name, but it was a small sound, swallowed up in the vast night forest. With mounting alarm, Ed searched the area.

Later, others did too. For four days, town authorities and volunteers, many of them classmates of the two boys, grid-searched the woods and surrounding fields. Police dragged the river. No trace of Robert Trimble was ever found. Had he run away? Been abducted? Official speculation was that the boy, having awakened in the night, perhaps to pee, had wandered away and, without his glasses, became confused and had fallen into the river. Wearing a jacket and boots, the cold water, and the fact that Robert wasn't a swimmer…

No one ever openly voiced the possibility that Ed had taken his friend out there with ill intent. And maybe it had been a testimony to the nature of their friendship after all, to the trust that Robert had had in Ed, that Ed never heard anyone mention Robert's strange phobia. By all evidence, Robert had shared that secret with no one else. As to the question that sometimes rose in Ed Cogan—had Robert somehow crossed that gulf of dreams he'd talked of?—he always wedged that idea away as quickly as it arose.

HALFWAY DOWN THE TRAIL TO THE RIVER, THE WIND COLD IN HIS face, Cogan became aware of his isolation. The world was invisible beyond the curtains of slanting rain. He squinted at his watch. Two minutes to midnight. The chopper would be returning soon. He should get back up on the high ground to be ready. No pressing need to go farther. Everyone was accounted for.

Most of the storm lights had gone dark, the generators having run out of fuel, but one was still going. He could hear it off to his right, upriver from where he stood. He moved in that direction.

The term was *hylophobia*, a dread of the forest, especially in the night, when the world grew formless, when you could become lost, or trees could take the shape of strange creatures that reached out with root and branch, and twigs could poke the eye and terrible evil lurked in knot holes and the rustling of leaves could stir a primitive terror.

The wooded trail was a quagmire, sucking at Cogan's boots. He trudged on. Winter lightning flickered. Brief flashes lit the ground, but then the trail grew even darker, and he was tripping over roots and rocks. The river roared, still invisible beyond the pelting rain.

Something crackled. Cogan blinked. He took the mobile radio from under the poncho.

"Cap—are you there? Come back." It was one of the soldiers waiting in the Humvee.

"Copy."

"Chopper inbound, three clicks out."

Cogan acknowledged and signed off.

Against the moan of wind and lashing trees, he was aware of rushing water. The flood crest was near. He started back up the trail but stopped. Listened. Had someone called him? He waited, but did not hear it again.

In the distance, beyond the high ground, a blinking strobe was visible in the scud. A single thin searchlight beam probed the dark like a silver sword. The chopper was landing. The radio sounded: "Sir, they're here." In the background, he could hear the *whup-whup* of rotors. "Chopper's here."

The surge was here, too. He felt a rush of cold air, bringing a dank smell of ice. There was a rending, metallic screech as the crashing wave ripped out the bridge supports. Seconds later came a roar as the bridge collapsed.

"Captain! Affirm." The radio voice was faint.

Cogan had given up any illusion that he had power over anything. In its place was a peculiar excitement. He set the radio aside. As lightning strobed around him, he leaned into the wind and staggered downhill toward the river.

He passed a silent pump. Its fuel gone, it sat useless as a stone. He came upon a feeble barricade of sandbags, the icy water already breaching it. Exposed roots along the bank looked more than ever like claws, noisily tearing the muddy flank of the river to a froth.

It occurred to him that in his preoccupation with memories, he had failed to respect the true magnitude of the current storm. It came to him now, too, though it didn't matter. It was as if his rational self had given way to something more tenuous and unknowable. More primal. Feeling a strange and growing sense of destiny, he continued to make his way through the slashing rain. After a while, he reached the elbow of the river.

That was where he saw it.

Being swept along amid the ice floes, urged by the flood, came a gigantic, uprooted tree. In the gloom, he could make out a lightning scar. It moved at foaming speed, broken-off branches upthrust and hissing, like the periscopes on a dark submarine. He watched, unable to take his eyes from the tree. He was standing shin deep in the overflow, feeling the water's eddy and pull. As the tree neared, the sound was like a snarl. He could make out the dense tangle of its roots—and something intertwined in the maze, only a bleached shape there in a blink of lightning, then gone.

A feeling came to him that he was staring across a chasm, utterly unaware of or prepared for what lay in between. Lightning flashed once more. This time there was no mistaking the colors, long weathered, in tatters now, the crimson high school jacket faded to pink, and above it, he was sure, a yellowed skull.

Cogan looked around for a branch, something to extend his reach; but there was nothing at hand. He took a tenuous step into the river.

An ice floe knocked his legs out from beneath him. He went under, gulping frigid water. He fought to regain his footing. Coughing, panicked, he surged upright, feet scrabbling to find the river bottom. But the current had hold of him. He tried to swim against the brown sediment-stained water, but his boots and uniform hindered him. The water swept over his head and sped him out and away from the shore.

Into the path of the enormous uprooted tree.

As it bore down on him, the flag of Robert Trimble's letter jacket flapping in the rush, there came the snapping of branches and limbs.

David Daniel is author of more than a dozen books, including entries in a prize-winning Alex Rasmussen mystery series, as well as a bestselling novel of the late 60s, *White Rabbit*. A new book, *Beach Town*, a collection of stories, will be published in April 2023 by Loom Press. He is a frequent contributor to the Boston Globe. Contact him at daviddaniel67@gmail.com.

THE TREES KNOW

Alyson Faye

Vines violate his body,
ivy infiltrates inside,
as he sleeps, eternally
so cold; snow-glazed
branches enwrap him
cradle and cushion him.
wood-cracks
bark-breaths
soil sighs
Once he was master
now, in his death,
see how the forest feasts!
Feral, riotous, rampant;
it will never let him go
wood-cracks
bark-breaths
soil sighs
Loam and clay
blood and bone,

it is all one.
The trees know
his name, whisper it . . .
snow-weeps
ice-groans
wind whistles

Alyson Faye lives in the UK, with her family and rescue animals, including her Irish-born Labrador, Roxy with whom she is often out on the moors. She is a tutor, editor, mum, dog-walker, and avid film buff. She often writes her dark stories and poetry in the wee grey hours. Her fiction has been published widely - most recently by *Space and Time* magazine, *Brigids Gate Press*, *Were-Tales*, *Musings* and *Daughter of Sarpedon* and by Black Spot Books in their award winning women in horror poetry anthology, *Under Her Skin*. Her poetry has won, and been placed in competitions and read on BBC Radio.

LIFE CYCLE

Jay Sykes

I
n a monochromatic landscape of frozen desolation, a
shadow made its way across the vision of every
unfortunate creature that shivered in the cold. Every time
some furry or feathery morsel of life tried to focus on the blurry
figure, the surrounding landscape swallowed it whole. Only
when she was so deep into the non-forest that nothing could see
her did Winter take her form.

Skin a patchwork of onyx and ivory, hair so pale it was
translucent, she was perfectly camouflaged against the dead trees
and snow. She dragged a burden, impossibly large for one so
spindly and insubstantial. She moved it in the manner of an ant,
dragging the corpse of a beetle one hundred times its weight. It
was implausible, but also inevitable.

Winter sighed. She finally allowed the cumbersome bag of
materials to thump to the ground in a grand clearing dominated
by a mighty elder. The tree of life was not her final destination,
and she needed a rest. She looked up, utterly overwhelmed, as
always, by the size of the trunk, the branches, the whole
anthropoid giant of vegetation. Stretching into the sky above her,

it elicited a sort of reverse vertigo: a feeling of falling upwards to the top and beyond.

She shook herself violently and focused on the network of roots reaching across the suddenly bare ground towards her. A strange heat pulsed through them, forbidding the snow from touching their tentacular forms. Winter forced her charcoal eyes out of focus, allowing herself to see the doorway only concepts knew the way through.

Squeezing through the barely there arch, her huge burden easily followed. She never questioned how the tree knew to let it through after her, it just always did. It took her a moment to get used to the view from the inside, where reality was no longer even a vague acquaintance.

She kept her mastery of her environment limited. Winter had no energy left for a self-indulgent crystal staircase of icy grandeur to bring her home. She managed a texture that was halfway between concrete and wood, alternating between stairs of different heights and a ramp, as she changed her mind regarding what was easiest to force herself to charge upward.

As she climbed, she passed the realms of others with influence over the natural world. Their homes faded into the simple rendering of her journey, giving a vague sense of who she was stumbling past.

The winds barely visited their own domicile, always whisking themselves into a frenzy over something or other.

The storms ventured out a few at a time to take their fiery disputes out on the Earth.

Night and day shared their one-person abode, leaving love notes for each other as they grasped and released the land.

Eventually, Winter found herself at the top, smoothly transitioning from climbing to winding her way along an uneven garden path. Her surroundings changed with each uneasy step. The world-between-worlds shuddered under the weight of her fellow seasons' dreams, although her mood coloured them for her consumption. It was always bleak. One moment she was stumbling through a rainstorm to a small stone hut illuminated by lightning, the next she was knee deep in sludge in a swamp that light would not touch, trying to peer through mangroves to some tumbledown excuse for a dwelling.

She paused, leaning the miserable sack of hard-won prizes against her legs. It weighed as heavily on her heart as on the rest of her body, almost crushing her twig-like ribs. She wrenched her focus away from the pain in her chest and tried to once more exert some real control over what she was seeing.

There were a few moments of psychedelic static, but then, out of abstraction emerged a simple bungalow in a parched grassy plain, featureless but for a network of dilapidated fences that never seemed to create any actual fields. The sun beat down out of a cloudless sky. It was uncomfortable, but Winter figured it was probably the best she could manage. She stumbled through the rest of her journey with relative ease, cursing fiddly locks on illogical gates as she went.

It took her three tries to open the doorknob. Her brain was sluggish and couldn't direct her arm to its destination. Once she succeeded, she wrenched her burden through the too-narrow door frame (almost ripping the hessian sack as she did so) and dumped it unceremoniously on the floor of the atrium.

"Is that you, darling?" chirped a sing-song voice from the voluminous kitchen.

"Of course, dear sister," Winter replied wearily.

"I was getting worried. You're so very late!"

Spring sashayed into view. She was a portly woman, with hair the colour of lemon peel and eyes like hungry puddles. Plucking open the sack with her pudgy fingers, she leaned over to examine the contents.

"Thin pickings this year, sweetie!" she tutted. "Never mind,

I'll just have to make them a little smaller." She picked up the sack as if it were a dandelion blossom and skipped to her sewing room to get to work.

Winter collapsed against the coat rack, so tired she could barely breathe. It was late, and every inhalation was like boiling water down her throat. But she needed something before she could sleep. It would keep her up all night if she ignored it. Pressing down hard to elevate her emaciated frame, she clawed her way to Spring's sewing room and scratched at the door. With time, it opened.

"Goodness, look at you!" cried Spring, horrified by Winter's bruised complexion and protruding bones. "You needed to get to bed days ago. What in heaven's name are you doing?"

"Thank me," rasped Winter.

"Nobody's going to thank you for killing, dearie, you know that!"

"Why not? You said it yourself, 'It's got to be done. I need the old ones to make the new.'" Winter mocked Spring's lilting voice as best she could with no strength.

"Because killing's wrong. That's why I don't do it," Spring cooed, stroking the tears away from Winter's face as she talked down to her. Suddenly, she was bouncy again. "Off to bed with you, lickety split!" she exclaimed, and slammed the door.

Winter rolled away from rejection and despair, and into Spring's roaring hearth in the hallway. Her screams almost woke Summer and Autumn. Almost.

———

THE NEXT NINE MONTHS PASSED WITHOUT EVENT. SPRING SEWED life so beautifully you couldn't see the stitches (despite her complaints about what she had to work with). Wet from her sweat, her creations teemed over the world, reclaiming what their own flesh had relinquished. When her bag was empty and all her handiwork lovingly sent forth, she trotted off to bed with her eye mask on her forehead and curlers in her hair.

On her way there, she gave Summer a good-natured pat on the shoulder as he was warming up for his stint and asked him to be gentle. He laughed and pretended not to know what she was talking about before somersaulting down the elder tree, ready to throw his usual gymnastic fits of tumultuous temper and burning euphoria. Some life was caught up in his mood swings here and there, but nothing serious, nothing you could really call killing. He was Summer after all, and with Winter coming every year, life would put up with a few forest fires and be grateful for the heat. When his task was complete, he fell asleep on the couch. Autumn had to carry him to bed when they got up.

They crept back downstairs for fear of re-awakening Summer and sang softly as they hovered into reality, calming the world's vibration a little, almost comfortably. They painted it the colours of art and poetry, inspiring the moody and the listless to turn their melancholy outwards. The wilting flowers of soulful hopes and dreams swelled to creative fruition like the apples bending branches in orchards.

Autumn also had a more serious purpose, running from town to town and forest to forest, helping everyone get ready for the oncoming slaughter. They tested the preparedness of each community with meteorological emergency drills and provided one last bounty before the approaching catastrophe. Yet no catastrophe came.

Winter never slowed the world to a near-stop with her icy contortion, never tortured with the still and the cold. All the creatures that should have frozen to death were left with their warrants unsigned, their threads uncut. They meandered in the no-man's-land between living and dying, twitching and flailing one minute, galloping and feeding the next.

Eventually, Spring rose from her slumber. Too tired to realise she wasn't shivering, she lit a fire in the hearth with sleep-filled eyes to warm the world. She took a few days to have her coffee as she waited for Winter to come stumbling through the door.

She sipped it luxuriously as the world burned.

JAY SYKES IS A NON-BINARY CREATIVE AND ACADEMIC FROM Tasmania, Australia. They delight in birthing works that disturb whilst maintaining a sense of wonder and beauty. So far, they have had written pieces accepted by Sirens Call Publications, *Science Write Now* and *The Last Girls Club*, among others. They also sell their artwork and handmade jewellery in historic Salamanca Place, and assault the audiences of their hometown with their dark comedic observations. They hope to continue spreading a vague sense of unease far and wide!

IN THE FULLNESS OF TIME

Steve Ingeman

I
t was spring, and new growth was just shooting from the cracks when Scritch saw a girl clambering up the slope, slipping on loose scree. Her shift was torn, her knees were scraped. She cried out in panic. Scritch saw waterfalls tumbling from her eyes and recognized in her a mirror of his own rushing cataracts. He understood in that instant, for the first time, that he was alone, and so he showed her a hollow between boulders, and he shielded the entrance with low-hanging branches. There she cowered, trembling and small, unlike the others who came after, who darted back and forth, and carried fire and shook clubs in the air, and who shouted and climbed over boulders and looked under things. Scritch lured them away with a rock falling here, a branch breaking there. Tumbling water masked the girl's sobs, and after a while they moved on and their clamor trailed away.

The girl, safe, emerged and observed her protector, craggy and ancient, shagged with pine needles and scuttling with bugs. She chose a flat rock by a pool and lay on it, face down, arms wide. She said her name was Ama. She spoke an oath, thanking

Scritch and blessing him, and bound herself to him. Scritch felt something swell inexplicably inside.

That night, Scritch provided lichen and moss to cover her, and piling aspen sprigs and mounding up the earth until she stopped shivering and gave in to sleep. In the morning, she scrubbed at her scratches in the upper pool, and the cool water eased her purple welts. Scritch marveled at the warmth of her skin and knew then that he'd been cold a long time. He gave her berries and nuts when her stomach rumbled.

Days passed and women snuck up from the village, covering their tracks, carrying clothes and food and incense. They dressed Ama in red and gold, crowned her with feathers and prostrated themselves at her feet. At night, under the full moon, they stripped and danced and howled like dogs. Their breath steamed white in the chill. Then the women gathered up their clothes and kissed Ama's hands and went back down before dawn.

In those early days, men would come creeping with knives and axes in the dark, moving quietly. But they would turn an ankle on loose stones, or a foothold would give way. They would cry out, giving themselves away. Discovered, they would flee in terror, and Ama would stretch herself against Scritch again and thank him, and he would tremble under her warmth.

"Look," he showed her. A little mulberry sapling sprouted from a cleft in the rocks where she had hidden that first night. Ama smiled and wrapped its tender trunk in red ribbon.

———

SHE CHANGED SO FAST. IN THE SUMMER, WHEN THE STREAMS slowed to a trickle and the trees buzzed with insects, Scritch found her suckling an infant. He was wonder-struck. Had he ever been so small and so helpless? Soon other children were skipping and clambering and kicking the dirt, dislodging loose rocks, sweeping away the fallen leaves. They darted like minnows. They splashed in the shallows.

"Caleb, slow down," Scritch said, always worrying after them, and Ama laughed.

"Caleb is grown, silly. That's Filippa."

Scritch was surprised but saw that she was right. He watched Filippa run and dive from the top of the falls into the deep pool, spraying water over and over. She was fearless.

By this time, men would come from the valley, not to do her harm, but to seek her skills. So many, in fact, that paths were worn in the low meadows, and they had cut stairs for the steeper climb. Ama mixed herbs, petals, and tiny animal bones for them. She sang incantations, brewed elixirs. Then she would lead them to the pool and take off their clothes, and take off her clothes, and draw tears from their eyes. She would send them home, humbled, but keep a part of them for herself, in her belly. And Scritch raised fawns for her, nurtured crayfish in rocky stream beds, ripened berries, and filled shallow pools with trout and salmon. His heart overflowed.

———

IN THE FALL, THE AIR TURNED. WET LEAVES STUCK, SLICK AND itchy, on Scritch's back. Gone were the sounds of the children who used to sweep away the pine needles and kick and run across the stones and skip the pebbles across the surface. Their feet had flattened weeds growing through his cracks, but Scritch felt unkempt now, disheveled, and he apologized for his appearance.

Ama laughed. "Aren't we a pair," she said. "I look like you now," and she touched her creased face.

Scritch looked around. "Where are the children?"

"They will visit sometimes," she murmured, as she rested in

the shadow of her gnarled mulberry tree, lulled half asleep by the gurgling stream.

Ama used to tell him that he was slow, but Scritch had learned lately to wait for her.

"There's a big bass in the lower pool," Scritch told her. "I know you would find it delicious." She was tending a small fire, warming some water.

"I am too slow now to catch a fish," she sighed. Then she turned thoughtful. She laid a thin hand on Scritch. "When I'm gone, will you be alright?"

But the question made no sense to him. Absence was incomprehensible when he felt so full inside.

———

WHEN AMA LEFT, IT WAS WINTER. THE WIND HOWLED THROUGH bare branches as hunters discovered her, desiccated and cold, and carried her down the slope with their hats off. Scritch hunched for some time, alone, under the snow. His back itched with loose rocks and fallen sticks. He had always felt solid and immovable, but now a chasm opened inside him. He sagged and shifted, and he let out a voiceless howl as the ground rocked and gave way. Boulders tumbled down into the town, smashing houses. The ice dam upstream shattered. Water spilled over the banks and swept horses and fences and men and carts away.

Villagers fled in terror. But Filippa gingerly climbed the stone steps, favoring her bad hip. She reached the old flat rock and lay down, breathless, next to the surging water. "Stop this," she snapped, and Scritch was somewhat chastened. "You should be happy. You had enough."

Scritch wasn't so sure. "I had warmth," he said, "and now I'm cold."

She waved that thought away. "Most mountains never know warmth."

His self-pity was persistent: "There was laughter, and now it's gone."

"You thought it would last forever?" she chided.

He was still seething and spasmodically pitching. But he had no response.

"Well," Filippa *hmphed*. "Now you know how people feel. All the time."

Her voice was gentle, though. She placed a hand on him and softly stroked his rough surface until the heaving started to subside. After some time, he stilled, except for an occasional hiccup.

"Will you stay?" he asked. His voice was cracking and snapping.

"Not for long," she answered. "A little while, though."

So she lay with him on a bed of cool moss and closed her eyes, humming one of Ama's old songs. Scritch's rage was extinguished, and he was left with a new and fathomless emptiness. So his waters slowed and split and trickled until they were just two rivulets running down his rocky face.

Steve Ingeman is a full-time librarian and former philosophy instructor whose fiction and non-fiction can be found in *The Journal of Popular Culture, Analog: Science Fiction and Fact,* and *Dark Recesses*, and others. He lives, works, and writes in the greater metro area of Washington, D.C.

I AM WINTER.

Elinora Westfall

She is everything I am not. She is supple as a snake. I am frozen.
She is the whisper of holidays and beach trips, BBQs and
laughter.
I am eerie stillness, the last bloom of white from dying blue lips.
I am winter. I
am cold. I am in darkness, flirting with madness, wires in my
veins, pulsing,
vibrating, killing me.
I am the splinters of skeleton trees in the pockets where my eyes
used to be, my
mind the fleeting glimpse of a wolf. She is a peacock, I am a
wild hare, running,
but never finding home in a wood full of eyes. She watches me.
Hiding.
Breathing.
I am the uncertainty of black ice, I am strong as the North Wind.

Elinora Westfall is a Australian/British writer of stage, screen, radio, fiction and poetry with work previously published in *Poetry Salzburg*, *The Rialto*, *Rattle*, *Sheepshead Review* and shown on Broadway and in London's West End. www.elinoralord.com

LAGNIAPPE

la·gniappe /ˈlanˌyap, ˌlanˈyap/
noun
NORTH AMERICAN
1 something given as a bonus or extra gift.

LIGHT THROUGH THE TREES

Mike Adamson

S he'd come up to the cabin with Jack a score of times over the years, treasured the open country and felt it their retreat from the ever-increasing insanity of urban life. Now to come back without him was both a coda to all that had gone before and the unwelcome shape of all to come.

Going through the motions of a funeral had been difficult enough, but Liz knew that was mostly play acting—it was for the relatives, for family expectations, the group expurgation of grief in the manner society prescribed.

Now, this, the pilgrimage to their cabin, was for her. Not even the kids could intrude upon her moment. Turning her face from society was entirely appropriate. Propriety had been satisfied in the last few weeks; now came her turn.

The cabin was hiking distance from the overlook above Cedar Springs. She took her time, drove carefully, with memories as her only companion. When she got out in the late afternoon in Cedar Springs, she knew she was deliberately placing a tough trek before her. She was well equipped—quilted jacket, knitted hat, hiking boots, thermals, backpack, a rifle, bear-bells to tinkle as she moved. The first snow had fallen, and the year was beginning to bite.

Challenge was the point. If Jack was gone, could she survive without him? If the answer was no, she preferred the wild country take her, rather than lingering alone as an aging curiosity, pitied even. She was just old enough to know there was no one else waiting for her out there, and just young enough for it to still matter. She slammed the tailgate, locked up, and put her keys in an inside pocket. She settled pack and rifle, tucked silver hair under her wool hat, and set off up the hiking trail around the hill behind the overlook. The silence of pine woods welcomed her.

Her breath plumed faintly in the long afternoon light, and fresh snow crunched under her boots with that once-heard never-forgotten sound. A few birds called, and the wind was gentle. Despite the beautiful day, without Jack at her side, ready with wit and affection, a whole dimension was gone from her world. Though, she wasn't entirely alone on this path. Jack's ashes were in her pack. She had two tasks: scatter his remains at the cabin, his last wish. And then, make sense of a world without him.

The winter sun was low now, the warming power of its rays spent. Sunglasses went into her pocket, gloves became a necessity. She stopped to rest for a few minutes, hearing the stillness, the silence of the world after the steady rhythm of her climb. It was a difficult slog with the weight. A high pass turned away through a saddle between hills. She would follow a stream to the cabin from there. But as the short day approached evening, she looked more at the fading rays than the track.

At last, she paused on the ridgeline and dropped onto a fresh-sawed tree stump to catch her breath and watch the sunset, the last act of the day, through the intervening forest. The swollen, orange sun kissed the horizon, bringing more feelings than she could readily understand. Those who survived near-death

experiences often spoke of walking a tunnel of light towards...
what? The next life? Eternal rest? Enlightenment? Rebirth?
She'd read of them all, and despite the faith placed in them by
legions, she only knew she was alone.

Sunset mesmerized her. Light rays through the vertical trunks
splayed and cast a million shadows, at the conflux of which was
the light. She reached out a glove toward it. She watched the sun
until the fiery eye closed and red clouds filled the woods with
their reflected glow. Then she hung her head and let the tears
come. There was no one left to pretend for, and nature neither
judged nor pitied.

Perhaps she should just sit here and let the cold have her?
The nihilism talking. Instead, she thrust to her feet angrily, if for
no other reason than because of her promise to Jack. She
stamped her boots for warmth, adjusted pack and rifle, and
pulled out an energy bar. Still a long way to go in the dark.

She knew the way blindfolded and used no flashlight, but let
her eyes acclimate to the night. As the light faded, her pupils
opened wide, and she saw the woods as the animals saw them, a
clear indigo sky casting just enough silver starlight for her to
make out the trail. Her flashlight was in her hand, but she
resisted using it to keep her night vision as long as possible. The
patina of snow reflected the stars well enough to see the trees
and trail.

Now she was alone in the dark, and the metaphor could not
have been stronger. It was, after all, why she was really doing
this. If she was actually *alone in the dark,* then she had better
learn what it meant, to know what she was really up against. She
put one foot steadily in front of the other and listened to the
jingle of her bear-bells. Stride after stride, breaking down the
final goal of reaching the cabin into many minor goals, into
single steps.

Liz was very tired now. She had to stop to rest more often,

and the cold was becoming more difficult. She had a thermos of hot coffee, but to find it would require the flashlight and would cost her night vision. Only a mile more to the cabin—she decided to press on.

The snow would freeze hard, and she must be careful tomorrow. She had her mobile and knew there was coverage up here. If she got into distress that she could not escape, she could always call for help. *If* she wanted to. The thought had been in her mind from the first moment: she might not actually want to return. It was very easy to go be with Jack, if it was what she really wanted. This trip was all about finding out.

The cabin was not far away now, a quarter mile farther, and she moved on under the frigid heavens, panting a little. She had never attempted this on her own, much less on a winter night. She peered up at the Milky Way, which offered her a glimpse of the bottomless universe, a single frame of a movie thirteen billion years in the playing.

When the cabin appeared ahead at last, relief flooded her tired body. The living part of her still understood its own value. She plodded the last hundred yards up a shallow gradient to the old log-built and shingled cabin, which snuggled back among pines. Now she drew off a glove, found the keys inside her jacket and unlocked the stout old door. She sent it back on groaning hinges and flicked her flashlight to bathe the interior.

Musty air—dust and time. She heeled the door shut and eased off the rifle and pack, rubbed her shoulders in the chill silence. On the rough timber table stood an oil lamp and matches, filled and placed there many months ago. Jack's last act on their previous trip had been to set things just so, knowing he was unlikely to return. A tear made its way down her cheek as she unscrewed the glass. She took up the matches and struck, lit the wick, and reseated the glass. She turned up the flame and clicked off the flashlight to save the battery. A second lamp stood on the mantle over the hearth and soon she had enough light to work by.

Lighting the dry wood in the hearth came next, a skill she had learned long ago. When the tinder blazed up and the main wood caught, she settled into her chair by the hearth to rest. She glanced over at the pack with a sad smile. "Jack, honey, we're home. And you never have to leave again."

Coffee from her thermos was welcome warmth, as she turned a can of hash into an iron pan. She put it on the hearth before laying the table with folded linen from a drawer. With the greatest reverence, she brought the ornamental container of Jack's ashes from her pack and placed him on the table, then found the bottle of wine they had left up here.

She opened it, poured two glasses and placed one by the container, raised her own and sighed. "All the way to the end, sweetheart. I never imagined it would come so soon or that it would only be for one of us." She raised the glass again, then drank, the wine biting a little.

The hash sizzled. She turned it onto a plate, took a fork and tucked in at the table, going through the motions. She understood the gesture for what it was: the inability to step away from what was familiar and wanted. The food was simple and tasty and took the last chill from her, so when she settled by the fire with another glass of wine, she felt human again.

Trials did not rob one of humanity, she knew. It could only be surrendered. Relief that this hadn't caused her to reach that point settled in. She sat with a long sigh and sipped the red, determined not to simply drink herself to sleep. Tomorrow, she would let Jack go on the mountain wind. His mortal remains would scatter, become part of the wilderness, to be dissolved by the rains and carried by streams, to feed life.

They had always been card players, and kept a deck up here. Cribbage was a game for two, of course, and it felt strange, if now apt, to play solitaire. She sat with coffee and played by the glow of the lamp, heard the night wind in the shingles and chimney, and went to the dark place she had not wanted to confront around the family.

Much as she loved them, they had their lives to live, productive ones, full of purpose and direction. She could not see a role for herself in them. There were no grandchildren—some suggested this was the problem. No anchor for her.

Discomfited, she stood, set the knitted draft-stopper at the foot of the door, and took blankets from a chest; perching a generous log into the embers, she wrapped up by the fire, hoping for sleep.

ASCENDING FROM SLEEP, SHE KNEW SHE HAD BEEN CALLED. A moment later, she was equally sure she was still asleep.

The sprite sat on the edge of the fire grating and looked up at her from eyes that blinked in the pure flame of its form. Limbs of stringy fire held their outline and antlers spread from a crown of shaggy locks in which the long ears of a stag were occasionally visible.

Liz blinked, felt her heart race as she came fully awake, but the dream vision did not recede, fade, or blur.

"Hello," it said, its voice the hissing of embers or wind in the chimney. "You've had a long journey to reach this moment."

Her heart rose into her throat. Liz moved convulsively, threw her blanket aside and stood, knocking her empty coffee mug from the arm of the chair so it broke with a sharp clatter on the floorboards. She bolted for the door, desperately turned the key in the lock, and was outside in the icy night in another heartbeat. The cold slugged into her like a solid wall and she stopped short, mind spinning. Was she dreaming? She must be...

Before her, a mounding of snow shuddered and drew together, hunched upward and little by little built itself into a vaguely human outline. Her breath was foggy before her as she panted, feeling sanity slip as the flurry arranged itself into an anthropomorphic figure. Antlers of ice grew like crystals from its brow, and eyes of cold blue flame opened. A hand gestured, a finger wagging in remonstration. "Don't be silly," the apparition said softly, in a voice like the wind. "Fire is your best friend." Hands gestured, shooing her back into the cabin.

Her wide eyes flicked back and forth over the white slope among the trees, wondering if an infinity of snow beings might dwell there, ready to rise before her. She backed up against the door, felt for the handle and eased inside, already shuddering badly. Her eyes did not leave the rooted being of snow until she closed the door. Once inside, she made herself turn and look at the fireplace.

The fire sprite was still sitting where she left it, and it shrugged with arms spread wide. "You wasted all that warm air." Words soft as the breeze. "Come back, before you throw your life away for nothing. If you want to know what sin is, you're doing it right now."

One faltering step at a time, Liz approached the orange glow of the hearth, panting shallowly. "You can't be real," she managed in a tight whisper.

"I'm as real or unreal as you need me to be," the apparition replied, flames crackling and rippling from feet upward to antlers. "If you need me to be a nightmare, fine, I'm a nightmare. It changes nothing."

Liz sank into the chair and drew the blanket close, shivering, and seemed to submit helplessly to the dream. "Whatever," she murmured. "I just want to wake and have this all gone."

"I will *not* be dismissed!" the sprite said sharply, rising from the grating to stand on the bricked hearth. It flicked a hand and a drop of flame spat onto the rug before the hearth, where it caught the dry fibers. Liz stirred from her shocked torpor, moved her blanket and stubbed out the flame with a boot.

Now she sat forward and eyed the being of flame as if really seeing it for the first time. It stood about two feet tall and had a long elegance of limb, as if built to run or dance. She could imagine such a being dancing in the swirls of flame from a well-built fire. Perhaps they did–and always had–if one only had the eyes to see them. "What is it you want?" Her voice seemed frail.

"Why, to speak to you, of course," was the curt reply. "You don't seem to appreciate the honor you've been done. Are you ready to talk?"

"Yes," Liz replied.

"Still wondering if you should live or die? Need some guidance?" The being stretched out an arm and leaned casually on a glowing log. "I know, Jack's gone. But his spirit is in this valley, it always will be. He's not gone *to us.*"

"Who are you?"

"Who indeed? That's the cornerstone of it all, really. Having to ask the question. Even humans who feel the living world around them are locked into the narrow band of seven colors they can see, the narrow range they hear—even though you know there's much, much more, you can't imagine it. Can you see the workings of life under a rock? Can you hear the hibernating fish under the ice? No, but you don't doubt they exist. Why is my kind so very difficult for you to accept?"

"Our legends are filled with your kind," Liz whispered. "We've learned not to believe in legends."

"Such a loss," the sprite murmured. "Time was, humans could see us, if they looked hard enough. Ghost-lights in the woods, the spirits of the air, life in the earth beneath us. Now just legends, for you to dismiss, dig up, and cut down." It paused for a long moment, then shook its antlered crown. "But that's not why I'm here. I'm here about you. What's all this shit about you contemplating relinquishing your life?"

Liz bristled automatically and sat forward with a flash of annoyance. "That's the privacy of my own thoughts, my vulgar little friend, and I'll thank you not to trespass."

The sprite wagged the burning finger again. "Attitude! A good sign!" It sighed. "It's hard to go where we're not welcome. Your mind is screaming all through these woods. Every spirit in nature knows what you're thinking." It folded rippling arms and rolled an ember back and forth with a toe. "We understand. Of course we do. Jack was part of this place and always welcome, and we'll take care of his essence. You have our word. But you're part of it too, if you only knew."

"Part of...?" Liz asked.

"Everything. Everything's connected, and you're part of the web. Each time you came here, each time you felt at home, you bound yourself more completely into the life of this place. And it doesn't want to let you go."

For a long moment, Liz hesitated as her heart thumped. "What does that mean?"

"It means, though we rarely make ourselves known to thick-headed humans, now and then we make an exception, and you're it."

The being looked up from beneath its magnificent tines of fire. "Don't throw away all you are. There's no need. You don't need to die to be with Jack, because Jack hasn't really gone anywhere. You're only a hand's breadth apart, if you could *see,* as we see."

"Can you… can you *make* me see?" The first tinge of hope lay behind her words.

"Perhaps. In time. But that's for another day. Today is for doing what you came here to do. *And no more."* All the sass and attitude were gone from the sprite now. "The first step is to understand, what you see is not all there is."

"I'm not convinced I'm not dreaming. How do I know this isn't just the ravings of an over-stressed mind?"

The sprite offered a weary shrug. "We're always here. And—one way or another—you'll realize the truth of things. Eventually."

After a moment, it stretched out a hand of transparent flame to her. She hesitated, at a loss to know how to respond. "Liz," the fire being said softly, quiet as the night breeze, "Liz, you don't actually think it'll burn, do you?"

She put out a hand, and the fire sprite took her fingertips in its grasp. The flames licked gently around her tissues like liquid, almost warm, almost cool.

"Remember," the sprite said as it held her gaze. Then, it released her and stepped slowly backward, vaulted over the metal grating and into the fire. Its essence held together for a few seconds, before dissolving in a swirl of ruddy flame, and was gone.

———

EMBERS GLOWED A DULL RED WHEN LIZ WOKE. SHE DREW A breath of cold air and blinked in the low light of the one oil lamp. She saw her broken mug on the floor, and when she bent to pick up the pieces, she noticed the black spot of the burn on the rug.

———

SHE LEFT THE CABIN JUST AHEAD OF THE WINTER SUNRISE. FRESH snow had fallen, yielding a shapeless mound where she'd seen the ice being formed in the night. With pack and rifle, she let her eyes acclimate to the early light, silver-gray through the clouds, and set off along another well-known path.

This one brought her up a gentle ridgeline to a point where she could see eastward over the valleys beyond. The east flushed brightly, staining the clouds yellow and white. The forest remained black before them. Liz held Jack's ashes and leaned against a tree to watch the dawn unfold. The rising day found the forest little by little, and when first light filled the glade by their home, she kissed the container, unscrewed the end, and let the breeze have the ashes. They flurried away, blew high and settled out as a dark stain across pure white.

"Farewell, Jack, my love. I won't say goodbye."

She went inside and busied herself with packing. Perhaps there were those who loved and needed her, if she could let herself see it. She straightened the cabin, mindful to leave things ready for next time.

Was it her imagination, or did a twist of flame seem to dance in the hearth?

Mike Adamson holds a Doctoral degree from Flinders University of South Australia. Mike has been a university educator since 2006, has worked in the replication of convincing ancient fossils, is a passionate photographer, master-level hobbyist, and journalist for international magazines. Short fiction sales include to *Metastellar, Strand Magazine, Little Blue Marble, Abyss and Apex*, *Daily Science Fiction, Compelling Science Fiction* and *Nature Futures*. Mike has placed some two hundred stories to date, totaling over one million words. Mike has completed his first Sherlock Holmes novel with Belanger Books and has appeared in translation in European magazines.

TRAILS IN THE SNOW

Marc Sorondo

There was just a half an inch of snow on the ground when Raymond met the devil for the first time.

He was walking home after a party, the last big party before the spring semester began. He'd left at just the right time—after the early birds, but long before the real partiers—so that he could have a few minutes to himself.

He'd looked out the window, seen it started snowing, and taken that as his cue. He had things to consider and a walk in the snow, and the cold air sobering him up a bit, seemed just the way to do it.

The snow fell in fat, puffy flakes that looked like down feathers, in miniature. It coated everything in a layer of white, and then it stopped.

Raymond walked, his collar turned up and his shoulders hunched against the cold, and considered majors, comparing his vision of his future with the one his parents had for him.

He kept his eyes cast down at the whiteness at his feet, but didn't see the track until he stood right before it. It was a hoofprint—its outline perfect, its interior cleared of snow to expose the dingy concrete sidewalk beneath. Raymond saw the trail of prints leading down the block a ways before veering off into the park that was off to his right. Curious by nature, the cold air not yet having sobered him back into a more cautious state of mind, Raymond followed the trail.

The glow from the street lamps at the periphery of the park did not penetrate far into the gloom at the park's interior. The pale, hazy light of a moon, filtered through wintry clouds, offered the only light. The hoofprints ended as abruptly as they'd begun, and where they ended, Raymond encountered an old man.

He wore baggy corduroy pants that looked grey in the obscured moonlight, an argyle sweater vest—its shapes all distorted to shades of grey as well—over a dress shirt with the sleeves rolled up his hirsute forearms, and a pair of ratty old dress shoes. He wore no coat or hat. The snow was a smattering of white speckles in his dark hair.

Raymond thought he looked like an aging librarian, one on the cusp of retirement. A perfect disguise.

The man looked at him and nodded, as if in greeting.

"Are you who I think you are?" Raymond asked.

"And who do you think I am?" His voice matched his exterior. There was a slight gruffness to it, the sort of voice common to old men who hadn't quite lost all of their youthful vigor.

"Old Scratch," Raymond said.

The man smiled at him. He had a wide, affable grin that showed teeth that were not quite perfect. His was a smile that people would say had character.

"There's a name I hardly ever hear anymore," he said. "Tell me, Raymond, what made you follow such an odd path in the snow?"

Raymond shrugged. "Just curious, I guess. Not everyday you find hoofprints in the snow in the suburbs."

The man watched him, oblivious to the cold. It was hard to be sure in that diffuse light, but Raymond didn't spot any goose bumps on his bare forearms. The man seemed to breathe, must have exhaled to speak, but there were no accompanying puffs of condensation in the frigid air.

Raymond waited for the old man to say something more.

He didn't.

"I was just walking home from this party. I needed a little time to think, so I figured a walk would be better than getting a ride from someone."

Scratch nodded as if he knew all this already.

"So, what's on your mind? Why did you need a walk on such a frigid night? A guy your age should still be at that party." He grinned and added, "Making mistakes you won't remember tomorrow morning."

"I have to declare my major."

"So. Pick what you like. Change your mind a few times. You kids change majors all the time."

Raymond shook his head. "Four years. If I'm in school any longer than that, I better be getting a master's. I'd like to get this right the first time."

Scratch nodded.

Raymond waited for him to say something, but when Scratch merely stuffed his hands into the pockets of his corduroys and stared at him, he went on. "Also, my parents want me to major in something safe. Mom wants accounting and dad wants statistics, but I think I'd rather focus on my photography."

"Mom and dad want stability for you, but you want to chase your passions," Scratch said, nodding to himself, seeming to mull it over.

"My professors say I have an artist's eye and a natural sense of dramatic construction."

Scratch smirked at that last bit. "Don't know much about photography, but I'm sure that's impressive. If I were you, I'd chase your dreams, but I'd minor in something stable, something that'll make mom and dad happy."

"Makes sense," Raymond said.

"Chase your dreams until you succeed or die. People who give up on them aren't as happy as those who just keep at it. The minor, though... pick something good. You'll be happy to be able to eat and pay rent, even if it means you're only taking pictures after your day job."

Raymond nodded as he considered minors. His parents would still complain, but not as much as if he'd focused solely on his photos. "That's it. That's what I'll do."

"Glad I could help."

"Thanks. You really did."

"See you around, Raymond."

"Yeah, see you around."

Raymond turned and followed the trail of hoofprints in reverse until he was out of the park. He looked back once he reached the street, but Old Scratch hid in the darkness.

A FEW YEARS LATER, A SLIGHTLY OLDER AND MUCH MORE SOBER Raymond walked home during a late-night flurry of impressively fat and fuzzy snowflakes. He was headed to his off-campus apartment—one he shared with several roommates—on his way home from Samantha's. Sam had offered to drive him, but he saw the snow falling through her window and decided he'd walk.

His route took him across campus. He was coming around

the corner of Meed Hall, planning on cutting across the tree-strewn lawn, when he spotted the first hoofprint. It was perfect, its inverted U-shape completely cleared of snow.

His sobriety did not dampen his curiosity, and, once again, he followed the prints. They moved in a gradual curve, leading Raymond towards a statue of a figure on horseback. There in the shadows, Old Scratch waited for him, his arms crossed over his sweater vest so that a dusting of white flakes had collected in the hairs on the backs of his forearms. He leaned against the base of the statue, and Raymond thought he caught the smallest suggestion of a smile as he came around the statue.

"Been a while, Raymond."

"You like the snow, huh?" Raymond said.

Scratch shrugged without uncrossing his arms. "If you believe what you see on television, it's hot where I live."

Raymond smiled at that but stopped short of a laugh.

"Seem to like it yourself. You always go for strolls when it's snowing?"

"Only when it's the right kind of snow."

"Or maybe only when you've got something on your mind," Scratch said, his eyes narrowing slightly as if scrutinizing Raymond, as if reading him.

Raymond nodded. "Her name's Sam... Samantha." He pulled the tab on his jacket's zipper, closing it up to his chest. "I think I'd be okay with her being *the* girl."

"Young and in love," Scratch said. "But you've got to keep something in mind. This…" He uncrossed his arms and held them out towards the campus that existed to the sides of and behind him. "This isn't real life. Give it until a year after you've graduated. A year of working a real job and paying your bills and all the other miserable bullshit that comes with being an adult in this day and age. If you're still going strong after a year, if you still like the idea of Sam as a permanent fixture in your life at that point, then you can start to think about doing something drastic."

Raymond smiled at Old Scratch's choice of words. It was, however, solid advice; he recognized that immediately.

"Can I ask you something?" Raymond said after a moment of quiet, during which the snow fell lazily around them.

"Shoot."

"You don't seem like a bad guy. Not at all."

"I appreciate that, Raymond. It wasn't a question, though."

"Why the bad reputation?"

Scratch nodded. "You don't actually know me very well. I'll admit that things are far more complicated than anyone ever wants to admit. We all have our roles to play, our jobs to do, and our reasons for doing them. That being said, just because I've been nice to you, that doesn't mean I'm necessarily nice, in general."

Raymond nodded again. "So wait a year?"

"At least."

"I'll do that."

"You won't regret it." Scratch crossed his arms again and adjusted his position—still leaned back against the base of the statue, but now with one leg bent and his foot against it like a cross between a retired accountant and the Marlboro Man. "See you around, Raymond."

"See you around," Raymond echoed as he turned to walk away.

———

THEY MET THAT WAY EVERY FEW YEARS, BUT ONLY WHEN THE snow was just right, with a thin coating of oversized flakes.

Raymond met Scratch once shortly after he and Samantha had gotten married. He'd admitted that his parents' vision of his future had been more accurate than his own predictions. His photography had become a weekend hobby, while he spent his week in an office utilizing his minor in statistics more than anything he'd learned for his major.

Scratch had smiled and admitted that the news didn't surprise him. "You'll still be happy you did it, even if it's never anything more than a hobby."

Raymond didn't doubt it.

THEY MET AGAIN JUST AFTER HE TURNED FORTY. THE KIDS WERE in their rooms—one reading, the other listening to music and drawing, having inherited Raymond's "natural sense of dramatic construction." Sam immersed herself in a mystery novel. He left to sneak in a quick jog.

When the snow started falling, he'd kept jogging until he saw the start of a trail of hoofprints that led toward the pond at the far end of the park. He found Old Scratch sitting on a bench overlooking a partially frozen pond.

They didn't talk about Raymond at all that night.

Instead, Scratch told him about how the town used to allow ice-skating on that pond, when it was cold enough. Then, someone made a bad call, and a little boy went through a weak spot in the ice. His mother went in after him, but just made the hole in the ice wider trying to get him out.

Several people working together finally got mother and son out of the freezing water, but the boy was dead by the time they pulled him out. The mother survived. She lost several fingers and her only child to the cold. And lost her mind shortly thereafter. Overcome by grief and rage and guilt, she killed herself the following winter.

Raymond was quiet for a while once the story was over,

initially waiting for Old Scratch to say something more. The grief-stricken mother's suicide didn't seem an acceptable ending, but neither said anything more for a time. The snow fell and caught in their hair, leaving a white coating on their shoulders.

"When something like that happens," Raymond said finally. "Something horrible like that… was that woman really punished for killing herself? Is she really burning in some Hell now?" Raymond asked.

Scratch sighed. "I'm not allowed to say. It's not my place. People aren't supposed to know what—if anything—comes before or after their lives. It's for the best, even if it's hard to see how sometimes."

Raymond looked at the snow as it hit the surface of the pond, where a wafer of ice floated on the cold water, and considered this rule.

"I can accept that."

"Good thing."

"I'll see you around then," Raymond said as he stood from the bench.

"I'll see you around, Raymond."

———

THEY CONTINUED TO MEET THAT WAY EVERY FEW YEARS, ALWAYS when there was a dusting of snow, just enough of it for him to hold the trail he was to follow.

Sometimes they discussed Raymond's life (Old Scratch didn't always give advice, but when he did, it was always spot on). Sometimes they talked about the state of the world or past events, like the story of the boy who fell through the ice and his mother.

A comfortable relationship grew, despite the infrequency of the visits.

A FEW DAYS AFTER HIS FORTY-EIGHTH CHRISTMAS, RAYMOND walked his usual route one cold night. His evening jogs tended to be mere walks more often than not these days. When it began snowing, he recognized the type of flakes: Devil's Snow.

Raymond looked for the trail, even when he knew it had not yet accumulated quite enough. He was eager to talk to Old Scratch. His advice had always helped him, had always cut through to the kernel of importance at the center of whatever knot he'd tied himself into.

If ever he'd needed advice, that was the night.

Earlier that day, his boss had called him in, sat him down, and fired him. He hadn't used that term, of course. He'd employed a number of euphemisms and corporate doublespeak, but Raymond had left the meeting knowing that his time with the company was running out. He had a mortgage, one child in college, and another headed there soon. He was supposed to be a breadwinner, but he didn't have a job anymore.

Finally, Raymond found the familiar trail of u-shaped prints. They led him into the park, and he didn't even have to look down to follow it to the bench overlooking the pond.

Scratch didn't turn at the sound of Raymond's footsteps crunching in the snow, but he said, "How've you been, Raymond?"

Raymond came around the bench, and his old friend looked up at him. "Never mind. Your face says it all."

Raymond sat. "You know, when we first met, I thought you looked old. I clearly remember thinking that you looked like a librarian that was getting ready to retire. Now we look about the same age."

Old Scratch laughed. He had a quiet laugh; it was part mirth and part sigh. "You don't look quite that old yet."

"Getting there."

"I do think you may have aged several years in the last few hours."

Raymond nodded. "I lost my job. I don't know what I'm going to do. Who's going to hire someone my age?"

"You've got a lot of experience. Your record speaks for itself."

"A kid fresh out of college could do my job. Would do it for a quarter of the salary, too."

Old Scratch looked out at the pond. It hadn't been cold enough for long enough to freeze it over. It was black and glossy as a pool of ink.

"Tell you what," he said finally, never looking away from the dark water. "I've always liked you, Raymond. I'm going to offer you a favor, just one, with no strings attached."

"Really? I didn't think you could do that. In stories, you know, there's always a catch."

Old Scratch nodded. "That's usually true, but I'm also not usually the one to offer things. Once people realize who I am, they're usually all too eager to trade something permanent for something fleeting. I think that's why I like you. You've never asked me for anything."

Raymond nodded. It had never even occurred to him to try to make a bargain with the devil.

"So what'll it be, Raymond? Anything you want, within reason."

"I never want to have to worry about money again. I don't need to be rich. I'd just like for it not to be a constant source of stress."

Scratch considered this for a moment. "Done."

"Thank you."

For a while, they shared the bench without speaking.

Then Raymond asked, "Does it bother you, always being portrayed as the bad guy?"

Old Scratch shook his head. "I play that role often enough. The simplest stories last the longest in people's minds and in their cultures. I don't mind."

THE NEXT DAY WAS JUST AS COLD, BUT THERE WASN'T A CLOUD in the sky. Raymond walked against an intermittent breeze that stung his cheeks and brought tears to his eyes as he headed for his office.

He was running late, and he didn't care. They were already letting him go. What would they care if he strolled in half an hour later than usual?

It would've been a pleasant walk on a warmer day. The sun was bright, and the sidewalk was far less congested than it had been while people were still rushing to work earlier that morning.

A powerful gust of wind sent a scrap of paper scrabbling towards him along the sidewalk. As it neared, a second gust drove it upward and into Raymond's chest. It held to his chest, as if by an invisible hand. He reached down and plucked it off, meaning to crumple it into a ball and toss it into the trashcan in front of his building.

Then he saw what it was.

He slipped the paper into his pocket.

RAYMOND IGNORED THAT SCRAP OF PAPER IN HIS POCKET ALL day. He worked, commuted home, had dinner, and did the dishes, and the whole time he was aware of it there. It was like carrying around a firecracker with a lit fuse. No matter what else he was doing, much of his concentration was on waiting for it to explode.

When he sat down in front of the television and finally pulled it from his pocket, he fought with himself. As he waited for commercials to end, part of him felt sure that Old Scratch was already at work, already making good on his promise.

The other part of him felt foolish for holding onto a piece of trash that had blown into him that morning.

Then the drawing began. He watched the numbers on the paper rather than the screen. As he listened to the pleasant but monotonous voice of the woman calling numbers, he mentally checked them off one by one.

They were all there, laid out for him in a neat row.

He'd just won over four hundred million dollars.

AFTER THE BOYS FINISHED COLLEGE, RAYMOND AND SAM bought small places in Cape Cod and southwest Florida. They spent all summer at the Cape and most of the winter on the Gulf Coast. Spring and an extended autumn that included Christmas was always at their home in New Jersey.

Raymond rented a small storefront near each vacation home, where he sold his photos to summer tourists and winter snowbirds. A successful year was one in which his photography business broke even–as rare as flying pigs and ice storms in Hell–but Raymond savored every moment focused on the art he'd neglected for so long. He loved photographing the sea, and the satisfaction of selling even a small framed photo filled him and nourished his soul.

Sam read voraciously and tried myriad hobbies until she found a few that stuck. The boys came and went as their schedules allowed, bringing girlfriends and then fiancées and later wives on their visits to the beach houses.

They used their wealth for good. He gave generously to any and every cause he found worthwhile: curing diseases, protecting the environment, feeding the hungry, providing clean water, educating children.

He gave his time with the same spirit of generosity. He donated photos for fundraisers and took on different roles with a handful of his favorite charities.

As time went on, however, a nagging idea formed in a back corner of his mind. He tried to ignore it at first, but the longer it sat there, taking up space on the cusp of his subconscious, the harder it was to ignore.

Though it had been a gift rather than a deal, though he'd used the money to try to improve the world in as many ways and for as many people as possible, Raymond couldn't shake the thought that he'd been punished for it somehow.

RAYMOND SPENT YEARS LEAVING FOR WARMER CLIMATES WELL before the snowy part of winter was underway and not returning until it was over. One year, the cold set in early. It was wintry for Thanksgiving, and the frigid temperatures lingered. Early in the evening just before Christmas, Raymond looked up from the present he was wrapping for his youngest granddaughter and saw fat, downy flakes of snow drifting past the window.

He finished wrapping the box and then told Sam he thought he'd go for a walk. She looked out the window and smiled. "You never could resist that sort of flurry. I used to think you'd grow out of it, but now I'm happy you haven't."

He walked over to her and kissed her where her greying hair met her forehead.

"Wear your hat and scarf. It's freezing out."

"I will."

He threw on his warmest cold weather gear—boots, coat, hat, scarf, and gloves—expecting he'd be outside for a while.

There was no trail of hoofprints to follow. He headed toward the park and the pond, their usual meeting place.

As he neared the bench, he could make out a familiar figure seated on it. Scratch sat watching the pond in the falling snow.

"I'd started thinking you wouldn't be here. You used to leave a clearer trail," Raymond said once he sat down.

"You used to need one," Scratch said. "We're past that now. You know where and when to find me."

"That I do."

"So, how're you enjoying life as a rich man? Giving a lot of it away, I see. I assume you've put stuff aside for your kids, grandkids?"

"Of course."

"But something troubles you."

Raymond nodded. "When you said there'd be no strings, that it was just a gift…"

Old Scratch smiled. "Ah. So it's that. I meant what I said. You have nothing to repay. You're in no debt."

"So I won't be punished? Once I'm dead, I mean?"

"You know I can't tell you that. It's a good rule; trust me. Do your best and trust that the system—whatever that is—will give you what you deserve."

Raymond nodded again. "I do trust you."

"I can tell you this without giving too much away. No one has ever been punished for something that I did. Even in most of the stories—not that they're always so accurate—people make their own choices, their own mistakes."

"I still say you get unfairly represented in those stories," Raymond said.

"You're biased."

AFTER SAM DIED, RAYMOND STOPPED GOING TO THE BEACH houses. He stopped leasing storefronts and looked at old pictures more than he took new ones. He kept the beach houses, but they were for the boys and their families now.

He had no need to visit them again. He preferred what he thought of as their *real* house—the place they'd bought when they got married, the home in which they'd raised their children. They'd spent some of the best times of their lives at the beach, but only one place really felt like home. Both boys had asked him to move in with their families after Sam died, or to at least consider moving closer. Raymond—though he loved the thought of seeing his grandkids every day—couldn't bear the thought of leaving that house.

He settled into new patterns and didn't mind the much slower rhythm of his life. He thought about the past quite a lot. Flipping through candid shots of Sam lounging on a beach in a blue bikini on their honeymoon, of Christmas mornings with little ones opening presents amidst a red and green sea of shredded paper, of first days of school and first dates, of birthdays and graduations.

He relived his life one important moment at a time.

He thought he'd lived a good life. Long before the money had made life easy, he and Sam had done their best with what they had. Most of the time, he'd learned from his mistakes and savored his triumphs. He was proud of the life he'd lived so far.

But his life's rhythm was steadily winding down, like a clock about to stop. He was ready for the next step. Still curious to see what came after—and hopeful that he'd get what he deserved.

RAYMOND SAW THE SNOW FALLING THROUGH THE KITCHEN
window, but he knew he'd never make it to the park. His days of
evening walks were behind him.

He pulled open the back door, and the snow blew in.

Raymond went to the front hall. He pulled on his boots and
tied them, his hands starting to shake as the temperature in the
house plummeted. He put on his coat and hat, wrapped his scarf
around his neck, and pulled on his gloves.

By the time he returned to the back door, a layer of snow had
built up in a u-shape extending into the kitchen. A series of
hoofprints began at the innermost reaches of snow and led
outside.

Raymond followed them, closing the door behind him as he
left.

Old Scratch sat in one of the Adirondack chairs in the
backyard. He remained unchanged as ever, wearing the same
getup that had called to mind an old librarian decades before.
Raymond knew that he now looked significantly older than his
friend. He slowly lowered himself into the empty chair to
Scratch's left.

"I was hoping to see you one more time," Raymond said.

"I wanted to see you off."

"You know, you're my oldest friend."

Scratch nodded. "Are you afraid?"

Raymond didn't have to think for long. "I'm not."

"Good."

"You probably can't say, but…" Raymond coughed out a
puff of condensation. "Will I see Sam again? Someday, will I get
to see my boys again?"

Scratch sighed. "I can't say."

Raymond nodded. "Trust the system."

They sat there for what felt to Raymond like a long while. They talked for a bit, but then they fell into a comfortable silence. After decades, neither of them felt a need to fill it. They could enjoy each other's company just watching the snow fall. Though he'd been outside for what seemed like hours, Raymond felt warmer the longer he sat. He had—on chilly nights at the very end of summer on the Cape—occasionally dozed in a chair set before the fireplace, and he felt that same warmth now. It made his eyes heavy.

Old Scratch turned to look at him as the weight of Raymond's eyelids became too much to hold, before he drifted off to sleep.

Marc Sorondo lives with his wife and children in New York. He loves to read, and his interests range from fiction to comic books, physics to history, oceanography to cryptozoology, and just about everything in between. He's a perpetual student and occasional teacher. For more information, go to MarcSorondo.com

STILL OF WINTER REVIEWS

We'll love to hear what you think—good, bad, or even ugly. It helps readers find us and decide whether or not to give this collection a try.

Or visit https://tinyurl.com/StillofWinterAmazonReview

Much appreciated!

ACKNOWLEDGEMENTS

Robin Knabel: A huge thank you to all the talented contributors in this book as well as everyone who took the time to submit to the collection. I'd like to thank Dair, my partner in crime, for her never-ending positivity and uplifting nature. I love being on this wild ride with you! A big thank you to my mom for always supporting me and my strange interests, for as long as I can remember. Finally, thank you to my amazing husband and kids. You get me. Thank you for your constant encouragement and your belief in me and my writing. I love you.

H. Dair Brown: Writers of "unsettling" genres, you are unfailingly the nicest and most generous people. Thank you for being so wonderful to work with on these adventures of ours. Many, many thanks to Robin, my sister-from-another-mister, for these Unsettling (Reads) hijinks! You're a fantastic (and delightful deranged) traveling companion on this creative journey. And, as always, so much love and appreciation going out to my friends and family. Thanks for reminding me that there's more to life than fiction. MJ and the Freds, you guys are the Center of Awesome.

ABOUT UNSETTLING READS

Unsettling Reads, LLC was founded by fiction authors Robin Knabel and H. Dair Brown as a place to offer their spoiler-free reviews and recommendations on **books from the Crime, Fantasy, Horror, Literary, Mystery, Noir, Sci-Fi, Suspense, and Thriller genres**.

If you picked up this book, you probably enjoy books that make you check for monsters under the bed (or perhaps even in bed next to you) before you go to sleep. Let Robin and Dair help you decide what to read the next time you're ready to sink down into the "safety" of your blankets and crack open **the kind of book that will make you shudder (and maybe even think) a little**.

They love to interact with their readers and fellow authors on Twitter, Instagram, and Facebook. That's where the truly unsettling stuff usually happens. Find them **@unsettlingreads**.

UnsettlingReads.com

ROBIN AND DAIR

For more information on what they're up to individually, you can find them online and on social media. (Okay, you'll definitely find Robin there. Dair's less great about social media.)

Robin Knabel | RobinKnabel.com | @LaConteuse
(Twitter) and @robinknabel (Instagram)

H. Dair Brown | HDairBrown.com | @dairlirious
(Twitter/Instagram)

Need to be unsettled monthly?
https://tinyurl.com/unsettleme

BYE BYE
FOR NOW...

Made in the USA
Monee, IL
23 February 2023

28529138R00204